D1557434

Welcome to the
SPOOKSHOW

Book Two

Tim McGregor

Perdido Pub
TORONTO

ISBN-13:978-1508806820

ISBN-10:1508806829

"An idea, like a ghost, must be spoken to a little before it will explain itself."

--Charles Dickens

August 17, 1994

MAMA WAS GOING through the horrors. Again.

It happened once a season, if not more, and there was nothing to do but wait it out. Billie knew better than to get in the way when the bad spells came on. Let Mama scream or throw things or cry or retreat to her bed for days. Billie had learnt this the hard way and had the scars to prove it. Run for cover and let the horrors run their course.

She wasn't fast enough this time. Snatched fast by the wrist, Billie was dragged back to the table in the front parlour.

"Do it again," Mama said, pushing the girl into the chair. "Run the cards."

Billie shook her head. "I don't want to."

Mama's hands shook as she pushed the deck forward. Her eyes were puffy from all the crying and her voice hoarse from shrieking. "Sybil Culpepper, do as I say. I need to be sure."

Billie quaked and kept shaking her head. "Please, Mama."

"Do it!" Mama's fist came down hard on the table. The deck jumped, causing the top cards to spill down.

The girl wiped her eyes and reached for the cards with the strange pictures on them. She cut the deck and laid down the first card. The three of swords. Same as last time.

Her mother's lips pursed at the reveal. "Don't stop. The next one."

Billie hated when mama made her do this. She hated the cards. Or the cards hated her. They never gave up good tells. Not that Billie understood what the pictures meant but mama always reacted badly. It was certain to ignite the horrors in her. She turned over the next card.

Her mother's hand began to tremble again. She nodded at the girl to go on. "Quickly now."

Mary Agnes was her mother's name but most people in town called her the spooky lady. Or the crazy lady. Never to her face, of course. Never when they came to the house to have mama run their cards or read the sludgy mess of leaves from tea. And they all came, sooner or later, sneaking up the steps, worried the neighbours would see. Mostly the women in town but some of the men too, with their urgent questions or desperate worries. Sometimes Billie would sneak down to the bottom step to listen but the questions were always the same. Will he ask me to marry him? Is she cheating on me? Will I get the money? Will she quit drinking? Should I leave him?

In town, these same desperate souls would barely utter a word to mama, a hair shy of openly shunning her. They talked about Mary Agnes behind her back, whispering nasty things about the spooky lady, and by proxy, about Billie too.

"That poor little thing", they would condescend. Or "The apple didn't fall far with that child, did it?"

Billie hated them all for being so two-faced but she hated mama more for letting it get this way. Why couldn't she just act normal? Or get a regular job, like at the grocery store or the insurance office near the taxidermist shop? Put the cards away and stop being the spooky lady. How hard could it be?

She suspected that Mary Agnes secretly enjoyed the fear she provoked in the townies. They gossiped about her because they were afraid of her, simple as that.

"What are you waiting for?" Mama snapped.

Billie flinched. Each card she laid down made mama shake even more, the tears glistening her eyes again. Billie put her hand on the deck but hesitated before laying down the last card. "Is it bad, mama?" she asked.

"Depends on the last throw. One way or the other. Do it."

It was going to end badly, Billie knew. The cards had run exactly the same as last time and her mother's quaking was rattling the wobbly table. She slid the last card from the deck, wondering if she was going to get hit this time, and laid it down at the bottom of the cross-shaped formation.

Mary Agnes ejected backwards as if pushed, knocking the chair to the floor. The whimper breaking her voice escalated into a wail as she backed into the window sill. Billie scattered the cards, flinging them across the table to dispel whatever it was they had foretold.

Mama shrieked at her to stop. The wild look in her eyes told Billie that the horrors had taken over completely and she wondered which hiding place she would use this time to escape the craziness that was sure to come. Would it be the attic or the dusty crawl-space under the floor?

The shrieking stopped without warning and the sudden silence frightened Billie more. Her mother held her breath and rushed to the window. Pushing back the faded curtain, she peered outside. This is what she said: "Oh God."

From outside came the sound of a car rolling up the driveway, the familiar crunch of tires over the gravel. Who was it?

Mary Agnes whipped about and, fast as a rattlesnake strike, snatched Billie by the arm. "Run, Billie. Hide."

"Who is it, mama?"

"Do as I say!" she snarled. "Hide in the place where I can never find you. Stay there. And don't make a sound."

"Mama—"

"Do it!" She flung the girl away and returned to the window.

Billie ran from the parlour. The hiding spot in the attic was upstairs, accessed by tugging the string on the trapdoor in the ceiling. The crawl-space was closer. She ran for it.

Closing the basement door behind her, Billie slid back the thin panel that covered the opening to the crawl-space. A cramped tunnel under the floor, used to store old mason jars and broken appliances that Mary Agnes refused to part with. Billie squirmed into the tight space and slid the panel closed after her. It was dark and it smelled bad. She tried not to think about the spiders or the earwigs that crawled about this darkened space.

She heard the thunder on the porch steps, then the lightning of the front door being kicked open. Mary Agnes screaming and the sound of something crashing to the floor and reverberating through the floor joists over Billie's head. And then the snarl of a man's voice.

Billie knew nothing of her father. The man had been absent most of her life and her mother never spoke of him. But she knew it was him stomping and bellowing in the kitchen above her. There was more crashing and banging and then it ended with a heavy thud that rained dust from the floorboards over Billie's head. Everything went still and her mother stopped screaming and then the male voice called out her name.

Billie, it bellowed. Billie, where are you?

Billie made herself very still as she listened to the footfalls stomp through the house, the voice hollering her name. She almost screamed when something touched her ankle. Clenching her jaw to keep her mouth shut, she kicked at it but it coiled up around her thin bone ankle and squeezed. So cold it hurt. Unable to turn around and see what it was, she pictured a snake wrapping itself around her leg but no cold-blooded snake was ever this cold. Whatever was in the crawl space with her, it too spoke her name but soft, like a whisper. Billie clamped her hands over her mouth to stay silent, wondering if it would be better to take her chances with the stranger tearing through the house.

The bellowing above ceased. Billie heard the scraping sound of something being dragged across the kitchen, then the clap of the screen door and something thudding down the porch steps. An engine rumbled to life, followed by the scattershot sound of gravel spraying as the car sped from the driveway.

Bashing out the thin panel, she scurried from the crawlspace but the grip coiled around her ankle pulled her back. This time she screamed and kicked out like she was on fire. It released her and she tumbled out onto the basement steps and peered into the narrow space. There was nothing there.

"Mama!"

No answer came. Barrelling into the kitchen, her shoes

crunched over shards of broken china. The checkerboard tiles of the floor were a collage of smashed dishes and shattered glass. She didn't want to look at the blood but the puddle of dark red pulled her eyes like a magnet. It didn't look real, there was so much of it. Flies were already buzzing over it.

The blood smeared across the floor like someone had mopped with it, from the sink to the front door. Leap-frogging the stuff to avoid stepping in it, she followed the trail out the front door where the blood tracked over the porch and down the wooden steps. The blood stopped there.

She didn't know what to do. She didn't want to go back inside the house. Billie was afraid that she would be blamed, that this was somehow her fault. So she ran. A third of a mile through the little town, running blind until someone spotted her. The police were called and Billie was settled onto the sofa, her aunt smoothing her hair back and cooing to her that everything was going to be okay.

Billie curled into a ball while the grown-ups fretted and paced back and forth. Her aunt Maggie could not sit still, impatient for answers as she straightened this object and fussed with that. The policemen came but they just seemed to stand around and tell her aunt to calm down. Billie's ankle stung and, remembering the snake she felt, checked to see if it had bitten her. What she found were bruises that looked like fingerprints on her skin and bloodied scratch marks, as if someone had clawed her sharp with their nails. Come morning, the scratches would become infected and her missing mother was never seen again.

1

THE MARK ON her ankle never went away. Even now at the age of twenty-nine, it was still there. White scar tissue left behind after an infection so bad that the doctor at the time feared it was gangrene.

Sometimes it still itched, a phantom pain from so long ago. Pedalling her way through the streets of Hamilton, she felt it as she pushed the bike through traffic. Exertion often brought it on and Billie exerted herself now, late as usual.

Fighting rush hour traffic on King Street was a losing battle. Too many cars and too many thoughtless drivers hostile to anyone on a bicycle. Swinging right, she cut through an alley to get on Wellington and try her luck on Cannon Street.

Jen's party had started half an hour ago and Billie had promised her oldest friend that she would help out running the shindig so that Jen was free to do the meet-and-greets. How pissed was Jen likely to be? Billie didn't even have a good excuse for her tardiness. She had biked over to Gage Park to soak up the first hot day of the summer and had simply lost track of time. She had lost track of everything actually. Another foggy spell had come over her sitting in the grass, when the outside world simply faded away. Lost time. She would snap out of the fog, wondering where the hours had gone.

An excuse wouldn't work, she realized as she chased down Cannon Street. Jen knew of her foggy spells. And Jen hated them, having witnessed more than her fair share.

"You need to focus," Jen had scolded more than once. Like everyone else in her life. "You can't just tune everything out, Billie. You need to stay in the moment."

Focus, or the lack of it, had been a constant companion all of her life. A recurring theme on every school report card until a learning disability had been recognized. Even then, the cause of the disability had never been diagnosed with any accuracy. Billie had gotten used to being written off as flighty or wool-headed so many times that she had even given up on herself. It was a different story hammering down the streets on her bike. The speed and muscle and heightened senses cleared away the fog like a strong wind and brought clarity to the fore. If only she could ride her bike forever, everything would be fine.

All journeys come to an end and Billie's ended before a brightly lit storefront on James Street. Retro patio lights strung over the entrance gave the shop a festive ambiance that matched the music streaming from the open door and the people milling on the sidewalk. A party in progress. Billie leaned her bike against the parking meter and slid the lock through the spokes.

"Billie!" came a voice at her back. "Where have you been?"

Billie snapped the lock shut and turned just in time to catch the tight embrace of a young woman in a floral print dress.

"Sorry, Jen." Billie leaned back from the hug and took in the storefront. "I got caught up. Did I miss anything?"

"Nah. People just started showing up. Let's get you a drink."

Letting her friend lead her inside where the music was louder and the air stuffier, Billie felt her angst over being late fade away. Jen had a charming way of disarming tension and dismissing anxieties among anyone in her presence and for that Billie was grateful. Aside from being the constant peacemaker, Jen Eckler was Billie's oldest friend. Their shared history stretched all the way back to the hormonal sewer of small town high school and had thrived ever since. To an outside observer, they seemed an unlikely pair. Where Jen's smile was bubbly with enough warmth to melt igloos, Billie's smile was a lopsided affair often misinterpreted as a sneer. This did, however, lend itself to an uncanny Elvis impersonation that Jen, if plied with enough cocktails, never failed to cajole out of her old friend.

"The shop looks great." Billie said, scanning her eyes over the interior. The Doll House was long and narrow with racks of dresses flanking one wall and a larger area in the back. "You were right about the lighting. Makes a world of difference. Intimate."

"Do you think?" Jen plucked a beer from the tin tub of ice near the counter. "I keep going back and forth on it. Thanks again for your help."

"I didn't do much more than slap paint." Billie clinked her bottle against Jen's champagne flute. She had donated more than a few hours of labour to help Jen turn an old shoe store into her new dress shop. After months of hard work and stress, the shop finally opened last week. A soft launch, to work out the kinks before tonight's official opening party.

"That was plenty and I totally appreciate it." Jen raised her glass and sipped. "You have a dress coming to you. I'll fit it for you too."

"Thanks." Billie's smile went lopsided as they both knew that she would never come in for a fitting. Her friend's dresses, both the vintage kind and the newer ones she designed herself, were gorgeous and colourful and eye-catching. All of which was the antithesis of how Billie dressed.

Billie surveyed the shop with its pink walls and black accents. Slapping pink paint on the walls, she thought Jen was crazy for going with the colour but as usual her friend had pulled it altogether in her arch style. Swanky and fun, with a wee bit of edge to it. "So," Billie said, "how does it feel to be an official business owner?"

"Exhausting." Jen plunked down on the church pew set against the wall. "I practically live here now. And Adam keeps complaining that I'm never home."

Billie took a seat beside her friend. "I'm sure it'll get easier when you work out the bugs. You hire anybody yet?"

"I can't afford to." The bubbly demeanor leaked out of Jen's smile as she contemplated the future. "It'll just be me for a while. Unless I want to borrow more money from dad. But I can't do that."

"Can't or won't?"

"Does it matter?"

"Is he here?" Billie asked.

Jen craned her neck to scan the crowd. "Probably in the back, fixing something."

"He never stops, does he?" Billie stood and sauntered for the door behind the counter. "I'm gonna go say hi."

"Okay, but don't disappear back there," Jen waved her flute at her. "Tammy and Kaitlin will be here soon."

Pushing through a drape of beads hanging over the door, Billie stepped into the chaos of the backroom. A clutter of hanging clothes and boxes of material narrowed the usable space to little more than a path to the end where the back door was propped open. Stepping out into the night air, she found a middle-aged man with a prominent gut wielding a cordless drill.

"Hey Mr. Eckler," she beamed. "The foreman blew the whistle hours ago. Time to punch out."

Mr. Eckler removed the galvanized screws clamped in his teeth and gave her a quick hug. "Hello Billie. It's good to see you."

"Put the work away, huh. Come join the party."

"Oh," he shrugged, nodding at the metal grate over the back window. "I just needed to get this grate secured properly. Can't be too careful, you know, now that the shop is up and running."

"Jen did a great job on the place. You must be proud of her for finally getting it up and running."

"I am," he smiled at her. "I am no matter what. I just hope she's ready for what's coming. Running a business is hard."

"I wouldn't know." Billie leaned against the rotting wooden fence. "But she has you to help her. Advise her and stuff."

"True, but only so far. At some point, you gotta sink or swim on your own. Otherwise what's the point? Hold that end up for me, would you?"

Billie held the grate in place while Mr. Eckler drilled the screws into place. "Tell me how you're doing," he said. "You swimming or sinking?"

She shrugged. She hated questions like this. As innocuous as the inquiry was, she still interpreted to mean 'what are you doing with your life'. Groan. "Neither, really. Doing the backfloat. Drifting around."

"Drifting? You still working at the bar?"

"Yeah. It's okay but it's just a job. Not a career, you know?" She wagged her chin in the direction of the shop inside. "Not like Jen with her designs and the shop. Or Tammy with her photography. I'd kill to figure out what kind of pursuit to make. To be honest, I'm almost jealous."

"Hang in there, kiddo. You'll find what you're meant to do."

Another shrug. Which she hated. She shrugged at everything. It was her default reaction to the world. Like nothing mattered. "I hope so. I just wish I knew what it was. How did you do it? Did you always know you wanted to teach?"

"Hell no," he laughed. "It was a temporary thing at the time. I was going to be a writer."

"Oh." Billie took a second look at her friend's dad. She had known him since she was seventeen but this was news to her. "So what happened?"

"I couldn't cut it. But teaching came easy. I was good at it."

She watched the smile drain from his face just then. It seemed odd, something she'd rarely seen in Mr. Eckler. His eyes had cast off somewhere else and Billie shifted her weight from one foot to the other in the uncomfortable silence. She wished she hadn't brought it up in the first place.

Jen's father seemed startled by his sudden wistful turn. Shaking it off quickly, he patted her shoulder. "We don't always get to choose our calling in life, Billie. Sometimes it chooses us."

She almost laughed. "You should write that down. It's good."

"Maybe I missed my true calling after all," he beamed. "Fortune cookie writer."

"Wouldn't that be a great job? Just coming up with pithy thoughts all day."

"I'm sure the pay is lousy." He cranked the chuck on the drill and removed the bit. "Say, how's your aunt doing? Does she like it out there at the beach?"

Her aunt Maggie, who had taken Billie in when she was eight years old and raised her like her own daughter, had moved out to the shore of Lake Erie after Billie moved to the city. "She loves it. She'd always bugged Uncle Larry to move out there but he wouldn't do it. So, when he passed, she packed up and moved."

"I should get her address from you. I'll stop in next time I'm in the area."

"She'd love that. She gets a bit lonely out there." Billie drained the last of her beer. "Okay, I'm going to get you a drink and you're gonna stop working. Deal?"

"Deal. Just not that Pabst stuff. I don't know how you kids drink that swill."

2

LATE FOR WORK, Billie cut the party early. Tammy and Kaitlin still hadn't arrived and Jen begged her to stay a little longer. Billie apologized, another late start and her boss would turf her sorry butt. Jen saw her to the curb where Billie unlocked her bike.

"We'll come by the bar after the party's over," Jen called out as Billie pedalled away. "Save us three stools."

Waving back, Billie said she'd try, knowing full well that reserving three stools was impossible. The ladies would just have to fend for themselves.

Work was a small north end bar called the Gunner's Daughter, a few blocks from the harbour. With its legal capacity clocked out at no more than fifty souls, it could, and often was, manned by a single bartender. The owner was a flint who seethed at seeing idle staff and kept the labour change thrifty. Which was fine by Billie, she preferred a one-man show anyway.

The bar itself wasn't much to look at, especially with the lights on. An old lunch counter from the city's steeltown heyday, re-purposed with little effort into a quaint watering hole. With the lights down low and candles on the table, it had a scuzzy charm. It was a place to meet before the night began or a stop along the way to some other place. The tables kept rotating, no lingering cheapskate hogging a stool for hours nursing a single beer. Billie liked the pace of it, people rotating in and shuffling out.

When the ladies arrived, there just happened to be three vacant stools but they weren't together. Jen said it was fine but Tammy was having none of it. She asked four patrons to slide one stool down and when they grumbled, she lied that it was Kaitlin's bachelorette party. The drinkers obliged and Kaitlin rolled her eyes at the shenanigans, like it was all beneath her.

"Set us up, Billie," Tammy drummed the bar top and turned to Jen and Kaitlin. "Jager bombs all down the line?"

"God no," Kaitlin sneered. Perched like a frail bird on her stool, she tried not to touch anything. "I'll stick with wine."

Billie's lopsided smile went large at the sight of her friends. "What about you, Jen?"

"Uh, just water," Jen said, waving her hand as if calling a time-out. "I've had enough."

"Don't be a pussy, Jen. It's you we're celebrating," Tammy sneered before nodding at Billie. "She'll have what I'm having."

"I gotta open up tomorrow. I don't want to do that bleary-eyed."

"Killjoy," Tammy spat.

Kaitlin surveyed the crowd. "We can't all drink like sailors, Tammy."

Billie got their drinks up, placing an extra tall glass of water in front of Jen. The poor girl's eyes were already droopy. Tammy was jawing up the patron on her right.

The four of them were an odd clutch of friends. Jen she had known for dog's years. Tammy, the photographer who lived like a rock star, they had met after moving to the city. Kaitlin, prissy and proper, came tagging along after Tammy one night.

"Here we are again," Tammy said, clinking her glass against Jen's. "Just like always. Cheers, Jennifart."

Jen held back. "Wait, Billie doesn't have a drink."

"Pour yourself one, kiddo." Tammy wagged her chin at the draught taps.

Billie waved the notion away. "I'm working."

"C'mon. Half a glass. Enough to make a toast."

"She won't let up until you do," Kaitlin suggested.

Billie relented, pouring three fingers of pilsner into a glass and chinking it against her companion's glassware.

"Atta girl," said Tammy. "Wait, what are we toasting?"

The bar had become a defacto meeting place for the ladies, on their way out somewhere or swinging back for last call. Which was great, Billie loved seeing her friends but she was on the other side of the bar while the three of them blew off steam.

They worked days, Billie told herself, you work nights. No biggie.

Still, it gnawed at her. Something had changed within the foursome, an unmentioned but acutely felt shift in their relationship. The three of them were busy charging ahead with life while Billie slogged it out four nights a week behind the bar. After a year of planning and prepping, Jen had finally opened her shop. Tammy was busier than ever, shooting photos for an ever growing list of clients. Kaitlin was getting married next spring, the first of their core group to take that plunge.

Billie was being left behind, the distance between her and the ladies growing farther all the time. They partied while she worked and she slept when they fought the morning commute. Time and circumstance were pulling them apart.

How long would it be before they parted ways altogether? How long before they stopped coming to this skeezy bar in favour of some more upscale place? The grimy charm was wearing thin, especially on Kaitlin. A flutter of panic rumbled through her guts at the thought of drifting apart and along with that came a hasty idea. "We should go away this weekend. To aunt Maggie's for some beach time. Like we used to."

Crickets. She watched all three of them stop cold, sentences dropping away unfinished. Excuses rushing in to replace them.

"Can't," Tammy said. "I got two shoots to do this weekend."

Jen gave a mock-pout. "I'd love a weekend at Maggie's but I can't. Not with the shop finally opened."

"I'm sure I'm busy." Kaitlin dismissed.

"Sure." Billie became busy restocking the clean glassware. "It was a stupid thought."

"It's not stupid. It just needs some planning." Jen stirred the ice in her glass. "I'd kill for a beach day at your aunt's."

Her aunt Maggie's house, situated on a mile long stretch of beach, had become a cheap getaway for them over the last few years. Aunt Maggie frowned on all the drinking but she adored the company. The woman fawned over the girls, referring to them as her wayward daughters. Billie was about to suggest another weekend when she noticed a man at the end of the bar flagging her down.

"What can I get you?" she asked the man.

He looked over the selection of taps. "What do you have that passes for decent lager?"

Billie set a glass under one of the taps. "I like this one."

"Ta," he said. "And a sidekick for it too, yeah? Single malt."

Billie hazarded a guess at his accent as she poured. English, maybe Irish. She wasn't good with accents. She felt the man watching her, triggering her radar for potential trouble. In a minute, he'd hit on her, trying to charm her with lame banter. It was a hazard that came with the job.

The man scanned down the other drinkers at the bar. "Your friends are carrying on without you," he said.

The trick to handling chatty men was to never give up anything personal. Keep it polite but vague. Never reveal any detail that they could latch onto and prolong the conversation. Billie replied "Everyone's a friend. Long as they keep drinking and don't bother me."

"Course," he said. "That means we're chums, yeah?"

Billie slid the drinks before him. "You're still on the bubble."

A round of laughter burst from the ladies, momentarily overwhelming the music. The man studied Billie as she watched her friends. "That happens to you a lot, doesn't it? Being left on the sidelines."

The question seemed barbed. She flung it back. "Nope. Too busy working."

"That's the part that mystifies." Loosening his tie, he turned and scanned the room again. "Why are you working here?"

"Everybody's gotta work."

"Sure," he said. "But why not do what you're meant to do?"

The glass she held under the tap slipped a little. Something was off. She had kept it vague but he seemed to latch onto something personal anyway. Without turning, she took a second look at him. A little older than her and not bad looking but something seemed off. Despite the tie, he didn't look business. His sleeves were rolled up, like he was used to getting his hands dirty. He seemed shrugged together at the last minute, like he'd just rolled out of bed in those same clothes and came straight here. The phrase 'snake oil' popped into her head.

Playing along would only exacerbate the problem but she couldn't help herself. Not after a question like that. "Oh. And what am I meant to be doing?"

"You're taking the piss now," he guffawed. "What is all this then? A cover? The Daily Planet with taps?"

She didn't know what he was talking about. Was that British humour or was he just a mental case? His smile was lopsided, she noted. Like hers. "I've been doing this awhile. And I like it just fine."

The pint was halfway to his lips when it stopped and stayed there as he blinked at her. The gape of surprise passed and his eyes narrowed on her. "You honestly don't know, do you? Here I thought this was just an act, you playing dumb and whatnot."

"Hey, mind your manners, chum. Or leave." Billie took a step back. This was giving her a headache and she didn't want to play his game anymore, whatever it was. If he was trying to pick her up, he had a strange way of going about it.

He rubbed his eyes, as if her headache was infecting him. "I've spent months tracking you down, luv. Don't tell me it was all for nothing."

"Five bucks for the pints," she said. "I'll spot you the scotch if you leave right now."

"Christ. That's quite a feat you managed." He reached into a pocket but instead of cash, he came up with a crushed cigarette pack. He shook one out, clamped it in his teeth and dug for a lighter.

"You can't smoke in here."

He glanced at the other patrons. "They won't say anything."

Everyone turned at the snap of his Zippo as he lit up but no one said a word. Even her friends kept mum, instead harshing looks at Billie to do something about it.

"Just so we're clear," he said through the smoke billowing around him. "You don't have something on the side? Another line of work?"

She wished the bar employed a bouncer. She wanted this creep gone but the pain in her head notched up the dial so fast she closed her eyes. It had been a while since she'd had a migraine come on so fast.

"Billie?" Jen's voice cut through the clatter of pain.

"Look at me." The voice with the accent.

Billie let her eyes slit open. The dull glow of the tea candles was blinding and too powerful. The creep at the bar materialized through the haze.

He took a lengthy haul on the damn cigarette, then wagged a finger at her and said "You don't know, do you? Jesus, girlie. How long have you been keeping your eyes shut?"

Her eyes were open. If only a slit, she thought. What was he talking about? Why doesn't he just go away?

She heard Tammy's voice. Something rude as she approached the creep, Jen crowding in as if they were about to take the creep down. Kaitlin, she wasn't surprised to see, stayed perched on her stool and watched.

The man downed the whiskey and rose from his stool, tossing a crumpled bill onto the bar. He looked at Billie and said "I'm not finished with you."

He made for the door, Tammy cursing him out the whole way. Jen came around the bar and gripped her elbow to keep her upright. "Easy," Jen said. "Are you all right?"

"I'm fine," Billie flushed. "No. I'm not. Watch the bar."

With that Billie spun around to the sink behind her and retched loudly into the stained basin. Three people at the counter collected their drinks and fled.

3

THE DRAG OF the wind cleared her head as Billie shot down the highway with the windows down and the music up. She almost felt normal again.

The migraine that came out of the blue the night before had been replaced with a numbing hazy sensation that Billie described as 'the fog'. The two had gone hand-in-hand her whole life, the headaches followed by a deadening numbness. She never seemed to get shed of them. It was partly to blame for Billie's poor schooling in the past, her inability to focus.

After ralphing in the bar, she assured Jen that she was fine and slogged through the rest of the shift. There was nothing to do except push through it, no matter how foggy she felt.

The fog was still there when she woke this morning. She thought back to the creep at the bar who had unsettled her, as if he had brought it on. She got all kinds of crazy at the bar, most were easily handled but once in a blue moon she caught a real humdinger who threw her off her game.

Drawing back the curtains she noted a serenely blue sky and decided it was time to get the hell out of Dodge. So what if the ladies couldn't make it. She'd go to Maggie's by herself. All she needed was some wheels.

Bruce lived on the floor below her, a crotchety ex-mechanic in his sixties whose eyesight was rapidly deteriorating. Bruce also owned the garage next door where he kept a collection of old cars. He and Billie had an arrangement. She agreed to do his shopping for him if she could borrow one of his vintage rides from time to time.

Answering her knock, Bruce squinted up at her. "Where's all the damn soup gone?" he gruffed.

"I don't know," Billie said, accustomed to the older man's bark. "You must have eaten it all."

"A dozen cans?" he scowled. "I think that Philipino woman down the hall sneaks in here when I'm gone and pilfers my cupboards."

Billie cocked an eyebrow at him. "Mrs. Santino? No way."

"Are you going shopping?"

"Not today," Billie said. "But I need to borrow some wheels. Can I take the Citroen?"

"No, you can't take the Cit." He reached over and took a set of keys hanging near the door and dropped them in her palm. "Take the Rover. I just replaced the manifold on it."

"Aw, come on, Bruce. When are you gonna let me take the

Citroen out?"

"When you're old enough," he grumbled, shooing her on. "Be careful with the Rover. And bring back some soup this time."

The Range Rover was bigger than what she was used to but once she was outside of the city, Billie had eased into it and rolled through the small towns on her way south. Drifting past fields of corn and tobacco, she hummed into Norfolk County and coasted onto the causeway of the sand spit. Her favourite part of the drive, a long stretch of pavement with the marsh on her right and the smell of the lake drifting in port-side. Everything felt different here, unlike any other part of the province. Long Point was a beach town built on a finger of sand jutting a mile out into Lake Erie. A summer town that came to life when the vacationers returned to dig their toes into the white sand of its immense beach.

Rumbling slow along the boulevard, Billie took in the newly renovated cottages and the older sun-faded homes of the permanent residents. Although the summer season had kicked in, it never got too busy for the place to lose its breezy feel. She pulled the Rover into the sandy driveway of the woman who had raised her since she was eight years old.

The screen door twinged open on its rusty spring and a short woman in her fifties stepped onto the faded stoop. "Hey kiddo," Aunt Maggie trilled in her sing-song way.

"Hi." Billie wrapped her arms around the woman and

squeezed. The familiar smell of lilac perfume hit her nose, triggering memories. Her aunt felt slighter in her embrace, a little less there than last time. "Sorry this is so last minute. I just wanted to get away."

Aunt Maggie brushed it off with a wave. "Anytime is good with me, you know that. What is that you're driving?"

"Another one of Bruce's toys. It's English."

"Hmm. They drive on the wrong side of the road there, you know." Maggie swept her niece up in another hug. "Let's get your stuff."

"I didn't bring much," Billie said, fetching a single bag from the backseat.

Her aunt's smile drooped a little. "You're not staying long?"

"Can't." Billie flung her bag over her shoulder and lifted out a grocery bag. "Here, I stopped at the fruit stand on the way."

"You didn't have to do that, honey. I have more than enough."

"The cherries are in."

"Ooh," Maggie said, peering into the plastic bag. "They came in early this year. Come on."

The house was small, a clapboard bungalow originally built as a summer home. The big windows at the front faced south onto the lake without letting direct sunlight into the house. Everything seemed the same, Billie noted, from the dried flowers strung over the kitchen window to the small crosses above the lintel of all three bedroom doors. Some small comfort to a place that resisted change. She dropped her bag by the door while Maggie rinsed the cherries and brought them out to the patio.

"I'd hoped you were bringing the girls with you," Maggie said, settling into a chair under the big umbrella. "It's been ages since I've seen them."

"They couldn't make it." Billie crossed to the railing and looked out over the beach. An expanse of near white sand stretching out in both directions. The sound of the waves immediately slowed her pulse with its deep rhythm. "They're all so busy these days. I hardly see them anymore."

"Even Jen?"

"Yeah. She practically lives at the shop now."

Maggie chewed up a cherry and worked the pit out. "I'm sure she'll have more time for you when she settles in. Starting up a business is tough. Good for her."

"I know." Billie felt a sting. Was her aunt rubbing her nose in Jen's ambition or was she just feeling overly sensitive about the whole thing? "It's just weird. I feel like the loser in the group now. The charity case."

"Oh, I'm sure they don't think that. Why would they?"

Billie turned her gaze back to the lake where a small boy was letting the string out on a blue kite. It held fast in the steady wind coming off the lake. "How's the knee?"

"It flared up two days ago. So bad I could barely get down the front step." Maggie dropped another pit onto the folded paper towel. A tumble of them piling up fast, staining the paper red.

"What about you? Any episodes recently?"

"I was on a streak," Billie replied. "Six months without an incident." The episodes her aunt referred to were the headaches and foggy spells that had plagued Billie for as long as she could remember. Misdiagnosed over the years as Maggie dragged her to one specialist after another looking for a cause or a treatment for a condition that, at times, left Billie as unresponsive as a shell-shock victim. Staring at the wall with a gaped jaw and a thread of drool running down her chin. The cause of the attacks were never determined. Bipolar, a chemical unbalance, attention deficit disorder; the list went on but none of the diagnoses ever stuck. In school, she had been written off as having a learning disability.

"Eat some of these before I polish the whole thing off," Maggie said, holding up the bowl of cherries. "What broke the streak?"

Billie plucked the stem from a cherry. "Came on last night. Bad one too."

"Do you know what brought it on?"

"Do I ever know?" Billie tasted a burst of tart sweetness as her teeth bit into the fruit. The triggers for her episodes remained elusive and arbitrary. When she was younger, Maggie used to document each one, trying to get a fix on what brought them on but no pattern ever emerged. Eventually she gave up, they both did. Billie thought back to the Englishman in the bar last night. If anything, he seemed to trigger it with his weirdo questions but that made no sense. The foggy spells were never instigated by a person, that much she knew.

Maggie smoothed the hair from Billie's eyes and tucked it behind her ear. A gesture so familiar and routine that neither of them noticed anymore. "You look a little pale. Are you sleeping enough?"

"I am. Honest." She couldn't help the sharpness to her tone. A tiny signal, shorthand for her aunt to let it go.

"Okay." Maggie brushed her hands with a flourish and pushed the bowl away. "Are you going for a swim?"

"I think I'll just get my feet wet."

"All right. You splash around, I will prep dinner."

"Let me do that." Billie watched her aunt push herself up out of her chair with what seemed like more effort than last time.

"Please," Maggie huffed. "I never cook anymore. Go. You can work the grill. Deal?"

"Deal." She noted the uneven dip to her aunt's step as she went back inside the house. The bad knee was getting worse and Billie speculated on how much pain Maggie was in. Her aunt had an inordinate tolerance for it and she disliked doctors. Especially since Uncle Larry died. Maggie was notorious for claiming that she was perfectly capable of remedying her own aches and pains and that suffering wasn't always a bad thing. The Catholic in her coloured these notions. Suffering was part of life. Don't complain, just carry on.

Leaving her shoes on the deck, she walked down to the water. The sand was already blistering hot and the cool water was a relief. She watched it lap over her ankles, feeling the sand push away under her heels. Out on the lake, a kite-boarder skimmed over the waves. Beyond that, the horizon line of water and sky.

A ripple buzzed overhead. Billie looked up to see a kite kamikaze dive into the beach. A sharp snap as it hit the sand. The boy she had seen earlier ran up and lifted his kite from the sand. It dangled from his hand like a broken puppet and his face soured like he was about to cry.

"Can you fix it?" Billie called to him.

The boy squinted up at her then went back to contemplating the flapping thing in his hand.

Billie waded up out of the water toward him. She could already see that the cross tree had snapped loose from it plastic mooring. "The wind can change her mind on you pretty quick out here. One minute you're sailing, the next you're crashed."

The boy said nothing and Billie wondered for a moment if he didn't speak English. Foreign vacationers were not rare to Long Point beaches. Planting her knees in the sand, she smiled at the boy to disarm any worries he might have. "Maybe we can put it back together."

The boy looked at her, then to the limp kite, and then back to Billie again, as if trying to gauge whether she was up to the task. After a moment, he held it out to her.

"I used to love kites." Billie took the bundle of plastic

material and sticks from him. Fanning it out, she inspected the illustration on the sail. A green dragon. "These pieces usually just snap back into place."

The spine and cross tree slotted together easily enough but the plastic cap that stretched the sail over the frame had slipped off one end. Pulling it tight to slip back on, the plastic sheeting ripped and the cap tore off completely. Billie's face fell this time. There was no way to fix it now.

"Ah shoot. I'm sorry. I guess I pulled too hard." She looked at the little boy and saw his face contorting, trying hard not to cry. Billie panicked, needing to waylay the boy's tears. "I'm such a klutz. I'll buy you a new one, okay? They have great kites at the corner store."

The boy took the kite from her hand and walked away.

"I'm sorry! Which cottage are you in. We'll ask your parents first."

The lad didn't even look back, trudging quickly across the hot sand with the broken kite trailing behind him. Billie didn't know what to do. Chasing after him might make it worse. She'd done it again. Trying to help, she had made everything worse and now this little guy had to go home and explain to his parents how some weirdo broke his toy. She kept her eyes on him, hoping to see what cottage he'd turn to. The pale blue one with the white gingerbread trim. The McNiven's place, often rented to vacationers during the high season. Maybe she could knock on their door later and explain the whole thing to the poor kid's parents.

Helpful to a fault. Something Maggie used to tease her about.

4

"RITA AND TOM moved on," Aunt Maggie said.

A late dinner on the patio. A seafood stew Maggie had wanted to try. Billie admonished her not to go to so much trouble but Maggie dismissed her objections, making a large pot of the stuff so the girl could take some home. They made dinner together, her aunt catching Billie up on the local news.

"I'm sure they got a pretty penny for it too," Maggie said as they carried plates out to the deck. "Despite all the repairs that place needed."

"I thought Tom was dead set against selling," Billie replied.

"Rita wanted to be closer to her grandchildren. And she wasn't going to take no for an answer."

Billie laid the plates on the wobbly table and ducked back to get their drinks. "Have you met the new owners?"

"No. The realtor assured me it was a family but that doesn't mean anything. It could be a family of neanderthals for all I know."

"I'm sure they'll be fine." Billie watched the steam rise from her bowl and tucked in. She nodded in approval. "Not bad. It's got some kick to it."

"Did I overdo it with the chili peppers?"

"Nah, its perfect," Billie said. "I like a good kick."

Maggie flourished her spoon in the air. "Do you remember the Morrisons? Doug and Emma?"

Billie nodded. "Yeah. Emily's parents, right?"

"Yes. Emily's getting married in the fall. And we got an invite to the wedding. October first. So mark it in your calendar."

"Wow. I never thought Emily would ever get hitched. She was so gung-ho on academia."

"I guess her priorities changed. Life has a habit of doing that." Maggie tilted her head to one side, like a thought had just occurred to her. "Say, how's that boy you were seeing. Ryan? The one I met at Christmas?"

Ryan was a self-absorbed poser who sucked the oxygen out of any room with his pathological need for attention. One who enjoyed twisted head-games to boot. Billie had walked away with a few scars after that encounter. "I'm sure he's fine," she lied. "He aways looked out for himself. We broke up in April."

"Oh? I'm sorry. He seemed like such a nice young man. Even with all those tattoos."

Billie plucked another mussel from the bowl and forked out the meat. "Do you know the people renting McNiven's cottage?"

"No. In fact, I haven't seen anyone there since the May long weekend. Why?"

"No reason." She wasn't in the mood to relate the story about the kite fiasco.

Maggie pushed her plate away and leaned back with a sigh. "So? Are you seeing anyone new?"

"Nope," Billie said. Ryan, or the emotional leech as she preferred to think of him, had left her drained and a little horse-shy. "Not really."

"No one on the horizon, even?"

Aunt Maggie, bless her heart, was only looking out for her. Having raised her since she was eight, Billie knew that Mags worried about her like any mother would. She would sleep easier if she knew Billie was with someone. She'd sleep like a babe if her only niece and ward was safely married off. "Nah. Just not in that head space right now."

"Just remember," Maggie said, "one bad one doesn't spoil the bunch."

Grasping for some cue to switch topics on, Billie looked up at the sunset. The sun had already dipped below the western treeline and dusk had painted the sky with mottles of dull pink and purple as night came on. Rising above the trees was a cloud of dots, darting and arcing through the air. "The bats are out," she said. "Dinner time for them too."

Maggie glanced up without interest. "Did I tell you I had one of the little devils in the house? God knows how he got inside. I was falling asleep in front of the TV when I heard something knocking around the window. Scared the hell out of me."

"What did you do?"

"Went after it with the broom," Maggie said proudly. Her aunt was no wilting flower when it came to wildlife invading her home. "It got tangled in the drapes. I tore the whole curtain down and tossed it outside. In the morning it was gone."

Billie raised her glass in mock salute. "You got grit. I would've ran screaming."

"So what happened with Ryan?" Maggie asked. "Did you break it off or did he?"

"Me." She kept her eyes from rolling at her aunt's persistence. "He was a bit of a Jekyll and Hyde. Nice in public, not so much behind closed doors."

"I'm prying. I'm sorry."

"It's okay." Another shrug rolled off her shoulders. She drew back a few strands of hair at her temple. "He left me with a few grey hairs. I couldn't believe it."

"We all go grey eventually, honey."

"I'm not even thirty."

"Your mother went grey at that age too."

Like a needle scraping across vinyl, everything stopped. Billie's glass froze halfway to her lips. "She did?"

Maggie stood up and began collecting dishes. "Do you want desert? I think I have a little ice cream in the freezer."

"What? Oh, no thanks."

Her aunt bustled back inside the house and Billie heard the tap run. She picked her jaw up from the table. Her mother was a topic rarely broached anymore. When her aunt had taken her in after that awful day all those years ago, Maggie had done so wholeheartedly, sparing neither hardship nor expense to comfort Billie and surround her with love. Sometimes too much love, if that was possible, smothering the girl at times and in those times Billie would push back or withdraw into her own world. It was something she would come to regret, realizing now just how much her aunt had sacrificed to somehow patch over the unfillable void left by an absent mother.

Maggie would have moved heaven and earth to protect her niece but the one thing they did not do was talk about her mother. The first two years under her aunt's roof, Billie had been unable to mention her mother at all, let alone actively discuss her. Billie had barely spoken at all that first year, communicating through an improvised shorthand of nods and shrugs.

The few real memories she had of her mother began to crumble, leaving Billie to wonder what was truth and what her mind had improvised to fill the gaps. Had her mom always been crazy, she'd ask aunt Maggie, or did having a kid make her screwy? She remembered people being wary around her mother, almost afraid of her. Even the people who came to the house. Was that part real, she'd ask, or had she just imagined it?

Maggie kept her answers short, neither elaborating nor expanding on the subject. Billie would stomp off in a huff, never stopping to consider that the subject of her mother's death was painful to anyone but herself. Later, Billie felt ashamed when she realized that within the scope of her own tragedy, her aunt had lost her only sister.

The facts she possessed were few. Mary Agnes Culpepper disappeared from her home in the small town of Poole, Ontario, the victim of a violent assault and abduction. Her body was never found. Her ex-husband, Franklin Riddel, was suspected for the crime but he too had disappeared. Mary Culpepper worked as a medium and tarot reader. She was 29 years old, survived by a daughter and a sister. There was no more information beyond that. No one was ever charged in the case of her disappearance.

She let it go after that and the memory of mom slipped further and further away. And now, out of the blue, this scrap of information. A detail, nothing more, but it rang louder than bombs. Her mother had gone gray before the age of thirty. She didn't live to see thirty either.

Maggie stayed busy in the kitchen and didn't venture out again except to say goodnight and gently suggest that Billie not stay up too late. Billie kissed her aunt goodnight and refilled her wine glass. The night air was warm and the strong breeze kept the mosquitoes at a tolerable level. After a while she fetched the heavy gauge flashlight from under the sink and settled back into her chair on the patio. Aiming the powerful beam of light up toward the swaying boughs of the overhanging willow tree, she watched the bats flash and dip through the artificial light like dark pixies from some unread storybook.

~

Awoken the next morning by a tap on her bedroom door, Billie propped up one elbow and tried to focus her blurry eyes.

Maggie stuck her head in the room. "I'm off. It's Sunday."

"I'm up." Billie swung her legs out of bed and waited out the dizzy spell.

"Breakfast is on the table." Maggie glanced at her watch then looked at her niece with a slight sparkle of hope. "I don't suppose you'd like to come to church this morning? It's been a while since you last took in a mass."

"Uhm, I'm okay. I'll just make you late anyway."

"I can wait."

"You go ahead." Billie shuffled up to the door. "Let me say goodbye. I gotta head back."

"So soon? I thought we had the day together?"

"Can't. I gotta work tonight." She gave her aunt a tight squeeze and peck on the cheek. "See ya later."

"You too. Bring the girls next time, huh? Tell them my door's always open."

"I will."

Her aunt left the house and Billie staggered to the kitchen table where a full breakfast was laid out. Bacon and eggs kept warm under a plate. Fanned out over the edge of the plate were three pieces of strawberry, sliced sideways to resemble little hearts. A small touch that her aunt had added to her plate since the day she had taken her in.

An hour later, Billie had dressed, cleaned the kitchen and climbed back into the borrowed Range Rover. She stopped at the corner store to look over the selection of kites they had. Wavering between one that had a red eagle and another with a stylized lightning bolt, she chose the eagle one and drove two blocks down the strip before turning into the driveway of McNiven's pale blue cottage with the white trim.

Clutching the kite in her hand, she knocked on the door but was surprised when Mrs. McNiven answered her knock.

"Oh hi Billie," Mrs. McNiven said. She held a broom, cleaning the cottage before the next set of renters arrived. "How have you been?"

"I've been good, Mrs. McNiven." Billie looked past the woman, trying to get a look inside the cottage. "You?"

"Busy. Summer season and all." The woman's eyes went down to the kite in Billie's hand. "What can I do for you?"

"I was looking for the family who's staying here. The boy, actually. Do you know his name?"

"Oh, they left last night. Late too."

Something dropped in her stomach. Billie looked at the bright red kite. "Damn."

"They seemed like a very quiet family. Not much for conversation."

"The boy. I wanted to give him this." She looked out at the road, as if she could spot their car. "I don't suppose they're coming back this summer for another stay?"

"Not that I know of, dear." Mrs. McNiven glanced at the kite again. "It's very nice. I'm sure the boy would have liked it."

"I'll never know. Thanks, Mrs. M."

The woman waved goodbye and Billie went back to the Rover. She stood there for a moment, unsure of what to do with the kite now. She tossed it into the backseat finally, climbed under the wheel and drove away.

5

BILLIE FLUNG THE trunk open and reached for a hard shell case of camera gear. "What's this event for?"

"Art gala," Tammy answered, adjusting something on her vintage Hasselblad. "It's their big fundraiser."

The parking lot at the pier was crammed with expensive cars. Billie and Tammy lugged the gear into the park where strings of paper lanterns floated over the tables and the flowers while the upper crust art patrons mingled about with champagne flutes in hand. The strains of Dixie jazz drifted across the harbour from a band playing under a gazebo on the wooden pier.

Tammy was here to shoot the event for a local paper, documenting the glitterati in their natural environment. Watching her friend work with a camera, Billie had developed an interest in photography two years ago. Another attempt to find a passion to follow, a vocation to pursue. It had ended up as a minor hobby. Still, she thought when Tammy asked for help, she might learn a thing or two.

"I'm gonna work through the crowd first," Tammy said as they strode into the thick of the crowd. "Then I'll get some wider shots from the pier when the speeches start."

Billie scanned the party-goers around her. Primped up and turned out in their finery, they seemed like an entirely different species. "How long is the reception part?"

"About an hour. Hold up." Tammy dug through the bag on Billie's shoulder and swapped out cameras. "Plenty of time to get what I need before the jet set get trashed. Where are you gonna be?"

"I'll plunk down over there," Billie nodded to the railing near the water's edge. "Out of the way."

"All right. I might need to change cameras again." Striding into the crowd, Tammy hollered back. "See if you can snag us some of that champagne."

Lugging the camera bag to the railing, Billie hunkered down on the concrete step. The breeze off the water was cool against her back, turning her sweaty skin clammy. She watched her friend work through the crowd.

Tammy was an adorable oddball but the one thing Billie admired about her was her passion for the photographic image. She was always experimenting or getting into complicated situations to find the most interesting angle. Sometimes dangerously so. Tammy had fallen from ledges, scraped her legs open on barbed wire and had her arm singed badly on a hot exhaust pipe. All of it dismissed as part of the job chasing the right frame. Her passion was infectious, which is what led to Billie's own interest in it. Tammy, it turned out, was the secret ingredient. Left to her own devices, Billie found her interest in cameras dwindled quickly away.

At the very least, she could cross photography off her list of potential vocations to pursue. One more down, a million more to go through.

A server with a tray of champagne flutes buzzed through the nearby tables. Billie tried to flag her down but the server ignored her, clearly marking Billie as a party-crasher.

"She pegged you as a fence-jumper." A man's voice, coming from her left.

Turning around, it took a moment for Billie to place the man's face. The creep from the other night. The English dude in the rumpled tie. "You need to tackle those bloody people if you want a drink," he said.

She got to her feet. "Oh come on. Are you stalking me?"

"Maybe. But not the way you mean." He raised his arms. Two flutes in one hand and a full champagne bottle in the other. "Can we talk?"

"Nothing to talk about." Billie hooked the camera bag back onto her shoulder, ready to stomp away.

"Hang about. Here, take one of these."

He held out the flutes to her. Billie didn't move but then he waved the glasses at her, as if it were urgent. She took one.

"Let me do-over the intros, yeah?" He tipped the bottle and filled the glass. It foamed up and ran down his fingers. "My name's Gantry."

"You suck at pouring champagne, Gantry." Billie shook the sticky wine from her hand. "What kind of name is that anyway?"

"The one I got stuck with," he grinned. "You're Billie, yeah? Billie Culpepper."

Again, a prickly sensation tingled her arms. Trouble. "How do you know that?"

"Wouldn't be much of a stalker if I didn't glean that basic information, would I?"

He was grinning but she didn't find it very funny. Listen to your gut, she scolded herself. "Look, what ever you're selling, I don't want it. Just leave me alone."

"I just want to talk,. He held up both hands as if to show that he wasn't hiding anything up his sleeves. "I swear."

Billie hesitated, then grumbled "You have two minutes."

"Alright then." He eased down onto the step she had just vacated and set the bottle beside him. "How much do you know about your mum?"

Not what she expected, to say the least. Who did this creep think he was, bringing that up? "What does she have to do with this?"

"Everything. Sort of starts with her." He fished out a cigarette and lit up.

A terrible thought popped into Billie's mind. "Did you know

her?"

"Nope. Never met her," he said. "So you don't remember much about her?"

"She disappeared when I a kid."

Gantry leaned forward, intrigued by what she had said. "How old were you when that happened?"

"Eight."

He mulled that over, as if something loose had clicked into place. "Yeah. That makes sense."

"None of this makes sense." She was getting bored of the whole mystery act he was putting on. "Look, if you know something, then just spit it out. I hate games."

"I'm not playing at one, luv." Gantry puffed a smoke ring. "We just need to take this slow. Because what I'm about to tell you requires an open mind."

~

Tammy checked the time on her phone and scanned through the schmoozefest playing out on the harbour lawn. She'd snapped over a dozen of the pretty people but none of them had any zap. Zap being the photo that would relay the tone of the event. Sometimes she got lucky and found the right person or the right mix of people that captured the event. Other times, she struck out completely and had to roll with what she had.

Plenty of people had twigged to the camera in her hand,

smiling or flipping their hair in a sly attempt to catch her attention. Photo sluts, as she termed them. The vain and the narcissistic who loved nothing more than to have their picture taken. These were the polar opposite of what she was looking for. She scanned the faces for someone who turned away from her camera. Ready to throw in the towel and move out to the pier for the wider vista shots, she stopped and craned her neck to see over the mob of teeth flashers. Paydirt.

The couple looked a little more real to Tammy's sensibilities. The woman was clearly part of the scene but more on the art side than that of a patron. She was beautiful but in a way that suggested something more than what she wore or how her hair was done. Her date was handsome enough but a little rough looking. He seemed bemused by the crowd around him, as if he'd wound up at the wrong shindig.

Tammy wormed through the stiffs toward her target, the camera raised up. "Hi. Can I take your picture? It's for the Meridian."

The woman immediately waved her off. "No thanks," she said.

Her date pulled her back and locked his arm round hers. "Oh come on. It'll be fun."

"No, it won't," she said. Then she turned to Tammy. "No offence."

"No worries," Tammy smiled. She kept the camera poised to snap the shot. The man was willing, his date just needed a nudge.

"Can I be honest? You two are the only interesting people I've seen all night."

"Go ahead," the man told her, keeping his date close. "Pay no attention to miss *'I-hate-my-picture'* over here."

The woman scowled but stayed put, humouring her date. Tammy got closer and started shooting. "What are your names?"

The woman was about to speak when her date suddenly jolted out of frame, peering off to something behind Tammy. He blinked, as if he couldn't believe what he was seeing. "Holy shit."

"What is it?" the woman asked, perturbed.

"Stay here."

The woman clutched his arm. "Raymond, you're off the clock, remember? Call the office, let them handle it."

"I can't." He gently pried her hand away. "Wanted suspect, twelve 'o clock."

Tammy glanced over her shoulder, trying to see what the fuss was all about but saw nothing out of the ordinary. What were they talking about?

"Who?" the woman demanded.

"Gantry."

Her face blanched and she gripped his arm tighter. "No. Call the office, let them handle it."

"He'll sniff the cruisers from a mile away and vanish again." The man pried himself away but looked his date square in the eye. "He's not expecting me. Call Odinbeck, tell him what's

51

happening."

The man hurried past Tammy and elbowed through the crowd. The woman was already dialling her phone. "Get me the desk sergeant on duty," she hissed into the phone, panic rising in her voice. "Tell them Detective Mockler has gone after a suspect. A dangerous one."

The term *detective* rang through Tammy's ears. The guy was a cop? She spun around to pinpoint said detective rustling through the throng of champagne-swillers, charging at the man they had both described as a suspect. The man they were talking about was standing near the rails by the water's edge.

And he was deep in conversation with Billie.

~

The man wasn't making sense and Billie couldn't decipher a word of what Gantry was saying. Pressure was building in her head, like a storm threatening to pour down and it threw a haze over everything around her. The fog was coming on, like it did last time she had spoken to this man.

"Stop. I need to sit down."

Gantry rose up and took her arm. "It's happening right now. And you don't even realize it. Do you?"

"Just shut up for a minute," she said. She tried to snap her thoughts back into place. He was about to tell her something about her mother, wasn't he?

A bark cut through the lazy air, sharp and startling. One word.

"Gantry!"

They both looked up to see a man charging up the path toward them. A brick wall of a guy with pure venom in his eyes. It froze Billie's marrow until she realized the menace was directed at the Englishman beside her.

"Oh shite," Gantry hissed.

"Step away from the girl, Gantry!" the big man barked. "Get down and assume the position."

Billie felt Gantry release her elbow. The air felt charged and electric, the threat of violence humming strong. Why was Gantry smiling?

"You look off-duty, Mockler," Gantry sneered. "You don't want to mess up that cheap suit, do you?"

The big man locked his eyes on Billie. "Miss, step away."

"What's going on?" she stuttered.

Gantry seethed through clenched teeth. "You just cost me work hours."

The other man moved in, slow and cautious. "Get on the ground! Do it now."

"Piss off."

Gantry feinted left then bolted right, knocking the glass from Billie's hand. The other man charged like a linebacker and lunged at the Englishman. Both men plowed straight into her.

Bille walloped hard against the railing, her head ringing off the metal, and then the railing crumbled away. Billie felt herself falling. Everything went very dark and very cold when she hit the water. The deep end.

Tammy booked it hard, calling her friend's name only to see Billie sail over the edge into the harbour. The two men tumbled over one another, fighting and cursing until the big guy she had talked to earlier bucked like a bronco. The skinnier man lost his balance and fell into the drink too.

"Billie!" Tammy ran to the edge of the pier where the railing had fallen away and looked down. The water lapped dark and still. Billie was nowhere to be seen. Unhooking the camera strap from around her neck, Tammy was kicking off her heels when she saw that the big guy had beat her to it. His shoes and jacket were left on the pier as he lunged over the side. His frame snapped in a graceful dive and he slipped into the water with barely a splash.

The man's date came up alongside Tammy and now both of them peered down into the black water but nothing moved. There was no sign of any of them.

6

SQUARES OF WHITE floated before her eyes. It was a long time before Billie realized that what she was seeing were ceiling tiles. The crappy soundproof kind you find in an office or a hospital.

Hospital.

Leaning up one elbow, the room swam with a seasick lurch and Billie flopped her head back down onto the pillow. Everything hurt at once and she wondered how badly she was injured. Waiting for the vertigo to pass, she unscrambled her thoughts. She was in a hospital room. She must have been hurt. How?

The fishy smell of Lake Ontario. Gantry. Then some bruiser appeared out of nowhere and knocked her into the drink. Just the thought of dropping into that polluted stew of cold lake water gave her the willies.

She patted the bed with her hands, looking for the button to summon a nurse. It dangled loose down the side of the bed. She pressed it. No tell-tale buzz or ping but she hoped it got someone's attention.

Eons later, a nurse whooshed into the room. She looked bored to tears. "Hello," she said. "How do you feel?"

"Like shit."

"I'm sure you do. Can you tell me your name?"

Billie glanced about the room. "Isn't it on a chart or something?"

"I want to know if you know your name, honey." The slimmest of smiles touched the nurse's lips. "Or your age, phone number? Details."

"Billie Culpepper. I live on Barton East. I'm twenty-nine."

"Billie?" The nurse frowned and reached for the chart. "Says here you're Sybil. Is Billie the short form?"

"Yes. What happened?"

"You drowned, honey." The nurse set the clipboard down and turned for the door. "Let me find a doctor. I'll be right back."

"Wait," Billie called out but the woman didn't reappear.

Drowned? Was the woman pulling her leg? Shouldn't she be dead? Maybe she was still asleep and this was just some stupid dream. The urge to go home was so immediate it felt like panic fluttering against her sternum.

It was a moment before she noticed that someone had entered her room. She hoped it was the doctor but the man's white smock marked him as another patient. He stood hunched over, staring at the wall as if entranced. Billie tilted up to see what was so interesting but there was nothing but a bare wall.

"Hello," she said.

The man shifted a little but didn't look at her. She didn't like him in her room. She always attracted the crazies. "Hey," she ventured. "Are you lost?"

"They won't let me outta here," he said. "Fucking doctors think they know everything."

"Call the nurse. She'll help you."

"I just wanna go home," he grumbled. "I fucking hate hospitals."

Okey-dokey. Now he was officially freaking her out and she wanted him gone. "No one likes hospitals."

"You should get out. While you can." He finally turned to look at her, rotating around toward the door, and as he did so, Billie saw the immense splash of red on his smock. So much blood it almost looked fake. It dripped from the hem, leaving droplets on the floor.

"Oh my God!" Billie sat up and screamed for the nurse, for anyone. The man shuffled slowly out the door and disappeared from sight.

The nurse came running, with another staff member on her heels. "What is it?"

"There was a patient in here. He had blood all over him."

"Where?" Her head bobbed around, as if the patient in question was hiding somewhere in the small room.

"Here! Not two seconds ago. You gotta find him before he bleeds to death."

"Oh for Christ's sakes," the nurse huffed and ran back into the hallway.

The remaining staff member approached. A young man not much older than herself. "Billie?" he said. "I'm doctor Sanjay. How do you feel?"

"Groggy. Did you see that guy?"

"Afraid not. Lie back for a second, okay?"

She did as he asked and tried not to blink when he shined a penlight into her eye. "Do you know what happened to you?"

"I got shoved into the lake by two meat-heads."

"You got a nasty bump to the head too."

Her hand shot to her head, feeling over the scalp until she felt a tender lump. Her hair felt dirty and greasy. "Ouch. Is it bad?"

"That's what we're trying to determine. Billie, you've been unconscious for three days."

"Three days?" That seemed impossible.

"There was very real risk that you might have slipped into a coma. But here you are, awake and lucid. Good."

The room felt colder. "The nurse said I drowned."

"The first attempt to revive you wasn't succesful. You weren't breathing. It wasn't until the paramedics arrived that you were resuscitated. You were brought here. Stable condition but unconscious."

"Resuscitated? You mean, like not breathing or anything?"

"Yes. I don't like to tell people this but you were officially dead for almost two minutes."

For a second time Billie thought her leg was being pulled but the grim look on the doctor's face negated that notion. The flesh on the back of her arms goosed into pimples at the idea of being dead. It was hard enough comprehending that she'd been unconscious for three days but dead too? That seemed ludicrous.

"Can I go home?" The moment she asked the question she thought of the patient who was just here. Bleeding and wanting to go home.

The doctor patted her arm. "We're going to hang on to you for one more night. Just for observation. With head injuries like this, you can never be too sure."

She sank further into the bed at the thought of being kept another night. She turned her eyes to the bedside table. "Is there a phone I can use?"

"Sure. You have some visitors here. Out in the waiting room. I think one of them said she was your aunt."

~

"So you've been at the apartment this whole time?"

"I certainly wasn't going to stay in a hotel," aunt Maggie said. "The prices they charge? I remembered where your spare key is hidden."

Settled into a chair alongside the bed, Maggie fiddled with

the crumpled tissue used to dab away her tears. They had streamed steadily the moment she learnt Billie was awake and poured forth stronger when she laid eyes on her niece in the hospital bed.

Billie shifted upright, sitting cross-legged in the narrow bed. A touch of dizziness lingered and details kept slipping away the second she'd heard them. "Wait. So, Tammy called you?"

"Jen. Tammy didn't have my number but she knew Jen would. I came straight away." The tissue was balled into a tight orb in Maggie's hand. She tossed it at the wastebasket but missed. "I've never made the trip into the city so fast. I'm surprised I wasn't pulled over."

"Must have been a shock, getting a phone call like that. I'm sorry."

"I'm just glad you're all right." Maggie plucked another tissue from the box. "So, between the girls and myself, we've managed to keep vigil here. We didn't want you to wake up alone."

"They've been here too? Jen and Tammy?"

"Kaitlin too. We took turns so one of us was here at all times."

Billie fell silent. The thought of her friends and aunt sitting here in the room made her want to cry. "Wow," was all she could say.

"You seemed surprised," Maggie said. "People care about you, sweetheart."

"Pass that over, would you?" Taking the tissue from her aunt, she shook off the tears. They made the dizziness worse.

"There was a man here too. He asked that I call him the minute you woke up."

Gantry was her first thought. "Tall guy? English?"

"No," Maggie said. "He said he was a police officer."

Timing can be everything. A knock on the door turned their heads. A man stood politely in the doorway. "Miss Culpepper?"

It took a moment for Billie to realize that the man was addressing her and not her aunt. "Yes?"

Maggie got to her feet and smiled at the visitor. "You got my message?"

"Yes," he said. "Thank you."

"I'm going down to that awful cafeteria." Her aunt turned to Billie. "Do you want anything, honey?"

"Iced tea?"

"You got it. Nice to see you again," Maggie said to the man as she quit the room.

The air went still. The man lingered in the doorway. Finally, he said "I'm glad to see you up. Your aunt was quite worried about you."

"You can come in," she said as he stood there. "Do I know you?"

"No. We sort of met three days ago."

She got a better look at him as he stepped inside the room. Thick boned and powerful looking but not overly-muscular.

Rough looking in a way but not bad. His nose looked crooked, like it had been broken a long time ago. "My memory's a little spotty right now," she said.

His head dipped down a notch. "I knocked you into the water. Accidentally, of course. I'm the reason you're in here."

"Oh." It was all she could think of to say. She tried to remember exactly what had happened but her memory was a confused jumble of images, none of which made sense. He didn't look familiar to her at all.

"I'm sorry." His eyes finally lifted from the floor to find hers. They were green. "Did the doctors tell you anything? Will you be all right?"

"They think so. Except for this lump on my skull." Billie clutched at the sheet bunched in her lap. She felt suddenly vulnerable on this narrow bed, clad in a thin hospital smock. "So? You are?"

"Ray Mockler." He strode in and offered his hand. "Hamilton P.D."

She felt her back stiffen up as she shook his hand. An old habit kicking in. "You're with the police?"

"Yeah. Detective, actually." He caught her reaction, the alert wariness triggering her. A reaction he saw on a daily basis. "I was starting to worry about you."

"You were?"

"Yeah. Second day and you still hadn't woken up? I tend to flip to the worst case scenario. Coma, or worse." He looked away again, as if avoiding her eyes. "Again, I'm really sorry I put you in here."

"I'm fine. Really." Billie forced her hands to be still. "So what happened? Why did you knock me into the drink?"

"I was trying to apprehend the man you were talking to. Is he a friend of yours?"

"Gantry?" Something clicked. Her initial wariness of the police officer paid off. "So that's why you're here. Because of him?"

"I needed to know if you were okay," he said. "If there was anything I could do."

She took a second look at him. He seemed sincere but she found herself focusing on that bent nose again. He must have had it broken. "Why are you after Gantry?"

"He's a suspect. Dangerous one too. How do you know him?"

"I don't," she shrugged. "He came into the bar where I work, started talking to me. Then he showed up at the party down at the harbour."

Detective Mockler scratched his chin, listening. "Was he trying to pick you up?"

"That's what I thought at first but no. I don't think so." She tried to remember her conversation with the weirdo but everything seemed scrambled up. "I don't know what he wants."

"What did you talk about at the party?"

Billie shook her head. "It's all foggy. He said he had

something to tell me."

"Which was?"

"I think that's when you barged in." She rubbed her eyes, the earlier dizziness rushing back in. "I need to lie down."

"Sure." His demeanour flipped. The cop mask dropped away. He came forward to settle her pillow back into place. "Get some rest. Listen, I'm gonna leave my card here on the table. If you think of anything else, will you call me? No matter what it is. No detail's too small."

"Okay." Her head hit the pillow and fatigue dragged her down like an anchor.

The detective lingered for a moment, as if there was something more to be done or said. He finally turned to leave. "Get well," he said.

"Hey," Billie said.

"Yeah?"

"What's Gantry wanted for? I mean, what did he do?"

"Murder," Detective Mockler said. "He killed two women."

He stepped into the hall and Billie listened to his footfalls drift away, unsure that she had heard him correctly.

7

"GUYS, THIS ISN'T necessary."

"Shush," Jen scolded as she unlocked Billie's apartment door. "This is no time to play the martyr."

Billie relented. She thought it was overkill for Jen, Tammy and aunt Maggie to see her home. She absolutely hated to be fussed over, loathed to be anyone's object of sympathy. She'd had a lifetime's worth of that when her mother had disappeared and she wanted no more. Still, when her vertigo crested on the stairs she was grateful someone was there to catch her fall.

Stepping into the small one bedroom she called home, Billie felt her stomach drop. The place was immaculate. In the three years she had lived here, she had never seen it so clean. There were flowers too. A simple clutch of bluebells dropped into the only vase she owned. "Maggie, you didn't have to clean up."

"I was here for three days," Maggie said. "What else was I going to do?"

Tammy dropped Billie's bag inside the door. "All this time I thought this was a dump, turns out it just needed a good scrub. Hey Mags, wanna come live with me for three days?"

"You get knocked cold, I'll see what I can do." Maggie moved on into the kitchen. "Are you girls hungry?"

Billie winced. "We can order in. I got nothing here."

"You have plenty," Maggie insisted. "I can whip up that nacho platter you girls like. Billie you must be starved."

"Maggie, tell me you didn't." Billie limped forward and swung the refrigerator door open. Rather than the bare racks of condiments and crusty takeout cartons Billie normally kept cold, her fridge was stocked with food. "You didn't have to buy me groceries too."

"What was I supposed to live on; ketchup packets and Corona?" Maggie bent at the waist to inspect the contents of the refrigerator. The interior bulb flickered on and off. "What can I make you before I head home?"

Billie tugged her aunt away from the fridge. "You've done more than enough. You're not going home now, are you?"

"If I leave now, I can make it home before sunset." Maggie hated the drive between her house and her niece's squalid flat. Even more so in the dark.

"Stay one more night," Billie pleaded. "We can watch a movie."

"I've been away long enough." Maggie cast her eye to the other two women in the room. "One of you is staying here tonight?"

Jen put her hand up, like the good student she'd always been. "I am. Tammy's gotta work."

"Okay. Give me a call in the morning." Maggie squeezed her niece one more time before collecting her bag and heading back out the door. "You gave me a real scare, honey. I'm glad to see you back among the living."

Billie watched her aunt hustle out to the stairwell, wondering what she would ever do without her.

~

"I bumped into Ryan yesterday," Jen said as she settled into the small table in the kitchen. "I told him you were in the hospital."

"Oh?" Billie stood at the counter, chopping black olives. "Why?"

Jen folded her hands on the table. "I thought he should know."

"What did he say?"

"He pretended to care," Jen said. "Said he'd drop by to see you. Then took off without asking which hospital you were at."

Billie nodded glumly. "That would have required effort on his part."

"What an asshole," Tammy concluded.

Since they had broken up three months ago, Billie's ex-beau had become a convenient topic of conversation. "Oh, don't be too hard on him. It's hard for him to think about anyone but himself."

Tammy came alongside Billie at the cramped counter. "Bee, why are you doing that? Go sit. We'll make the grub."

"You?"

"I can cook." Tammy mocked being offended. "A few things anyway. Go sit."

Billie shooed her away. "I've been on my back for three days. Need to move my limbs." The mention of her aunt's nachos put her in the mood for it. A staple of their getaway stays at Maggie's house, it was comfort food and comfort was what she wanted right now. Plus it was dead easy to make. "So where did you run into Ryan?"

"He came by to see the shop."

Sliding the tray into the oven, Billie aimed for nonchalance. "Oh. Is he seeing anyone?"

"He was with someone but I didn't ask."

"Who cares?" interrupted Tammy. "Good riddance to bad rubbish. Move on, Billie."

"Just curious is all."

Jen snapped her fingers. "That reminds me. I know someone you should meet."

Tammy groaned. "Don't even go there, Jen."

"What? He's a really nice guy." Jen dismissed her friend's negativity and appealed to Billie. "A graphic designer. Remember Ted from the Meridian? He works with him. I think you'd like him."

Despite herself, Billie asked "What's he like?"

Tammy rolled her eyes. "Billie, don't fall for it."

"He's nice," Jen said, trumping her friend's protest. "Sweet too. Big into volunteering."

Tammy's hands shot up. "I rest my case."

Billie raised an eyebrow on her photographer friend. "Do you know him?"

"Being set up is a waste of time. It never works. It has to happen on its own." Tammy swung the fridge door opened and peered inside. "And don't even get me started on 'nice guys'. Puke."

Jen sneered at that. "You have to be practical about it. Set parameters, have a goal. Otherwise you're just wasting time with loser after loser."

"Jennifer," Tammy laughed. "Only you could make romance as boring as looking for a job."

"And if you wait for it to happen, it never will. That's all I'm saying."

The debaters settled into the dust of a deadlock and both looked up at Billie for the tie breaker. As usual, Billie floundered at dropping the gavel on a decision. "I think you're both off your collective rockers."

"Typical Billie." Tammy scrounged into the fridge. "Why don't you have anything to drink in here?"

Jen bobbed her head up. "Who was that guy hanging around

the hospital? The one asking about you?"

"He's the guy who knocked me into the drink," Billie shrugged. "He's a cop."

Tammy interjected. "He's also the guy who fished you out of the drink. He saved your life."

Billie straightened up. "I thought you pulled me out?"

"He beat me to it. Dove in like a shot after you. He musta been a lifeguard at one time."

"Oh." Billie pulled the window open to get some air but the old sash only went up half a foot before sticking. Tammy's news didn't sit right with her, about detective Mockler saving her life. He'd said he had felt responsible for putting her in the hospital but now she owed him her life. Who wanted a debt like that?

"Charming," said Jen. Then, with a skein of sarcasm levelled in Tammy's direction she said, "Maybe he's single."

"She can do better than that," Tammy gave back.

"You know I'm standing right here," Billie said, annoyed that these two geniuses at romance were going to fix her love life for her.

"Hey, chief." Tammy nodded at the oven. "Put out the fire, would ya?"

Smoke billowed from the faulty door of the old oven. Billie shrieked and yanked it open, spilling more foul smoke into the kitchen. Using a dishtowel to lift out the hot tray, Billie flung the smoking mess of nachos into the sink and ran the water. The stink of wet ash added to the noxious smoke, all three women waving their hands about to clear the air.

Billie regarded the blackened, soggy mash. "Jesus. I can't even do this right!"

"Don't sweat it." Jen opened the fridge, ready to make lemonade from the situation. "We'll fix up something else."

Tammy was already on her phone. "We're ordering pizza." Tammy said, already on her phone. "Billie, what was the deal with that cop guy crashing into you anyway? Was he after someone?"

Billie thought back to Gantry and what the detective had told her about the slippery Brit. A reticence to answer her friend was inexplicable but sudden. "He didn't say."

"You should sue," Tammy huffed. "Make off with a big settlement. Maybe next time the big galoot will look where he's going."

After Tammy left, they cleaned up the mess in the kitchen then withdrew to the couch to gab for a while. An hour later, Jen had drifted off under a blanket while Billie flicked through channel after channel of unwatchable dreck before settling on the local news. The news anchor droned on in a monotone but nothing of what he said filtered through. Billie tried to gather up the broken fragments of memory to piece back together. Little of it made sense.

What had Gantry been going on about? It felt important but the memory of his words slipped away like shy ponies every time she closed in on them. She retrieved her laptop and settled back onto the sofa without waking Jen. Typing Gantry's name into a Google screen came back with nothing useful. A few hits on Facebook but these John Gantry's were in the States. One in France too.

She added the terms British citizen and murder and wanted suspect to his name but the results were nonsensical and without meaning. Adding the term Interpol made no difference. The man was a ghost.

Closing the laptop, she contemplated going to bed but didn't want to be alone. The blanket Jen was huddled under was big enough for both of them. She burrowed under it and closed her eyes.

8

TASK ROOM THREE had sat unused in the Division One building for weeks now and Mockler didn't foresee it being needed anytime soon. His superior, Staff Sergeant Gibson wasn't due back in the office until tomorrow. That gave him enough time to plant roots and gear up. By the time Gibson returned, he'd have the cold file warmed up and she might let him keep the task room. If he was really lucky, she might even be swayed enough to grant some extra manpower.

He shook his watch loose from the sweaty cling to his wrist and checked the time. It was after shift change, when the day team moved out and the graveyard shift settled in. Hustling down to the evidence room, he signed out the boxes he needed and lugged the stash back up to the unused task room in a hurry. No one paid him any mind.

When Odinbeck poked his head in the room, Mockler had the photos pinned to the corkboard and was scrawling notes on the whiteboard. "The hell you doing, Mockler?" gruffed Odinbeck. "Day shift's long gone, man."

"Extra credit."

"Brown-nosing Gibson is tricky business, boyo. She can smell that a mile off."

"You speaking from experience?" Mockler jotted another bulletin point onto the whiteboard. "If you don't wanna help, find someone else to harass."

"I am helping, dumbass. If the Inspector sees this shit again, she'll tear you a new one."

"Not this time," Mockler mugged. "Hot hit, old file. She'll love it."

"You're a glutton for punishment, man." Odinbeck turned his attention back to the open bullpen behind him then swung back with an even wider grin. "Looks like we get to test that theory."

Mockler kept his back to his colleague. "How's that?"

"Because she's right here."

Mockler spun around to find his superior darkening the doorway of Task Room Three. Staff Sergeant Thea Gibson topped out at little more than five feet, far shorter than the two men she faced but she wielded the presence of a giant. She folded her arms as she surveyed the sprawling mess in the room. "Detective Mockler, what have you done to my task room?"

Odinbeck just grinned like an ape, lapping up every moment of his colleague's distress. Jabbing a thumb in the direction of the corckboard, he said "The kid's itching for a gold star on his homework."

Gibson's cold stare was somewhat legendary among the officers of Division One. Levelling her lethal glare onto Odinbeck vaporised the grin right off his face. "Don't you have bad guys to catch, Odin? Or paperwork, at the very least?"

"I'm on it, Sarge," Odinbeck grumbled.

"Because if not, I can find a broom and you can make yourself truly useful around here."

The detective hurried along, moving with a quick step that belied the basketball-sized lump that hung over his belt. Mockler knew better than to gloat so he kept his grinning on the inside. "Sergeant. I didn't expect you back till tomorrow."

"Clearly." Gibson stepped further into the room and leaned over the table to squint at the frames of paper tacked to the cork. "That's not what I think it is, is it?"

Mockler already felt the quicksand under his feet. "There's a perfectly good reason. He's back—"

Her hand went up to cut him off. "I know all about it. Did you think I'd just let you commandeer the room because your ghost showed his face again?"

"I almost had him this time. He was in my grip."

Sergeant Gibson's glower hardened. Mockler had seen tough-as-iron cops wither under it and now he felt its heat. "You also railroaded a civilian into the harbour and put her in the hospital," she said.

There was no getting around that one. Mockler steeled

himself for the flaying about to come. "I screwed up."

The Sergeant leaned against the table. "You don't get off that easy. If that young woman files a lawsuit, I'd have no choice but to throw you to the wolves."

"Understood." Mockler felt the noose slacken from his neck. "I spoke to her, the woman who was injured. I didn't get any sense that she's looking to sue."

"Why did you do that?"

He felt the noose tighten again. "She was talking to Gantry."

A flicker of interest passed over his superior's face. "Is she a friend of his? Girlfriend?"

"No. She says she doesn't know him."

"Do you believe her?"

"Yeah. I do."

Gibson rolled her eyes to the ceiling and sighed. "So you knock this young woman and Gantry into the water. You fish her out. What happened to Gantry?"

"He didn't bob up," Mockler said. "I suppose there's a chance he drowned."

"We should be so lucky." Gibson swept her hand over the corkboard. "This has to come down. Immediately."

"But he's here. I saw him."

"I get that. But that doesn't entitle you to a task force. You add him to the open files on your desk. You do not pull an Ahab on this again. I can't afford it now."

It was his turn to sigh. This wasn't the reaction he'd hoped for.

"Detective," Gibson warned. "Are we clear on this?"

"Crystal." He watched his boss march out of the room, then called out. "Hey, how was the conference?"

"An excruciating waste of time," she called back. "Go home, Mockler."

He tore down the material from the corkboard and tossed it back into the box. The centrepiece of the evidence display was a still shot taken from a security camera eleven months ago. Grainy and fuzzed out, it showed John Gantry smiling up at the camera cheerily as if someone offscreen had said 'cheese'.

As much as Mockler despised the smug look on the bastard's face, he found the snapshot to be motivational. "Fuck you too, amigo," he said.

~

The scratching sound wouldn't stop, grating Billie's nerves until she opened her eyes. She was still on the sofa, Jen fast asleep on the other end and their legs tangled. Raising her head from the cushion, she listened for the sound.

Of course it stopped the moment she opened her eyes. The apartment was still, the only noise was the muffled hum from the street outside. Laying her head back down, the noise returned the instant she closed her eyes.

Scratching. Like cat's claws on wood but when she lifted her head this time, the sound didn't vanish. It was coming from the front door.

Someone in the building must have gotten a new cat, she thought. It was clawing at her door to get in. Newly adopted and left in the hallway, the tabby must be mistaking her door for that of its owners. Easing off the sofa without waking her friend, Billie padded silently to her apartment door. The scratching ceased as she approached, the shadow under the door moving away. Turning back the bolt, she cracked the door open a few inches.

The hallway was empty. Dim, lit by only one of the four sconce lamps running the length of the corridor. There was no cat. Nothing at all to see. Spooked by her approach, the cat must have bolted away. Easing the door home, the scratching sounded again.

There. Further down the corridor, where the sconces were dark, something moved in the gloom. It was too dark to see clearly but she could see that it was bigger than a cat. Someone's dog? No one in the building owned a dog. Unless it was a stray pooch that had somehow gotten inside.

Opening her door all the way, Billie tiptoed into the hallway. "Hey pooch," she whispered, wanting to simply get its attention.

When its head raised up, she saw it was no dog. A child. A little boy, hunkered down on the floor.

"Hey," she whispered, not wanting to spook the tyke. "Are you okay?"

The boy shifted around but she still couldn't make out much of him in the darkened hallway. Had he been locked out of an apartment? He didn't look familiar to her. There was only one family with kids in the building, the Santos on the second floor. They had two girls, eight and twelve. Maybe his family was visiting someone in her building. Or he was lost and had wandered inside.

She took two more steps. "Hey, are you lost?"

The boy scampered across the floor to the opposite wall in a peculiar crawling motion, like he didn't know how to walk. He turned to her but all she could make out were his eyes, twinkling in the dark.

Another step. "Where's your mom?"

A shriek rang through the hall, unnatural and startling. A brief flash of his face as he jerked back but his features seemed all wrong and then he scurried away like an injured crab. The boy had no legs. Wet stumps cleaved at the thigh, leaving a smeared trail of blood on the dirty floor.

Her heart froze and her brain hiccupped in disbelief. What had happened to him? Had he been in an accident, hit by a car, and crawled in here? She padded after him but the boy had vanished, scuttling away with surprising speed. The hallway ended at the door to the back stairwell, no boy in sight.

Where had he gone? Feeling a wet slap, she looked down to find her bare foot in the bloody trail. She hopped back.

The scratching noise returned. At her back. She spun round to find the boy scuttling behind her. Twisting back, he looked at her with his sparkling eyes and then crawled away on his hands, dragging his darkened stumps behind him.

Her apartment door stood wide open. The half-boy skittered inside and the door swung closed with a heavy thud.

This isn't happening. This isn't real. Her legs felt paralyzed, her feet rooted to the floor.

Shaking it off, she ran to her door but it wouldn't open. She pounded it with her fist. "Jen! Jen, open the door!"

There was a crash from inside the apartment, like glass breaking. She rammed her shoulder into the door and it popped open, spilling her inside. As she hit the floor, something moved in her peripheral vision but it was on the ceiling. Scampering away like an enormous spider, it was gone before she locked on it.

She screamed Jen's name again. How could she sleep through this racket? Dashing for the sofa, she skidded to a cold stop.

Jen hadn't moved, dead asleep. The boy with the stumps was perched on the arm of the sofa. One thin hand reached out, touching Jen in a way that made Billie shudder.

"Jen!" Fear boiled over into rage and Billie dove for the kid to shove him away. He shrieked at her and something sharp cut her arm as his dirty fingers clawed her skin. He toppled over the back and a dark shadow skittered from the room.

Jen thrashed about, groggy but alarmed to find Billie on top of her. "Ow! What are you doing?"

Billie climbed off and ran to the foyer. The door remained open, beyond it the dim corridor. The boy was gone. So too was the bloodied trail he had left on the floor.

9

"IT WASN'T A nightmare."

Billie folded her arms in frustration. The adrenalin had burned off, leaving her insides feeling cored out like an apple. Why wouldn't Jen believe her? "It was real."

"I'm sure it felt real," Jen said with her head tilted slightly. A gesture meant to convey empathy or sometimes pity, depending on the circumstances. "Nightmares often do. That's why they're so scary."

This was their third go-around of the events that had awoken Jen. Billie knew she hadn't dreamt the whole horrid experience but when Jen asked for proof, there was none to be found. No tell-tale blood smears on the floor or shattered glass on the floor. The only aspect that remained were the angry red scratch marks running down her arm. She held her forearm aloft again. "Then how do you explain this?"

"Maybe you did it in your sleep. Or I did it when you

clobbered me. I got hurt too." Jen yanked her sleeve up to reveal a welt on her left arm. "You whacked me good here."

The logic was tedious, eroding Billie's strength faster than sandpaper. She could already feel herself shut down, withdrawing into herself like she always did. Old habits and old dogs, she thought. Unwilling to learn new tricks.

"Look," Jen soothed, the sympathy tilt deepening by two degrees. "You just spent three days knocked out. A head injury no less. You can't walk away from that without some lingering affect. Right?"

"So my brains are scrambled?"

"I dunno. Head injuries are nothing to laugh at. Or maybe it's the meds they gave you."

Billie's face soured. "I wasn't on any meds. Just some painkillers."

"Maybe that's it. Or that combined with the injury. I don't know." Jen blew her bangs from her eyes. "All I know is that I see no sign of any home invasion by some amputee crab-boy."

Silence settled in like dust across the room. Stalemate.

Jen caved. "Let's just get some sleep. We'll figure it out in the morning."

Billie looked out the window. The sky above the trees was already burning with a pink glow. "It is morning."

Jen's face fell as she registered the time on the clock. "Then brew some coffee, cause I gotta open the shop in a few hours."

"Fine." Billie got to her feet slowly and opened the chipped cupboard door to get the coffee tin. She stiffened when she felt her friend's hand on her shoulder.

"Hey," Jen said. "I didn't mean to be so harsh. I'm still half-asleep and can't think straight."

An olive branch. Billie smiled at her. "It's okay. I'm not myself right now."

"Do you mind if I take a shower? I need scalding hot water to wake up."

"Help yourself. Check the dresser. I might even have some clean clothes too."

~

Vexed was how she felt. Vexed was also a word she loved to use but rarely did because it often only occurred to her once the moment was gone. Jen's scepticism still stung long after she had left for the shop and Billie couldn't shake it. Alone in the apartment, the quiet was too much and she kept seeing after-images of the creepy child from last night in every dark corner. She needed to get out of the house.

The promise of the bike did not disappoint. The moment she glided away from the curb, she felt better, lighter. The clammy gooseflesh that had clung to her skin fell away under the warmth of the morning sun. Focused on the road ahead with her senses on full alert, her mind cleared. She hadn't been on the bike for a week, almost forgetting how cleanly it swept out the cobwebs inside her skull.

Zipping through intersections, she guided the bike clear of the shadows to keep herself in the sunlight. She wanted that warm sun on her. It was an anti-septic that scoured away the taint from the previous night. The morning traffic had other plans for her as the cars seemed to clutter around her to block every route and slow her down. Veering across Barton Street, she took a back alley detour until the water hemmed up on her north side. Coasting through a gate, Billie rolled onto the grass at Pier 4 Park, a stone's throw from the place where she been knocked into the cold water. The rusting fence she had broken through was still down but webbed with yellow caution tape.

Leaning the bike against a picnic table, she stretched her back and her muscles groaned. Three days in a hospital bed had turned her limbs to mush. She plunked down on the bench seat and looked out over the park. A couple were spread out on a blanket to her left and two nannies pushed strollers on her right, speaking rapidly in Filipino. The lake stretched out before her, its dark surface rippling with sunlight.

Picture perfect, if one didn't count the man crawling up over the breaker from the water below. Sopping wet, his clothes hung heavy on his frames like dark streamers. His skin was so pale it seemed blue and he shambled forward like he was drunk. What Billie had at first thought were streamers of torn clothing, she could now see were thick tendrils of seaweed. The man was tangled in them, as if he had swum up from the icy bottom of

Lake Ontario.

Her sweat turned cold, the clamminess coming back instantly. There was something wrong with the man's eyes, all white and clouded over, like the water-logged gaze of a dead fish. His jaw moved, as if trying to speak but all that came out was a gurgling sound and a trickle of black water flowing over his blue lips. His dead eyes fixed hard on Billie and he stumbled forward like he had a bone to pick with her.

Billie shot to her feet. Why wasn't anyone else reacting to this? The picnicking couple continued to moon over one another and the nannies chattered on as if they encountered seaweed-tangled men all the time.

This wasn't a gag and it wasn't a joke. Seaweed man wasn't some casual swimmer who had taken a dip off the pier. There was something terribly wrong with him, wrong in the same way there had been something wrong with the half-boy last night. And no one could see the man with the dead eyes but her.

The gurgling slosh issuing from the man's throat grew louder the closer he came. As rubbery as her legs felt, Billie snatched up the bike handles and ran it up off the grass to the broken pavement. A quick glance over one shoulder revealed seaweed man tacking his course to follow. She pushed off and pedalled away.

She coasted to a stop after three blocks and clung to the chain-link fence to keep upright. The lateral muscles in her legs burned with pain and her lungs hurt. Was she losing her mind?

Was Jen right about the head injury? What if it had shaken something loose, causing her to hallucinate?

No answer came before another freakshow started. A little girl stood on the curb across the heavy stream of traffic. Waving to Billie as if she knew her. Here too, something was off. Her clothes were all wrong. Pinafores and a frock, her hair pinned under a bonnet. There was a chance the little girl was simply dressed up in a costume but this was dispelled when the girl walked straight into oncoming traffic. No car slowed or even blew its horn, roaring past the tiny girl in her pinafores like she was invisible. The updraft of the vehicles tussled the girl's hair but somehow she managed to narrowly avoid being struck dead by the cars.

"Hello," the girl said as she stepped up onto the curb in patent leather shoes. "That is a very nice bicycle you have."

The girl's smile was big and would have been beautiful if it were not for the fact that all of her teeth were smashed in and a bloody foam was spilling over her lips.

Billie pushed away, forcing her burning legs to keep pedalling. She heard the little girl calling out to her, pleading with her not to go away.

Jen, she realized, had been right all along. The head injury. There was no other explanation. Something in her brain had gotten scrambled after being clobbered, drowned and unconscious for three days. Now she was seeing things that weren't there.

The hospital was back downtown, uphill at a slight grade all the way and murder on her faltering legs. Plunging back into the downtown core meant fighting traffic again but the alertness focused her thoughts onto a single task and kept the panic pushed down. Even when she spotted the bonfire on the corner of John and Cannon, only to realize that it was a man on fire. The flames rippled up over him in a localized inferno but neither the pedestrians nor the cars noticed him. The burning man flapped his arms, not in an attempt to douse the flames, but rather to flag her down as she glided in his direction. Billie swung behind a city bus to avoid the hallucination and pedalled on.

When the hospital came into view, she wondered if the doctor she had spoken to would be in. She tried to remember his name. Sanjay? Didn't matter. They'd have her chart, know her history. It didn't matter who she saw, as long as someone could help stop the acid trip freak parade in her head.

Coasting up the ambulance ramp to the Emergency Room entry, she glanced around for somewhere to lock the bike. Then her skin went instantly cold and when she looked up, Billie wanted to cry.

The freak parade came out to greet her. A handful of them at first, wandering outside the ER doors, muttering to themselves or staring into space. Some of them were in hospital gowns, the thin material stained dark with blood and other bodily fluids. Others were mangled or bent or torn like they'd stumbled away from horrible accidents with their shattered bones and torn flesh. They all turned their eyes toward her in unison, all becoming aware of her in the same moment.

There was no help for her here, she thought. No refuge from the madness clogging up her brain and throwing these wretched mirages in her vision.

More of them were coming now, spilling out of the Emergency Room doors. Shambling or limping or crawling as they bottlenecked at the entrance and stumbled out into the sunlight. Every pair of eyes locked onto Billie, every broken body shuffling in her direction. Dozens of them now and more coming still.

Keep moving, she thought. They can't hurt you if they can't touch you. Billie wiped away the tears as she turned the bike around and rode away.

10

THE GRASS WAS soft as she sprawled onto the wide span of lawn, the bike on its side where she had let it fall. Billie rolled onto her back and looked up at the clouds. The smell of freshly cut grass was a nostalgic comfort but it did little to dispel the nightmares she had fled.

They were everywhere, this pageant of ghastly freaks and broken bodies. All of them creaking after her like she owed them something, unseen in their wretched state by the rest of the world. With nowhere safe from them all, she had kept cycling, kept moving, to avoid being touched by them. Hurtling down King Street, she cut south on Prospect to avoid a ragged man clutching his own severed head before spinning east again on Main. The buildings thinned on her right as the dark expanse of Gage Park opened up and she slowed her pace. The park appeared empty. No surprise for this time of day but more than that was the fact that the freak parade ended here too. An oasis from the nightmares, she swung into the park and rumbled across the open field. No pedestrians, normal or otherwise. Hewing up near the bandshell, she dismounted but her legs jellied under her and she sprawled into the grass.

The quiet enveloped her as the sun set overhead. With the racket of the city muffled behind a wall of trees, the only sound that reached her ears was the chirping of crickets. The questions came on fast and urgent but the pain in her legs drowned them all out. If she closed her eyes, she could almost drift off to sleep here in the cooling grass. Almost.

"Running away won't help, luv!"

Her eyes snapped open. The voice boomed over her, amplified as it was. Two stage lights had come on in the choral stage, making the aquamarine of the old bandshell appear otherworldly. A figure stood center stage, a dark silhouette against the pastel glow.

Another freak had found her out but she couldn't move a muscle if she tried. "No more," she pleaded.

"You been running long enough," the figure bellowed. "Time to face the truth. Before you screw yourself up royally."

An accent tinged the syllables. Gantry.

Billie dropped back onto the grass, relieved that it wasn't another twisted nightmare. It was just Gantry. Just a man wanted by the police for murder. "Go away!"

A lighter flicked then smoke bubbled under the hot lights. Gantry sat down on the floor of the stage, completely content to be alone under the empty sound shell. "You figure out what's happening to you yet or do I need to spell it out?"

She didn't respond. Maybe if she said nothing, he would just go away.

"If it's any consolation," his voice echoed. "You're not going mad. Those nasty things are real."

Billie jerked upright. He knew? She turned to the theatre but the bandshell was empty. Smoke wafted lazily under the lights.

"Bit of a shock, yeah?" Gantry stood in the grass before her. "Seeing those nasty things. Is that grass wet?"

She blinked. "What?"

"The grass. Is it damp? I hate sitting in wet grass."

"You know what I'm seeing?" she panted.

"I do. I can't see 'em. But I know what they are." He eased onto the grass. His face soured. "It is damp! Christ."

She hadn't noticed, slick with sweat as she was. She watched him grimace as he dragged on his cigarette. "It won't kill you," she said.

"No but it's hard to be serious with a soggy bum, isn't it? Here." A plastic bottle of water was in his hand. "And you and me, we need to be serious for a bit."

Creaking up into a sitting position, she looked at the water bottle but didn't touch it. Was it laced with something? How dangerous was this guy? He looked harmless enough in his rumpled tie and messy hair. "What do you want?"

"Right now, I need you to drink some water." He tossed the

bottle to her. "Dehydration makes you foggy. I need your mind clear." He tapped a finger against his brow. "How's the noggin? You took a nasty hit."

She unscrewed the lid. She didn't realize how parched she was until the water hit her throat. "No thanks to you. That detective said you're wanted for murder."

"Mockler?" He laughed. "Of course he did. If he ever manages to unscrew his head from his arse, he might be dangerous."

"So he's wrong? You didn't kill someone?"

"It's complicated." He looked up at the bandshell, eerie in its aqua-marine glow against the darkening sky. "I love this place at night. When there's no one around like this? Living or dead."

Water spilt down her chin. "What?"

"Haven't you figured it out yet? Jesus." Smoke blew from his nose like some lame dragon. "You can see the dead, Billie."

Billie watched him take another drag and waited for the laugh, the punchline to whatever joke he was telling. No laugh came.

"That's what those things are, luv. The spookshow that came out to greet you. They're not an hallucination, nor a symptom of a bump to the head. They're dead. You can see them. And they can see you."

"I have to go."

"Sit tight," Gantry said. An order, not a request. "Haven't you ever wanted to know why you've felt different all your life?

Why you're always on the outside of things? There's a reason for it."

"Please," she said, rubbing the bridge of her nose. "I've had a day full of crazy. I don't need anymore."

"You have had a day full of dead folks, not crazy." He aimed a finger in her direction. "What murders me is how you've managed to block it out all these years. That's a powerful sense of denial there."

She swept her eyes over the field but there was no one there to call to for help.

"Denial comes with a price though. Devil's bargain, innit? Those foggy spells you get. The migraines. That's them, trying to get through to you. But you put up a wall a long time ago and blocked it all out. Why? Was it your mum's murder? Did it happen after that?" Gantry smoothed a hand down his rumpled tie but it did nothing to straighten it. "My guess is your aunt had something to do with it. Maggie's a peach, isn't she?"

The warning bells she had ignored earlier began ringing a five alarm special. "How do you know about her? Or any of this? You don't know me."

"But I do, luv. I do. I had a little chat with aunt Maggie when she was staying at your flat. She's sweet, I'll give you that, but a bit too devout Catholic for my blood. How anyone can still pray to that papist claptrap is beyond me but, well, that's religion for you. All ritual, no brains." He stubbed his cigarette into the dewy grass and reached for another. "My guess is that she drilled it out of you. Your talents. She recognized it early on after she took you in and it scared the hell out of her and she smothered it all under all the holy weight of the Roman Church. Am I right?"

"I don't know what you're talking about."

"A lot of people have it when they're kids, seeing spirits and what have you. But it gets educated out of them as they get older, just like Santa Claus and then that's the end of it. You, you're a different story. Your ability is strong."

It sounded insane and she was tired of the craziness, of being hounded. "So why now? Why am I seeing it all now? Did the bump to the head knock it loose?"

"Not the head injury. More the fact that you were dead for two minutes or so. Maybe the coma afterwards. A filter broke, letting your radar shine through." Gantry raised his hands, palms to the sky as if offering something to her. "The question now is, what are you going to do about it?"

"I'm going to stop talking to crazy men in the park." She got to her feet slowly, the pain in her lats somewhat bearable. "That's what I'm going to do."

"You can't put the genie back into the bottle now, Billie. You need to learn how to deal with the spookshow out there. Or they will drive you to the nuthouse." He unfolded his legs and got up. A pop sounded from his knee. "Same way it drove your mum there."

Lifting her bike from the grass, Billie froze. "You're an asshole."

All he did was shrug. Guilty as charged.

She turned the bike around and walked away. "Stay away from me, Gantry. If I see you again, I'm calling the police."

"Learn it the hard way, then. No skin off my nose." He watched her march away, then hollered out. "You can tune 'em out, Billie. Like turning off a radio. But you gotta learn how first!"

Billie quickened her pace, steering back toward the lights on Main Street, without bothering to look back.

11

SHE CYCLED THREE blocks before the freak parade came out again to greet her. Slowing down before a red light at Wellington, a figure ambled out from the shadows. Keeping her eyes on the cross light, she gauged her pace to anticipate the green. She did this all the time to avoid stopping altogether but now she had extra motivation.

Unwilling to witness yet another gruesome injury, Billie kept her eyes on the traffic light. The figure slowed, as if unsure of its goal. The red turned to green and Billie rolled through the intersection. The ghastly figure seemed lost all of a sudden, staring off into the rush of passing cars as if he'd forgotten what he was after.

The tactic worked. Staying in motion, she clocked a woman standing in the middle of the street wailing at the sky. The city didn't lack for its share of disturbed people but this woman had unearthly red eyes. Billie ignored her, avoided eye contact. The spooky woman turned toward her but hesitated when Billie didn't look back.

It worked but for how long? Coasting up to her building, she locked her bike to the railing and hustled inside. After murdering her leg muscles on the stairs, she passed into her apartment, annoyed at herself for leaving the door unlocked. Switching on every light in the place, she found her bag on the coffee table and rummaged through its overstuffed contents. Receipts and coin and stale tubes of chapstick spilt onto the table until she plucked out a business card. The embossed name read: Detective Raymond Mockler, Hamilton Police Services.

She dialed the number on the card, sweeping her eyes over the apartment. Everything remained still and quiet but she couldn't shake the feeling of being watched. The last thing she wanted right now was to run across the creepy amputee boy from last night.

The call picked up. A man's voice. "Mockler."

"Hi, uh, detective? It's Billie Culpepper. We spoke a couple days ago. At the hospital?"

"Oh hey," the detective said. "How are you feeling?"

"Better, thanks." Billie stuttered. Having never called a police detective before, she was unsure of the protocol. "Uhm, how are you?"

His voice seemed to laugh. "Most people don't ask me that."

"Oh. Should I be more official or something? I wasn't sure if I should call."

"No, it's fine. Appreciated. Most callers just lay into it, you know? No time for niceties. What's up?"

A shudder of self-consciousness passed over her, feeling suddenly foolish. She had no idea why. "Well, I wasn't sure if I should call but you said you wanted to know. I ran into Gantry again."

"Where?" The detective's tone changed instantly. All business. "How long ago?"

"Ten minutes," she said. Something blurred in the corner of her eye but when she turned to look, there was just the kitchen. Nothing else.

"Stay put. Give me your address."

Noise creaked from the bedroom, like someone stepping on the old floorboards. "Can we meet somewhere else? I don't wanna stay here right now."

"Where?"

She blanked for a moment, then blurted out a suggestion. "You know the garden at Saint Clements? Near the fountain?"

"Be there in five," he said and hung up.

Billie slid the phone into her back pocket. Why had she picked that spot?

She hurried back out the door, remembering to lock it this time.

~

"Are you all right?" Mockler asked. "You look a little pale."

The garden of Saint Clements church was rigorously maintained and well lit and, for those reasons, almost always free of vagrants, crazoids and bored teens. She had circled the fountain at the centre of the garden six times before confirming that it was free of any hallucinatory nightmare people. Detective Mockler arrived two minutes after she did. He must have blown through a few traffic lights to get here so quickly.

"I'm fine," Billie said, trying to shrug off the jitters that had prickled her flesh for the last twenty-four hours. She had nothing to fear from the officer but felt the compulsion to not appear guilty all the same. Cops always had that affect on her. "It's been a weird day."

"Why don't we sit down." He led her to the wide marble lip of the parched fountain. The water had been turned off a long time ago, leaving a dark scum on the bottom of the pool. "So. What happened?"

Billie related the story to him as briefly as possible, omitting a few details. "Then I called you."

Detective Mockler hadn't said a word through her recap of events and remained silent for a long moment afterwards. "Back up a moment. What exactly did he say you could do?"

She had meant to omit the part about Gantry's assertion that she could see ghosts but it slipped out in the retelling. She had, however, skipped the fact that she had been hounded by a horde of refugees from a George Romero movie. "He said I had this ability. To see ghosts."

"Ghosts?" His eyebrows shot up. "Like the moaning and rattling chains and stuff?"

"I guess. I don't know. Crazy, huh?"

"That's Gantry," Mockler said. "He's got a thing for the occult."

Her eyes widened this time. "Occult? Like devil worship stuff?"

"He claims to be a paranormal investigator. A bullshit ghost-buster, if you'll pardon my French." He pondered the gardenia hedges before them before turning his gaze back to her. "And he just showed up out of the blue like that?"

She nodded. "Do you think he's stalking me?"

"What do you think?"

"Seems like it. How else would he have found me at the park?"

Mockler propped his elbows on his knees. "Is there someone you can stay with for a few days? A friend or family?"

"You think he knows where I live?" That hadn't occurred to her but it sent a shudder down her backbone now.

"Why wouldn't he? If he's tracking you, he knows exactly where you live."

"Is he really dangerous?" She chewed her lip, hoping for her mounting fears to be quelled. "You said he was a murder suspect. How?"

"I can't really go into it."

"Give me something," she blew rough. "How concerned should I be? What did he do?"

Mockler stewed for a moment then sat up straight. "Two thousand and twelve, a girl died in what appeared to be some kind of bizarre ritual. Gantry was the main suspect."

"Where did this happen?"

"Here, in town" he said. "But there was a similar incident in London the year before. Gantry was involved in that too."

A sobering thought. Just how deranged was John Gantry? "So he's out there killing people?"

"That's the working theory. Disaster seems to follow this guy around."

"Like what?"

Mockler shook his head. "I've said too much already. Just know that he's dangerous. And wily. For someone on an INTERPOL watch list, he slips through borders like nothing."

Billie folded her arms and became still. Beyond the fenced-in garden came the barking of a dog somewhere in the night. The breeze was warm with humidity but Billie felt goosepimples chill her arms.

A figure bled from the shadows of the oak trees on the far side of the gardens. Billie didn't need to see his face or any details to know that he belonged to the freakshow. He didn't come any closer or even move. He just stood and watched her.

"Hey," Mockler said. "Are you okay?"

Billie had never been good with a poker face, her emotions

flashing loud and clear across her features. She tried to look nonchalant. "Yeah. Everything just seems kind of scrambled right now."

"You've been through a traumatic event. It will pop up like this, out of the blue. It's normal."

"Nothing feels normal about this," she whispered.

"I meant the after-affects. Flashbacks, fear paralysis. That part is normal." He dug out his phone, looked at the display and slid it back into his pocket. "You should talk to someone. A counsellor. Talking through it seems to help."

"Whatever. I'll be fine."

"Hey." He turned sharply. Locked eyes with her. "Don't dismiss it. It'll come back to bite you in the ass if you do."

His insistence startled her. She felt pressure on her wrist and, looking down, found it gripped in his hand. "Okay."

"Sorry." He let go of her wrist.

The hiss of traffic filled the awkward silence spreading out like a puddle. Looking to kill the dead air, she said, "Is that what you do? Talk to a counsellor?"

"Sure." His nod shifted into a shrug. An evasion.

"That was vague," she said, calling him on it. "You don't follow your own advice, do you?"

He smirked. "No. I don't. It's easier to dole out than to take it."

"You're a hypocrite then."

"My secret's out." He looked out over the garden. "There are counsellors on call for the force. We're obliged to talk to them. I hate it."

"You don't like blabbing all your secrets to a stranger?"

"It feels forced. Like I'm meant to perform. There's a weird pressure to let it all out. Quickly too, before the hour's up."

"Well, you've convinced me. I'm sure to go now."

A slight grin creased his face. "Do as I say, not as I do. As my old man used to put it."

"So it runs in the family, huh? Being a hypocrite." Billie almost smiled back. The suffocating gloom she'd felt earlier lifted by a degree or two, bantering with the police officer. It surprised her. She normally felt uncomfortable around police officers but Mockler didn't seem like one at all.

"It's a family tradition, hypocrisy. I'll be sure to pass it on to the next generation."

"That's sweet of you. Mine's insanity, apparently."

"What?"

"The family tradition. Insanity. Getting the crazies, as my aunt says."

"That runs in a lot of families," he said.

"My mom was the real deal. She was known as the crazy lady in town." Billie blinked at her own words. She never talked about her mom. To anyone. It just slipped out this time, like it was nothing. Just another tidbit of bantering conversation.

"She took her craziness serious, then. What town was this?"

"Poole."

Welcome to the Spookshow

"Never heard of it."

"Nothing to hear about it."

"She still live there? Your mom?"

"No. She's dead."

"Oh."

Like a balloon deflating from a slow leak, the lightness of the moment evaporated with her words. She had squashed the conversation with a brick of bad news. Why had she done that? To get a reaction out of him?

"I'm sorry to hear that," he said softly. "How old were you when it happened?"

"I was just a kid." His condolence knocked about in her head for a spell. Not the words but the tone. Hushed and even. Was it habit with the detective? "How many times have you had to say that? In your job, like?"

"Say what?"

"That you're sorry for someone's loss."

He shrugged. "Never kept score."

"Maybe you should," she suggested. She still didn't understand why she felt the urge to goad the officer.

"Who'd want to?" Turning, he studied her for a moment. "How many times have you heard it?"

"At a certain point it becomes meaningless." Again, the weird urge to thwart the conversation. She had done this as a teenager, lobbing grenades into a friendly chat just to watch the conversants squirm as it went off. So why now? What was she

105

after?

"I see," he said, continuing his study of her. "At what point does it provoke hostility?"

She was about to say 'touché' but something hooked the corner of her eye. She had almost forgotten about the phantom figure on the other side of the garden but now it sidled closer, like a greedy dog looking for table scraps. A wave of cold air emanated from it, chilling her shins. She stood, the ache in her legs zapping up her muscles. "I have to go."

"Do you have a roommate?"

She leaned back. Why was he asking that? "No," she said. "Why?"

"Is there someone you can stay with? A friend."

"I'm fine."

"Billie, your hand is trembling. Stay at a friend's house. Just for tonight." He got to his feet. "Come on. I'll give you a lift."

She folded her arms to hide her shaking hands. "I have my bike."

"We'll toss it in the back. Let's go."

"You don't have to do that."

Stepping around the dry fountain, he took up the bicycle and wheeled it to her. "Don't argue with me. Get your wheels and let's vamoose."

The gravel of the pathway crunched under her feet as she followed him out to the parking lot. The shadowy figure under the wisteria vines tilted after her and she quickened her pace.

12

JEN COULDN'T MAKE coffee to save her life.

The smell of it hanging in the air as it brewed roused Billie from a dead sleep. Anticipating that first strong sip, she sat up and blinked her eyes, wondering who had rearranged her living room before remembering that this wasn't home. She had asked the police detective to drop her at Jen's place.

"Morning, sunshine."

Jen swept into the room with two steaming mismatched mugs and settled onto the floor before the coffee table. For reasons that Billie could never fathom, Jen Eckler was a morning person. Always chipper and eager to start the day.

Billie grunted, still getting her bearings. "Thanks for letting me crash."

"My door's always open," Jen said.

Billie rubbed her eyes to get them to adjust to the light but it was hard to tell which had more wattage; the sunlight coming through the window or Jen's smile. Jen never woke up puffy-faced or baggy-eyed, which used to irk Billie to no end until she accepted the fact that some people were just radiant no matter what the hour. That was Jen.

"Sorry you had to take the couch," Jen smiled. "Next time I'll make Adam sleep out here."

"It's fine." Billie swept her tangled hair up into a bun and pinned it in place with a pencil from the coffee table. "Is he still asleep?"

"He left already. He starts early on Tuesdays."

Billie picked up her mug and looked at it. A yellow happy face. "I'm not making you late am I?"

"No but I need to get moving. You're welcome to stay. Go back to sleep if you want."

Billie chewed on it but the thought of being alone wasn't appealing. "Nah. You want some help at the shop today?"

"Sure!" Jen brightened even more.

Billie could see the gears turning in Jen's head as she anticipated an extra set of hands at work. She might regret it. Blowing off the steam, she sipped the coffee and tried not to make a face.

Jen's smile dampened. "That bad, huh?"

"You lowered the bar this time." Billie set the mug down. The liquid inside was brown and it was hot but any similarities to coffee ended there. "What time does Mulberry's open?"

Jen rose to her feet with a graceful swoop. A lifetime

studying dance lent a fluid movement to her every move. "Six. Let's hurry, before they run out of croissants again."

~

The spookshow that had tormented her the night before had abated in the warmth of the morning sun. No mangled shamblers or creepy children to scare the wits out of her. With a dash of strong black coffee on her tongue and the bright sun overhead, the world tilted back onto its normal axis, leaving Billie to wonder if she had imagined the terrors from last night.

That still didn't explain Gantry.

"I don't get it. What does he want with you?"

Billie took her friend's cup as Jen unlocked the door to the shop. She had related the details about Gantry's appearance last night but left out the part about the spookshow.

"I don't know," Billie said. "A bunch of kooky stuff. I think he just likes spooking people." She was already regretting mentioning it at all.

"Well what did the cop say? Is he dangerous or just a loser?"

"He just wanted the details." Billie scanned the interior of the Doll House. Everything was displayed with a sense of grace and style, which pretty much summed up the shop owner. Peeking into the cramped back room told a different story. Boxes were piled haphazardly and caster-wheeled racks were pushed against the wall. "Is this the mess you mentioned?"

Jen sighed. "I have no room back here. Makes me panic just looking at it."

"What about the basement?"

"I hate it down there."

"You don't have a choice," Billie decided. "This mess is gonna tumble over and bury you."

"Did the cop tell you why he's after this Gantry guy? What did he do?"

"No," Billie lied. She felt little compunction to it. Jen was her oldest friend, one that she spilled everything to but something irked her about it now. Ten minutes ago, she had wanted to share the whole crazy thing to Jen but now, an inexplicable urge came hard to pull it back. To not reveal anything more of this. As weird as it was, the experience was hers and it would stay that way.

"Cops," Jen stated, shaking her head in regretful dismay. The dismay doubled up as she looked over the mess of her backroom. "Okay, give me a few minutes to open up, then we'll tackle this chaos. Deal?"

"Go ahead."

Jen ran off and Billie opened the door to the basement. The uneven steps scaled down in a steep grade to the bare brick cellar built over a century ago. Jen was squeamish about things like bugs and cobwebs. It was no wonder that she avoided the dungeon-like basement. She'd just have to get used to it, Billie concluded. Still, something unpleasant seemed to roil out of the opened door, like a bad smell drifting up the steps.

The lighting didn't help matters. A naked bulb, improperly wired into the exposed floor joists overhead, gave a harsh glare directly under it but lengthened the shadows in the rest of the space. Carrying a box down the trechourous steps, Billie surveyed the floor to plan out the storage space. The only person who'd been down here was Jen's dad. Some of his tools were left on the decrepit workbench under the only window. A trail of sawdust had been tracked in a pathway from the bench to the stairs.

"Dad promised he would fix this up. Put up drywall and stuff."

Standing on the bottom step of the wooden stairs, Jen refused to go any further. Like a bather at the end of a dock, reluctant to jump in.

"That would be an improvement." Billie swept up the sawdust with a straw broom. "You're gonna need shelving to keep stuff off this damp floor. But we can move the boxes down here for the time being."

Jen scanned the floor joists overhead. "I asked Dad about putting a proper ceiling up but he said I'd just lose head space because the ceiling is so low."

"You can always paint it. Stark white might brighten it up. Keep the dust down too."

"Anything would help," Jen said. A shiver rippled through her. "I hate being down here. I feel physically ill."

The basement was dank and smelled of dust and old brick. Something about the dark corners and exposed pipes discouraged any loitering. Jen was always a wuss about such things but Billie had to admit that she felt it too.

"Maybe there's mold down here." Billie scanned the pipes running the length of the room and her first thought was asbestos. It was all too common in old buildings like this but she didn't want to spook Jen any further. "Something toxic. You could get a building inspector in here."

"That's what I thought but Dad advised me not to. He said the wiring is all wrong and an inspector might shut the place down on me. I can't afford that right now."

A bell chimed from the floor above. The old fashioned kind that hung over the door, announcing a visitor. Jen loved the way it sounded.

"I'll be right back." Jen turned and hustled back up the steps.

The floor over Billie's head creaked under every step, the old boards loud and crackling. Billie leaned the broom against the wall and reached for the dustpan on the bench but it wasn't there. She could have sworn she just put it there. Stepping back, she spotted it in the middle of the floor.

Going to fetch it, the broom fell over and hit the floor with a whack that startled her. Dismissing it, she reached for the dustpan but it was gone.

Billie straightened up. It was just here, she whispered to herself. Her skin suddenly felt clammy.

A noise. The dustpan on the far side of the room. Scraping across the gritty floor all on its own.

Disbelieving her own eyes, Billie nonetheless watched the tin pan spin into the darkest corner of the basement where all the pipes and duct work fed to. Barely visible in the gloom was the old boiler, disconnected but left to rust in the corner. The cast iron grate across the barrel looked like teeth.

A synaptic disconnect flared as Billie stood frozen to the spot. Her legs were itching to bolt up the stairs but her mind was puzzling out the impossibility of a dust pan moving under its own volition. Her heart already knew what would unfold if she took a closer look but, as in most crisis moments, Billie made the mistake of letting her brain overrule her instincts as she crossed the floor to the dark corner.

The dust pan remained where it lay, a banal tool of boring housework. The closer she came to it, the colder her skin felt and her heart clanged in protest.

The old boiler clinked, the iron drum vibrating as if the rusty parts inside were clanking back to life. Another clang and the round door creaked open on its rusty hinges. Darkness within, where an inferno had once burned to heat the building above. Noise tumbled from the aperture, as if something was moving inside it. Trapped.

Fingers emerged and gripped the lip of the opening. Dark as charcoal, the flesh carbonized to the bone. Behind the burnt hand came a flash of eyes, twinkling in the pitch dark of the boiler.

Billie back-pedalled for the stairs, the sudden vertigo knocking her unsteady. She pounded her feet on the steps as loud as possible to avoid hearing the dry crackle voice coming from inside the cast iron belly of the boiler but some of it filtered through.

Please, it whispered.

Please don't burn me anymore.

I promise to be good this time.

13

"DON'T GO IN the basement."

That was all Billie had said as she fled the shop. Jen, busy helping a heavily-tattooed woman decide between two cocktail dresses, stood open-mouthed as Billie hurried out onto the street, clanging the bell over the door. Jen cracked a joke to her customer about having a flaky employee, hiding her shock at Billie's bizarre escape.

The terror dissipated with every step she put between herself and the awful thing in the basement. The humidity had shot up, cloying in her lungs as she tried to cool down her breathing. It was all too real.

Any notion that she had dreamt or imagined the terrors from the other night were immediately quashed after seeing the blackened hand slither from the boiler. The thing's awful voice would not go away. She hadn't hallucinated these things, the freak pageant was not the byproduct of a head injury. She could see the dead. Just like John Gantry had claimed.

As much as she disliked the idea, she needed to talk to Gantry again. She needed to understand what it meant. Marching briskly down James Street, the thought occurred to her that she had abandoned Jen with a ghost in her basement. Could it hurt her? What was she supposed to do about it now? Gantry hadn't said anything about that but she had no way of getting in touch with the slippery creep. He just popped out of the ether when she least expected him to.

Billie stopped in her tracks. Should she go back and warn Jen? To do what, exactly? Close the shop? Move? Jen had never mentioned any weird incidents or spooky stuff. What was the term for it? Unexplained phenomena. More to the point, what exactly did the restless dead do? Rattle chains and moan, like in the movies? Move the furniture around and pop lightbulbs? Even if Jen hadn't experienced anything odd, she knew in her gut that something was wrong. That explained Jen's reluctance to go into the basement. It had nothing to do with dust and cobwebs.

She needed answers but without Gantry, Billie had no idea where to turn.

~

The web, as usual, spewed up too much information. Pages and pages of ghost hunters and psychics, ghost sightings and self-professed experts in paranormal phenomena. The first half dozen sites she clicked through were so amateurish and gaudy that she closed the laptop and pushed it away.

Home was the last place she wanted to be now that she understood the truth about the spookshow. It meant that the disturbing half-boy from the other night was real and she did not want to run into him again. Stepping back inside, Billie turned on every light switch and opened all the curtains to let in as much sunlight as possible. She had a notion, true or necessarily delusional, that the spookshow only came out after dark. Either way, it felt safer with the lights on.

The cold sweat left her skin feeling grimy and it was difficult to think straight. A scalding hot shower and clean change of clothes, then maybe she could sort this out.

It was the quickest shower she'd ever taken, one eye constantly on the door. The shower head was old and a third of the nozzles were blocked but the jet spray scalded away the grime from her skin and she hated to end it so quickly. Towelling off and scooting to the bedroom, she banged the dresser drawers and hummed loudly, as if constant noise would keep anything nasty away.

Madame Ostensky

The name had popped into her head while showering. Not so much the words but an image. A sign hanging over a door, swaying slightly in the breeze. *Madame Ostensky - Spiritualist & Psychic.* Underneath that, a symbol of an eye within a triangle. She had passed this sign a thousand times or more without ever paying it any mind. Part of the unchanging landscape.

Was it crazy to think Madame Ostensky might have an answer to any of the questions buzzing through her head? It was no crazier than sifting through pages of nonsense on the web. Snatching up her bag, she checked the inner pocket where she kept her cash. Lots of bills. One of the advantages to working in a bar was always having cash on hand. Locking her door, she wondered how much the psychic charged for a reading.

The sign looked the same as ever. It hung on its iron hinge, motionless from the lack of any breeze on a humid day. The letters slightly faded from the sun. The curtains were drawn in the front window as if no one was home. In all the years she had passed by this door, Billie had never seen anyone go in or out of the place.

She squinted up at the sun-faded sign, reading the smaller print. Established 1973. Jesus. How old was Madame Ostensky? She'd been in business for over forty years. Billie hesitated, her hand hovering over the doorbell. Then the door swung open.

A little girl appeared behind the frayed mesh of the screen door. "Mama said come inside or move on," the girl said. Her dark hair was cut into bangs that draped just above two impossibly grey eyes. "Don't linger outside the door like a Jehova's Witness."

The girl looked no more than eight years old. She had to be Madame Ostensky's granddaughter.

"Thank you," Billie smiled. She opened the screen door and the little girl stepped back to let her inside.

The interior was gloomy with the window curtained. A sitting room to the left and a foyer that led to the back where the sound of a radio played.

"You can wait here." The girl motioned to the chair before a long table that Billie assumed the Madame used for clients. The table was empty save for a vase of freshly cut hydrangea and a tacky-looking crystal ball set into an iron stand.

The girl crossed to the sitting area where she hunkered down on the floor. Before her was a mess of drawing paper and artist-grade pencil crayons. Taking up a dark green pencil, the girl went back to her drawing.

Behind the table was a doorway strung with beads and when the beads rattled, a woman appeared. Dark-haired and grey-eyed like the little girl, the woman was stunning. Wiping her hands on a dishtowel, she motioned to the empty chair. "Have a seat. I'm Marta."

"Billie. Nice to meet you." Billie sat clumsily, entranced by the woman's face.

"Esme," the woman said to the little girl. "Take your stuff into the other room, okay?"

"I don't want to," the girl said without looking up. "How do you spell 'eternity'?"

"Sorry," Marta said to Billie. "I'll shoo her out of here."

Billie shrugged. "She can stay."

"Mom. How do you spell it?"

Billie waited while the woman spelt the word out. "She's your daughter?"

"Yes. And stubborn as her father." Marta set the hydrangeas to one side and placed her hands on the table. "What can I do for you?"

Billie hesitated. "Are you Madame Ostensky?"

"Not the original one. That was my grandmama. We shared the same gift so I decided to keep the shop open." The woman reached into a drawer and came up with a deck of cards. "I keep meaning to get a new sign out front. So, do you like the tarot?"

"No," Billie said, trying not to bristle at the sight of the cards. Too many bad memories. "Can I ask you something? What do you mean by gift?"

"The sight. The ability to get a sense of another person's spirit. The past and the present of that spirit. And if I'm lucky, a hint at its possible path forward. Does that make any sense?"

"I think so. So you inherited it from your grandmother?"

"Yep. She taught me everything I know. My mom had it too but she didn't want it."

Billie leaned back. "She rejected it?"

"She just chose not to use it, you know?" Marta nodded at her daughter. "Same with Esme. She has a bit of it too but doesn't like it."

Billie turned to look at the girl. Esme's tongue protruded as she furiously coloured inside the lines. "How come?"

"It scares her. So, I don't think she'll continue in the family business."

"Can you sense it in other people?"

"Most of the time," Marta said. "You mean like you?"

For a second time, Billie was taken aback. "You can sense it in me?"

"I felt it before you came through the door. It's strong with you." Marta leaned back, her gaze turning cool. "Are you here scoping out the competition?"

"No." Billie took a breath. "I've been seeing weird things lately. Someone told me that I have a gift too. That I can see the —"

"Wait." Marta cut her off. She rose quickly and crossed to the little girl. "Esme, go play in the other room."

"But I'm not finished."

"Take it into the other room. Hurry." The woman bundled up the paper and crayon box and shooed the little girl through the beaded doorway. When she turned her attention back to Billie, she did not look pleased.

"You let one in."

"What?"

"I don't allow them in here," Marta said, returning to the table. "Not where my daughter is. Get it out of here."

Billie still didn't follow. "What did I do?"

"One of the dead followed you inside. I can feel it in here. Is this a stunt?"

Billie spun around in her chair and scanned the room. Something darker than the gloom hovered near the door. It shifted about, as if politely waiting to be invited in. "Oh God."

"Get it out of here, please," Marta bristled.

"I didn't know." As her eyes adjusted to the dark form, Billie saw an old woman draped in black. A laced shawl draped over her head, like the little old Italian ladies she used to see, draped in perpetual mourning. "I don't know how to get rid of it."

Marta stood up again, anger flaring hot in her eyes. "Go open the door."

Almost idly, Billie noted how Marta's beauty didn't fade when her face hardened. It simply took on a different aspect, an otherworldly comeliness. Tearing her gaze from Marta to the old woman near the door, she felt her knees go wobbly. She didn't want to go anywhere near the spooky-looking woman.

"Do it," Marta ordered.

Billie sidled to the door, keeping as much distance from the dark figure as possible. The old woman stared at her with something like hatred in her tiny eyes. Billie pulled the front door open and stepped back.

"You are not welcome here," Marta boomed in a clear and loud voice. "This is my house and I did not invite you in. Leave now and don't come back."

Billie watched in silent wonder as the old woman hobbled like a penguin toward the open door. Her wrinkled face turned to her and she spit at Billie before moving outside.

"How did you do that?"

"How do you *not* know how to do that?" The Madame marched past Billie with a small jar in her hand. Tilting it, Marta poured a white sandy substance over the threshold of the front door.

"What is that?"

"Salt."

"What does it do?"

"Keeps them out." Marta screwed the lid back on and shut the door. She folded her arms. "Are you telling me you don't know about this? How to deal with the spirits?"

"That's why I'm here. I don't even know if it's real or if I'm seeing things."

The woman shook her head. "That makes no sense. You're like a magnet to those things. A powerful one too. How have you dealt with this so far?"

"I haven't. This is all new." Billie looked at the salt sprinkled across the doorway. "Does that actually work?"

"How can this be new to you? No one just snaps their fingers and becomes a medium."

Billie backed up, seeing the anger flash hot in the woman's eyes. "Hey, a week ago everything was fine. Now I'm seeing freaky shit and this weirdo English guy shows up, tells me I can see the dead—"

Marta cut her off a second time. "What English guy?"

"His name's Gantry."

"John Gantry?" The medium flapped the dishtowel in her hand, shooing Billie out the door. "Time for you leave. Goodbye."

"Wait. You know him."

Marta sighed impatiently. "He's dangerous. Stay away from him."

"How is he dangerous?"

"Goodbye."

The dishtowel kept flapping at her. Billie snatched it from the woman's hand. "Please. The guy's stalking me."

"John Gantry is a manipulator. He has no power himself so he uses people. Those with power. Keep your distance."

"Power? For what?"

Marta Ostensky narrowed her eyes in cold scrutiny. "There is a network of people who work in this realm. An economy of outsiders. And this economy is run on power or manipulation. Gantry falls into the latter. He'll use you up and chuck you in the trash, all the while making you think it was your idea."

Billie stammered for a moment, trying to parse the woman's words but none of them made much sense.

Marta ushered Billie out and closed the door. "Don't come back here."

The door thumped closed, leaving Billie stranded on the broken concrete stoop with a dumbstruck slant to her mouth.

14

MARTA OSTENSKY made it look so easy. She told the spook to go away and it did.

Was it that simple? She didn't understand the salt trick but maybe she didn't need to, as long as it worked. Jen was still in danger with that thing in the cellar. How long before it crept up the stairs to find her? She would just go back to the little shop on James Street and do what Marta had done.

Madame Ostensky's harsh ejection still stung. But Marta knew things. While Billie groped in the dark, the medium down the block had flipped on a light to guide the way. Only to take it away when she learnt of Gantry's involvement. How did Marta know the slippery Englishman? The woman's anger was hot and Billie wondered if there wasn't some history between them. A jilted lover?

Returning home, she scurried into the kitchen for the salt and pepper shakers, an old old rooster and a hen set that she had scored at a flea market. Both were empty. Scrounging the cupboards she turned up a box of sea salt. She shook it, wondering if the type of salt mattered. Nothing sifted inside the box, nothing spilling from the little metal pour spout. The contents had hardened into concrete. Tearing the top of the box away, she took a knife and stabbed the hard salt to break it up.

White clumps spilt over the floor as she stabbed at it. Could she really go through with this? The last place she wanted to go was back down to that creepy basement but the thought of Jen being alone with that thing spurred her on. What if she pleaded with Marta to come with her? To help get rid of the thing.

A noise from behind her broke the train of thought. Holding the knife, Billie stopped to listen but the sound was gone. Crossing back into the living room, she clenched the knife tighter in her fist. Like that would help if that disturbing crab-boy returned, she mused. Something caught her eye on the floor near the entrance. A manila envelope had been slipped under the door.

The fish-eye perspective of the peephole revealed nothing. An empty hallway. Shaking the envelope, two pieces of paper slipped out. Both newspaper clippings. One was dated two years ago. Victim found in bizarre scenario, read the headline. Police had been called to an abandoned tenement building where the remains of a young woman had been found. According to a local man who had made the discovery, the scene had been decorated with candles and symbols of witchcraft. Police would not comment on any questions about a ritualistic murder but rumours of a devil-worshipping cult spread quickly.

A photograph in the article showed a number of police officers, both uniformed and plainclothes, outside of the tenement. Billie squinted at the grainy newsprint image. She couldn't be sure but one of them looked like Detective Mockler. A much younger version of him anyway. If it was him, he appeared to have aged a lot in the intervening years.

She opened the second article. A page torn from the Weekly World News. Buried under a story about alien abductions was a small piece claiming that British police were covering up evidence of a devil-worshipping cult operating within London's east end. The article pointed out police denials about the murder of a young woman in Hackney having anything to do with Satanic rituals. The article conjectured that the death was the result of a botched exorcism. Police refused to comment. The date on the article was nine months prior to the first newspaper clipping.

Both articles pointed back to John Gantry. The local incident must have been what got detective Mockler on Gantry's tail in the first place. The other incident was in England, where Gantry was clearly from. Was this meant to be proof of Gantry's guilt? She leaned into the peephole again but the hallway remained as empty as before.

Madame Ostensky, she thought. Who else would have slipped this under her door? How the hell did the psychic even know where she lived? Maybe that was a silly question. She was, after all, a psychic.

She'd have to puzzle it out later. The thought of Jen alone with that thing in the basement was unbearable.

~

"What happened to you?"

Jen was surprised to see her friend return after such an abrupt exit. Marching back along James, Billie sweated out an excuse to explain both her mad dash out and sudden return. It was lame but it was the best she could come up with.

"Sorry. I needed to run home and get some things." Billie adjusted the bag slung on her shoulder.

"What things? What's wrong with the basement?"

Billie crossed her fingers. "Electrical problem. Loose wires. I had to go get some tape. I'll fix it."

"Since when are you an electrician?" Jen asked, scepticism writ large in her eyes. "And why didn't my dad see it?"

"I knocked something loose when I was moving the boxes down there. Don't worry, I'll fix it. It's just dangerous to leave it as is."

Jen took out her phone. "Should I call Dad? Maybe he should do it."

"Don't bother. He doesn't need to drive in for this."

"Oh," Jen said, lowering her phone. "Thanks. I guess that

explains the lights flicking off."

"The lights?"

"They've been flickering on and off since you left. The laptop's been acting screwy too. Would bad wiring affect that?"

Something cold slithered down Billie's spine. Had she angered the thing in the boiler?

"I guess so," she lied. "You never know with these old buildings."

"Let me see if it's working now." Jen crossed the floor of the narrow shop to the desk. Lacking a proper cash register, Jen used her laptop as a stand-in.

Billie chewed her lip. She had no way of getting Jen out of the shop to seal the doorway with salt. With Jen busy at the desk, this might be her only chance. She quickly dug the box of salt from her bag and started pouring a line of it across the threshold of the open door. Halfway through, she stopped. She was doing this too soon. Didn't she have to get the ghost out first, then seal the doorway? Putting salt down now might trap it inside. Did it work that way?

"Damn it."

"What did you say?" Jen called from the back.

"Nothing." Billie kicked the salt away but it had settled up against the rubber weather seal. Shoving the box back into the bag, she hustled past Jen for the basement door. "I'm gonna get started, okay? Back in a flash."

Jen looked up from the laptop. "Do you want some help?"

"Nah. You mind the shop."

The bell over the door chimed. Two women stepped inside, scanning the racks. That would keep Jen occupied. Billie headed down, closing the door after her.

The single bulb brightened when she hit the switch. Standing at the bottom of the stairs, Billie peered into the darkness of the far corner. The old boiler hunkered there in the shadow like some rusty octopus.

Her foot crunched something on the concrete floor. Looking down she saw a mess of pennynails and glass shards strewn across the grit floor. Had she knocked it from the windowsill when she ran out of here? She didn't remember doing so.

Overhead, the old hardwood floor creaked with every step taken. Billie could track exactly where Jen and the two customers were by the squeaks above. A little dust drifted down, filtered by the light of the bulb. She heard Jen's voice, wondering about the mess spilt all over the front entrance.

Shit.

A trace of smoke lingered over the damp smell of the basement. Nothing moved. Billie inched closer to the dark corner and then stopped. The boiler door was shut, the grated vent closed. What now, she wondered. Call the thing out? Wait for it to appear again? Give the boiler a kick to wake it up?

She waited long enough to feel silly standing there under the light of the dusty bulb. The straw broom stood against the wall and she took it up in both hands and moved into the dark corner.

The straw end was frayed and bent and she whacked it against the hull of the boiler. The cast iron boomed in a low rumble.

Nothing moved, nothing happened.

"Hey."

She felt silly addressing an old hunk of metal.

"You don't belong here. You are not wanted."

Taking a step back, she expected the little door to fling open or a valve to pop off but nothing happened. Had it moved on already, knowing it wasn't wanted?

"Hey! This place belongs to my friend. Her name is Jen and this is her place now. You are not welcome here. You need to leave."

A rusty creak sounded. The vent in the grate slid back. The lever handle tumbled and the door swung open slowly.

Billie gripped the broom like a baseball bat, ready to swing at anything that moved. Nothing did. A sour smell drifted from the open door in the boiler, that was all.

Another step closer, craning her neck to see into the belly of the boiler. Darkness.

Something whispered in her ear. Close enough for her to feel its breath.

It's cold in there.

She jerked back. The thing, whatever it was, stood right beside her. Its flesh charred to a blackened crust, flaking away in pieces as it moved.

"Get out!" she screamed at it.

Its hand shot out quick, latching onto her wrist. The thing's flesh was hot and it burned and she could not yank her arm free.

"Get out," she said but the conviction was lacking. "You have to leave!"

It leaned forward, like it wanted to whisper something intimate. In the dark hollows of its eye sockets, there was a tiny spark of red.

Come see, it hissed. *Let me show you.*

And then it dragged Billie toward the boiler. In the open door of the iron hulk, fire roared up. Hot and angry.

The pain in her wrist was unbearable as the thing's grip burned through to the bone. She could smell her own flesh sizzling and she dug in her heels but the charred figure kept dragging her to the raging fire inside the boiler.

She screamed at it to stop, to go away.

It's cold, it replied. *Stay with me.*

"Billie?"

The pain eased up as her wrist was released. The burned up thing was gone. Billie fell to her knees.

Jen was crouched at the top of the stairs, bending low to see into the basement without going down all the way. "Billie, what's all the screaming about?"

Billie was speechless, gasping for breath. Her wrist stung like hell, the flesh red and blistering from a bad burn.

"Oh my God," Jen stammered, hammering down the steps. "Is that fire?"

Billie turned to see the flames riffling up from the door in the boiler. Low hanging cobwebs melted where they hung from the floor joists.

Jen hurried down and rushed to her friend. "What happened?"

"Jen, get out of here."

The bulb overhead exploded, raining brittle shards and filament onto them. Sparks sprinkled from the outlet. Jen covered her head to protect herself.

Billie swung back to see the burnt figure leaning over her friend. It snatched Jen by the hair and the stench of burning follicles came on strong and sour. The thing hurled Jen at the boiler and the cast iron rung dully as her head smacked off the metal.

Jen slunk to the floor like a broken puppet. The thing in the carbonized flesh turned its hot eyes to Billie and leered with an obscene grin.

Something snapped at the sight of Jen going down for the count. She ran at it, shoving the thing into the boiler door. It shrieked and Billie's palms burned but she kept shoving, pushing it into the boiler. Screaming at it to go away and no one wants it and ordering it to go to Hell where it belonged and a hundred other things besides.

A new sound echoed around her, the thud of feet pounding down the rickety stairs but Billie never got the chance to see who it was before everything went dark.

15

RED LIGHTS STROBED against the picture window of the the Doll House. Two police cruisers, one pumper truck and an ambulance lit up the street. People gathered on the sidewalks to watch.

Billie sat on the bumper of the ambulance, watching the paramedic treat the burn on her wrist. A uniformed officer stood on the curb while two firemen clomped out of the shop in their bulky gear. Her memory was scrambled, like it had been after the incident at the harbour. She had no recollection of how she had gotten out of there or what had happened to Jen.

"Where's Jen?" she turned to the paramedic, a young man with a shaved head. "Did you get her out?"

"She's right over there." The paramedic nodded to where Jen sat on the curb, another paramedic bent over her.

"Is she all right?"

"Yeah. Nasty bump to the head but she'll be fine. Hold still."

Billie raised her free hand and gave a little wave but Jen wasn't looking. Jen's boyfriend, Adam was seated on the curb next to Jen. He wiped away a tear on her cheek and she leaned into him. Her head rested against his shoulder and something twinged inside of Billie, witnessing it.

She had gotten her friend hurt. In her ignorance and haste, Billie had rushed in without a clue as to what she had hoped to do and when everything went haywire, Jen had taken the punishment. It could have been much worse and the thought made Billie shudder. She didn't know the dead could lash out like that. Looking down at the blistered red mark on her wrist, she had no idea that they could hurt you.

And what of the thing in the basement? Was it still down there?

"Can I talk to her?"

"Sure." The paramedic looked over the dry wrap around her wrist one last time. "This is loose, so keep it from snagging on anything. Okay?"

Billie promised she would and the paramedic walked her to the curb where Jen sat nestled into her boyfriend.

"Hey," she said to Jen. "You okay?"

"Yeah. But I'll have a goose egg in the morning." Jen nodded slowly. "What happened?"

"I was about to ask you that."

The young man comforting Jen looked up. Adam had been Jen's beau for longer than Billie could remember. "The cops said it was an electrical fire," he said. "Bad wiring in the basement. Did you try to fix something down there?"

"Guess I screwed up." Billie studied Jen's face, looking for any hint of what she had witnessed. Hadn't she seen what was haunting the basement of her shop? "How did you get hurt?"

Jen shrugged. "I don't remember. I came down to check on you. Then I saw sparks. The rest is a blur."

Jen hadn't seen the scorched ghost, only Billie had. There was a sting of disappointment to that. If her friend had seen the thing, then Billie could actually talk to someone about the disruption to her life. Someone who was normal, at least. A friend.

"I'm gonna take Jen home," Adam said to Billie. "Do you want me call someone to come help you? Maybe Tammy's free."

"Aren't they gonna take you to the hospital?" Billie asked.

Jen shook her head. "They don't need to. They told Adam to wake me up throughout the night, just to make sure I don't have a concussion."

"I'm glad you're all right." Billie watched another fireman exit the shop and return to the pumper truck. "How bad is the damage?"

Jen rose gingerly to her feet. "They won't say until they know more."

"Can't be that bad," Adam said, looking back at the shop.

He was right. From the curb, the shop appeared undamaged. The only thing that looked out of place were the two firefighters chatting inside.

"Let's get you home," Adam said as he led Jen to his car. Turning back to Billie, he said "You sure I can't call someone for you, Bee?"

"I'm fine. Just take care of Jen, kay?"

"I always do."

Jen gave a limp wave goodbye and Billie watched them walk away. Adam eased her along like she was made of glass, opening the passenger door and helping Jen settle in. It was tender and sweet but difficult to watch as Billie stood alone on the street surrounded by strangers in uniforms. She hated pity and despised self-pity most of all but she let herself indulge in a moment of it now, wondering if there would ever be someone who would take care of her when she needed it the way Adam cared for Jen. It seemed unlikely.

Shaking it off, she turned to go back to the ambulance and almost collided into someone headed her way.

"Billie?"

She looked up from the tie she had almost barrelled into. Detective Mockler smiled at her.

"Hi," she said.

His eyes fell to her gauze-wrapped wrist. "What happened?"

"Just a burn," she dismissed. "What are you doing here?"

"I heard your name on the squawk box. I came to see if you were okay."

"You did?"

"How bad is this?" He took her hand and raised it gently, scrutinizing the gauze. "The call over the radio said it was a fire. What happened?"

"A fire broke out in the basement. I got singed on something."

"Jesus, this isn't your month, is it?"

Billie shrugged. "Just unlucky, I guess."

"I didn't have anything to do with this one, I swear. Did the ambulance boys let you go?"

Everything keeled left as a sudden dizzy spell knocked her off balance. She braced herself against the side of the ambulance. "I need to sit down."

Mockler settled her back onto the bumper then addressed the paramedic with the shaved head. "Hey, you've treated her already. Is she okay to go home?"

The paramedic said she was but a uniformed officer stepped in. "I still need to get her details, what she saw," he said to Mockler.

"It can wait. She needs to get out of here."

"Sure," the officer said without a fuss. "Friend of yours?"

"Yeah."

Billie listened to the exchange as the dizziness ebbed away. That familiar fog settled in, dampening everything around her. She felt the detective's hand on her arm.

"Up we go," he said. "I'll take you home."

~

Billie watched the street pass by the passenger window as Mockler turned onto Murray. She glanced over the interior of his car but aside from a binder on the backseat, the car was clean and devoid of any mess. The interior of one's car, she'd found, was always telling of its owner. A mess on the floor or a tchotchke dangling from the rearview mirror but Mockler's car was completely empty. Not even a stray pen rolling around on the floor mat. The lack of it suggested fastidiousness. Or a pathological austerity.

"Do you always keep your car so clean?" she asked.

"This is a work vehicle. The guys in the motor pool keep 'em clean. My car's a mess."

That was a relief. Overtly clean people made her uncomfortable.

He cut right onto Hughson and swung back onto Barton. "How have you been? Back to normal?"

She looked at him and, for a moment, contemplated telling him the truth. How, since getting out of the hospital, she's been seeing dead people everywhere and how they're tormenting her. How they scare the living daylights out of her and, oh yeah, apparently she's had this ability her whole life but didn't know it until he knocked her into the cold harbour and she almost drowned.

"Fine," she said. "Right as rain."

He grinned. "You're a lousy liar."

"I know. I'll work on that."

"Have you talked to anyone yet? About what happened?"

"A few people," she answered, deciding not to mention that one was a wanted criminal and the other a psychic medium. She looked at him again. "Why do you care anyway?"

"You seemed troubled last time we spoke. That's all."

"You feel guilty."

His fingers drummed the steering wheel as he mulled it over. "Not guilty, exactly. Responsible?"

"I absolve you of your guilt," she said, making a dismissive sign of the cross. "Maybe you have a white knight complex."

"I gave that up for Lent."

She laughed, despite herself. Free from the scene of flashing lights and emergency vehicles, detective Mockler seemed like a different man. Relaxed and easy in his own skin. Gone was the flinty edge he maintained on the job. Not for the first time, she caught herself glancing sideways at him and, again, reminded herself that she didn't like police officers.

Still, she thought as the streetlights rolled by, something was different here. Despite the gnawing ache in her wrist and the frantic terror she'd experienced, she felt calm for the first time in days. Could it be his presence? It made no sense. Maybe the knock to the head had driven her over the edge into complete mental breakdown.

It seemed plausible.

"Which building is yours?" he asked, slowing to a crawl.

"Just up here," she pointed. "The sleazy tenement."

Mockler pulled to the curb and leaned over to her side to peer up at the building. Her description wasn't far off the mark. The brick monolith leaned over the sidewalk like a toothless tombstone. Used up and spent, spared the wrecking ball out of nothing more than apathy.

"Looks homey," he said.

"No need to be polite," Billie said. She climbed out of the car. "It's ghetto, through and through."

"I wasn't being polite. I grew up in a building just like this."

Her brow arced with suspicion. "Sure you did."

"Six blocks from here. A redbrick shanty over on Sanford. Just me and mom."

"No guff? We were practically neighbours," she said, pushing the door closed with the wrong hand. "Ouch."

"You should stick that arm in a sling. It'll keep you from using it." Stepping around the car, he looked up at the building. "If you have a towel or something, I can rig it up for you."

Habit prompted her to refuse. She hated asking for help, or admitting to needing it, but she thought ahead to the empty apartment waiting for her. The idea that it might not be as empty as it used to be made her break the habit.

"Sure," Billie said, digging for her keys. "That would be helpful."

He cracked a joke about the three floor walk-up, one she'd heard plenty of times before. Unlocking the door, she apologized in advance. "Pardon the mess."

She waved him through and followed him inside. The mess wasn't as bad as she had feared, even lit bright as it was.

He looked over the living room. "Do you always leave every light on?"

"I do now." The place wasn't half so scary with the detective here, she noted. Too bad he couldn't stay. "Can I get you something? Beer? Cup of tea?"

"Just a length of material. Something light, about yay long." He measured a distance with his hands.

Rummaging through the hall closet, she came back with a length of gauzy material. God knew where it came from. "How's this?"

"Perfect." Folding it, he slipped the material under her arm and fitted the ends around her neck. "Pull your hair out of the way. Is that comfortable?"

"I think so." She couldn't quite tell. Too distracted by his proximity, his hands tying the knot at the back of her neck. Tiny crackles of electricity each time his fingers brushed her skin. Crazy notions swam through her head.

"How's that?"

Billie let her arm go limp. She could see how the sling would keep it still. "Good. Thanks."

He took a step back. Her free hand fussed with the fabric.

"I'll get out of your hair," he said, crossing back to the front door. She scrounged for something to say, some reason to stall him but couldn't find one.

Mockler passed into the corridor and stopped. "You'll need to give a statement about the fire. I'll have someone call."

"Okay." Billie looked down at the threshold of her front entrance. She thought of the salt Marta had used earlier. "Thanks for the lift home."

"Give me a call if you need anything."

She watched him disappear down the stairwell and then closed her door. The apartment seemed desolate now with only herself to keep it occupied.

Until the noise came from the kitchen. The sharp crack of glass breaking on the floor.

Her legs wanted to run after Mockler but she steeled herself to peek around the corner.

Gantry stood at the sink, one hand pressed over his bloodied nose.

"Can't you keep that little fucker caged?" he groused. "Creepy little bastard. He tell you what happened to his legs?"

16

"GET OUT."

Her heart threw its rhythm at the stranger in her kitchen. Billie took a step back. Had Mockler already left the building? He may have hit the sidewalk by now. She could holler at him through the window, tell him that the suspect he was after was in her apartment.

"Sorry about the towel." John Gantry dabbed at his bloodied nose with her dishtowel. Three deep drops of blood dotted his shirt. "That little shit packs a punch."

Billie swept the room, wary of anymore nasty surprises. "How did you get in here?"

"Did I get it all?" Gantry wiped his face one more time and then looking down, saw the bloodstains. "Ah Christ, look at my shirt."

Billie slipped her phone from her pocket. "I'm calling the police."

"Put that away. We need to talk."

Her thumb lingered over the keys. Gantry opened the fridge and bent over to examine its contents. Reaching inside, he came away with two cans of lager. "You're outta beer."

"What do you want?"

"Came to check on your progress. See how you're dealing with your newfound talent." Flopping into a kitchen chair, he popped the tabs on the cans and pushed one across the table toward her. "Settling in nicely, I see."

She stayed put. Any move to sit or linger would just prolong this. "You can shove your 'talent' nonsense. I want nothing to do with it."

"Little late in the day for that now, luv. You're stuck with it. And you have a boatload of catching up to do, yeah?"

"How do I get rid of it?" she said. "How do I turn it off?"

He snorted up beer with his laugh. "It's not a lightswitch, Billie. You're stuck with it. Like I said, you gotta learn how to deal with it."

"You're bleeding again." She snatched up the dirty towel and tossed it at him. "What happened to your face."

"I startled that little legless bastard when I came in. Is he always here?"

Her back went up, eyes scanning the corners of the room. "Is he still here?"

"He scampered. Who is he?"

"How should I know?"

"You're the one who can chat with dead people, remember? Ask him."

"That's the last thing I want to do. How do I get rid of him?"

"Telling him to 'fuck off' might work. The trick is to say it with conviction. Sit down already."

She took the beer he had opened for her but stayed on her feet. "I didn't know they could hurt people."

"Some can," he shrugged. "They stick around long enough, they learn how to manipulate the physical world. Those are usually the nasty ones."

Billie leaned back against the counter. Was she really discussing ghosts? With a wanted criminal in her kitchen no less? Her shoulders drooped. "I just want everything to go back to normal."

"I always wanted to be taller." He fished his cigarette pack from a pocket and shook one out. "But it just isn't in the cards, is it?"

"You can't smoke in here."

He snapped the lighter and lit up. "The thing is, Billie, is that there's different types of dead folks out there. Some are harmless, some are lost. But some are nasty. By the same token, there are different types of mediums too."

Smoke billowed up toward the ceiling. Billie slid a dirty dish across the table for him to use as an ashtray. "Do I really wanna hear this?"

"You should be taking notes. Some mediums can see the

harmless ones, the newly dead or the ones who got lost. The common ones, who just haven't crossed over or buggered off or whatever the hell dead people do when they move on—"

"Move on?" she interrupted. "You mean they go to Heaven?"

"I have no idea. They just aren't here anymore." He flicked his ash into the dish. "Now, the mildly talented mediums can see a bit more. But the really nasty phantoms, well, you need to move up the pay grade to find a seer who can pick out those ones."

"The job pays?"

"Don't be cute. The point is, I think you're one of the powerful ones. Lots of people have second sight, or whatever you call it, but they see forms and shapes. Or they just sense the dead person in the room. The rare seer? They can see them clearly. For what they are. And communicate with them."

Billie pulled out a chair and finally sat. "And you think that's me?"

"Bingo."

"And what exactly am I supposed to do with this talent? Besides being scared witless half the time."

"You talk to them. Find out what they want." Gantry stubbed out the cigarette. "Most mediums, the good ones, learn how to utilize their talent. They know how to open themselves up to it, to the dead around them. And they learn how to shut it down. Or turn off their radar so they won't be bothered by them."

"You just said it's not a lightswitch."

"It's not an exact science, Billie. It's feeling and intuition, like."

Billie ran a finger through the wet ring of condensation left on the table. Patience was normally a strong suit of hers. Sometimes she felt as if she'd been waiting forever for her life to start but this was not what she had in mind. Gantry's mystery-man routine was wearing thin, his riddles and supernatural mumbo-jumbo becoming tedious.

"Then tell me how to switch off my radar or whatever it is," she said. "I want nothing to do with this."

He shrugged. "I don't have a clue how that works. I'm not a medium, am I?"

"What are you, then?"

His mouth frowned in a comical way as he turned the question over. "Me, I'm more of a day-trader. Listen, I know this is hard to deal with but you can't walk away from it now. It's too big. It's like that bit from the Spiderman comics, yeah? About how power comes with responsibility."

"I have no idea what you're talking about."

"It just means you can't squander your talents."

"This doesn't sound like a talent," she said. "More like a disability."

"It's all a matter of perspective, innit?"

Billie wiped the table dry with her hand, set the can down and then raised it again. The water ring returned. "I tried to get rid of one. My friend got hurt. The place almost burned down."

"You bit off a bit more than you can chew that time."

"What was I supposed to do? That awful thing was haunting Jen's shop—" She cut herself short after using the word 'haunting'. Had she bought into all this?

"That's why you need to sort this. Get in front of it before it gets out of hand. Otherwise it'll drive you barking mad." He looked at his watch. "I gotta run."

"How?"

"That part I'm a bit foggy on." He rose and crossed to the doorway. "But a place to start would be to find out how you've suppressed your ability for so long. You've always had it. But now it's woken up."

"The knock to the head," she said quietly.

"I think it had more to do with being clinically dead for a few minutes."

With that, he left the kitchen and made for the front door. Billie blinked for a few moments before getting up.

"What's all this?" Gantry held the manila envelope with the newspaper clippings. "Where'd you get this rubbish?"

"Somebody slid it under my door."

"Why is this shite always so badly written?" He snorted and tossed the sheets away. "See you around."

Billie scooped up the loose clippings. "Is this stuff true? This is why you're wanted by the police, isn't it?"

"There's a grain of truth in there. The rest is bullocks."

The fine hair on her arm crackled again. "You killed

someone? In some Satanic thing?"

"I didn't kill anyone. It was an exorcism that went bad. The woman died."

Any patience Billie had left evaporated. Now she was just angry. "Come on. An exorcism?"

"Something took hold of that poor girl. I tried to help her." His eyes dropped to the floor. "I failed."

His darkening face made her pause. "So you're not some devil-worshipping serial killer?"

"Give me some credit, Billie. I wouldn't be caught dead with that pack of wankers."

"Then why is detective Mockler after you?"

"What? He's gonna believe me? He's got copper tunnel vision." Gantry stepped out to the corridor then stopped. "We're becoming quite chummy with Mockler, aren't we?"

She held the door open. "I wouldn't say that."

"Watch yourself there, Billie. Murder cops aren't the most stable bunch."

Gantry stuck another cigarette in his teeth, flashing a wide grin before he disappeared down the stairwell.

17

THE SPINE OF the binder was split from over-use, the edges frayed from familiarity. Opening it one more time would lead only to frustration but Mockler did it anyway. The typed reports flipped past, his notes cribbed into the margins on so many pages. Leafing past it all, he turned straight to the crime scene photographs. He had studied these pictures countless times before but their gruesome images still took him aback. The violence of it all.

The woman's body lay on the bare floor of some squat on Bleeker Street. Her left arm was bent back so unnaturally that it appeared fake, a trick of the light or a prosthetic effect from some horror movie. The right leg was broken at the knee and angled in a way it was never meant to. He remembered having difficulty describing the position of the body in that initial report. Although the victim lay on her belly, he couldn't state that she was face down. Like the rest of her, the poor woman's head was all wrong. The neck had been snapped and twisted all the way around. Her face looked up to the ceiling, even though the rest of her was face down. Detective Inspector Mike Schavinno, who was primary on the investigation, shook his head at the sight and asked Mockler to write up the description of the body for him. He didn't have a clue how to describe what he was seeing.

The woman remained nameless, another frustrating aspect of the case. Clad in only a thin smock, there had been no identification found at the scene. No wallet or bag or any other clothes. White, five-ten with medium length dark hair, the victim's physical details matched with no known missing persons in the Hamilton-Wentworth area. She remained nameless, which only added salt to the horror she had been subjected to. Mockler remembered a vow he had foolishly made at the time. That he would give the deceased back her identity and pluck her from the limbo of countless other Jane Does.

Turning the printed photos over revealed the victim at different angles. The close-up of the woman's face still haunted him, the way her eyes were stretched wide in terror but her pupils were all wrong. Dull white in colour, as if all the pigment had been burned out of them. The bleached-out eyes gazed straight into the camera and Mockler couldn't help the creeping sensation that she was looking directly at him. He flipped the photograph over.

The rest of the pictures were of the room itself. A large circle had been painted on the floor, with a five-pointed star within its circumference. A pentagram. Four of the five points of the star were capped with candles. At the fifth point, which compassed north, was a clay bowl of water. The pentagram measured fifteen feet in diameter and the dead body lay crumpled in the southeast corner of it.

The paint had also been used to splash words on three of the walls. The language of the scrawled words confounded both detectives until a professor from the university was brought in to take a look. It was Aramaic, the professor reported. A dead language not spoken since the time of the Romans. The meaning of the Aramaic continued to elude him however, as the professor could not translate the message. He said the words made no sense at all. It appeared to be a string of random words.

The fourth wall, which faced south, was plastered with pages torn from the Bible. They were all the same pages torn from different editions of the New Testament. Mark 5: 1-20. The story of Jesus encountering a lunatic in a graveyard and how he cast out the demons that had driven the man insane. Forced to abandon the hapless man, the demons entered a herd of swine and the pigs lept over a cliff to their deaths. Never a religious man, Mockler could make no sense of the bizarre tale or how it pertained to the victim found on the floor.

One significant article of evidence had been found on the victim herself. A name had been burned into the flesh of the woman's back, as if singed into the skin like a cattle brand. A single word:

GANTRY

Speculation ran rampant when they uncovered that awful wound. Was the perp marking his territory? Who was Gantry? Detective Inspector Schavinno ran out the bill for overtime as he worked his unit, Mockler among them, in the search for the individual identified as Gantry.

What emerged was a vague sketch of a shadowy British national named John Gantry. Even then, the details they had were few and their sources questionable. Known psychics and mediums, the owner of an occult bookshop in north end and the head of a Satanic church based out of a Quonset hut up on the mountain. These people seemed to know Gantry more by way of reputation than actual interaction. Working from the scant details, Gantry appeared to be some kind of investigator of the paranormal. A fixer of all things supernatural. Got a haunted house? Call Gantry, he can clear it (for a fee, of course). Cursed by an enemy or rival? John Gantry can fix that too. For an extra fee, he can even redirect that curse to boomerang back to the person who issued it.

A con-man through and through, Detective Schavinno concluded. Mockler agreed. A shifty fraud willing to swindle desperate people with his voodoo schtick. With the investigation of the victim in the pentagram, he was now a murder suspect. Sightings of the suspect came in all over the city but the more man-power Schavinno threw at the search, the more elusive Gantry became. 'Spooky' was a term whispered in the staff kitchen. 'Creepy shit' could be heard in the motor pool whenever the Gantry file was discussed. Schavinno shut down the gossip and worked his unit harder and Mockler put his shoulder to the task so intensely that he didn't make it home for days. Schavinno's health began to fail when the search entered its fifth month.

Reaching out to British police provided a few significant details. A big red alert flared up when the Hamilton squad learned of a homicide in England with eerie similarities to their own file. A young woman murdered in the east end of London in what appeared to be some kind of devil-worship ritual. The dead body broken and bent, the pentagram with the candles. The victims were also similar in appearance. White, dark haired, twenty to thirty years of age. No tell-tale name had been burned into the victim's flesh but the London police uncovered a much more solid article of evidence about the perpetrator of the crime. The victim had been identified as Ellen Marie Gantry. Wife of one John Herod Gantry.

The break in the case reignited the Hamilton squad but faded out as the London police force had found Gantry as slippery as they had. He appeared to have slipped off the grid sometime in the last decade. An inactive national insurance number, no driver's license, no income reported, no bank account, no known employer. Hearsay and gossip from less than reliable sources within London's occult community. Gantry appeared to have operated as some kind of paranormal 'fixer' before vanishing altogether after murdering his wife.

Ellen Gantry was as normal as houses. A brief stint at London Art College, followed by a freelance career as an illustrator. Aside from a marriage licence, there had been no legal connection to John Gantry. Even that was sketchy, as no one could figure out how someone without an actual identity had gotten married. His name was printed on the marriage certificate, that was all.

The London Police service did, however, provide one key piece of information to the Hamilton file; a photograph of John Gantry. The same photo that Mockler had hung on the evidence board. The smirking visage of a thin, rakish man who appeared to be winking at the security camera as it snapped its shutter. The photo was distributed throughout the Hamilton units and then things sort of went to hell after that. Sightings of the man popped up everywhere. A sighting on James Street, near the armoury in Hamilton. The next week, a sighting in Camden Market in London. It seemed as if the suspect was travelling constantly between Canada and the U.K. every week, which proved curious for a man without a passport. It was downright embarrassing to border security on both sides of the pond.

The sightings died down, the case grew cold. Inspector Schavinno was forcibly retired after blowing the budget on the investigation, leaving only detective Mockler to carry the ball on it. Nobody else wanted to touch the spooky case and the incoming sergeant, Thea Gibson, dampened any further investigations without new leads. Mockler rotated back into the shift, supporting the primary detectives on new case files.

Nothing happened after that, until September of 2013 when Mockler came face to smirking face with John Gantry.

Driving back to Division One after canvassing the Welland block in a stabbing incident, Mockler took a detour and drove past the abandoned tenement where the Jane Doe had been found. Something about the case was prickling his skin and without thinking about it, he steered the car back to the old building where it had all started. Intending to simply drive past it, he noticed a flicker of light in a third floor window. The shanty brick edifice had been without power for more than three years, yet a glow of light bled from the upper floor. Eyeballing the third floor windows, he realized the light was coming from the same room where the victim had died.

Going around back, he found the plywood boarded over the rear entrance had been broken open. After calling it into Division, he slipped through the opening and crept up the stairs. Voices echoed down from above, muffled and unclear. More than one person. Coming onto the third floor landing, he could make out one voice clearly. Male, with an English accent.

He stopped and checked his gut. His hand dropped to his side to reaffirm the firearm clipped to his belt. Most days, Mockler left it at the office. He had drawn his weapon a few times while on the job but had never discharged it while on duty. Letting off a tiny sigh of gratitude for clipping it on today, he unlatched the strap and drew it slowly from its holster. The question facing him now was whether to go in or wait for back-up.

Judging from the voices, there were at least two individuals inside the aparment. An awful stench hung in the air, one he would find difficult to describe later when typing up the incident report. The smell of smoke combined with an acrid sulphur smell and the tang of rot. When the hallway lit up with flashes of light, Mockler moved in.

Sidling up to the doorway, he quick-peeked inside to establish one individual near the window. He swung about with the weapon in both hands, barking at the individual to hit the floor.

John Gantry sat on a plastic milk crate near the cracked glass of the bay window. His shirtsleeves were rolled up and his tie was tugged loose, sweat stains darkened his shirt. Both hands were dirty like he'd been digging in soil. The weapon Mockler thought he had seen in the occupant's hand turned out to be a tall can of lager. Two empty cans lay crushed at his feet, like the man had come for a picnic in this abandoned tenement.

Gantry didn't startle or even look surprised. He took a swig from the can. "Well if it ain't the filth."

Mockler repeated his demand in a loud, clear voice to drop everything and get on the ground.

"Put the piece down, yeah?" Gantry said. "I don't want to get shot today."

Mockler scanned the room quickly. It was empty. "Where's

the other person?"

"No one here but me, mate." Gantry sipped his beer, heedless to the police detective's demands.

"I heard a second voice in here. Who else is here?"

Gantry didn't answer. Mockler scanned the room again, the walls dark with graffiti but the room remained void of another person. Something crunched under his heel and he looked down to see bones on the floor. It wasn't unusual to find animal bones inside a derelict property but these were bigger than anything left by a rat or raccoon. His first thought was that they were human.

There was a lot of them, strewn over the floor, but not in a random mess. Femurs and ulnas were laid out on the grimy linoleum in a pattern that chilled his blood. A pentagram. The candles were there too, placed at the points but where a bowl of water had sat at the northernmost point of the star, there was now a human skull. The hollow eye sockets rippled with light cast from the wicks.

The whole tableau was a horrorshow. Mockler had been in bad situations and had seen terrible things in his job but this unnerved him in a way that was entirely new. He wasn't a man prone to flights of fancy or delusion. He worked with facts and human weakness. Things that made sense, even when it came to how one human being could murder another. Although he would leave it out of his written report, the scenario he had stormed into felt evil. He didn't know any other way to describe it.

He ordered the suspect to identify himself.

The Englishman shook a cigarette from a crushed pack. "Me? Pope Pius. But my mates call me Pi. You?"

The gun in the detective's hand lowered a notch, drawing a bead on the man's knees. "I'm detective Mockler, Hamilton Police. And you, mister John Gantry, are under arrest. Now get on the floor before I knock your brains in."

"Can't, detective," Gantry blew out the smoke. "I'm late as it is and you're cutting into my work hours."

"Fine with me, asshole." Mockler felt his trigger finger itch with an irrational urge to pull. There was no one else on the scene yet. How easy would it be to claim the suspect charged at him, forcing him to fire to protect himself. The limey asshole could bleed out on the floor for all he cared.

Rationality won out as he rushed the suspect, eager to throw him to the floor and get the restraints on. Gantry remained seated on the milk crate, in a weak defensive position and Mockler had already sized up the skinny creep. No contest.

The man was slippery and he was fast and Mockler never did figure out exactly what had happened. He'd rushed Gantry only to find himself flat on his back, the dry bones crunching underneath him and the Englishman's boot stomping his guts in. And he could kick hard for such a scarecrow. Enraged, Mockler swung the barrel of the gun up fast and fired.

The trigger piece locked, the round jammed in the chamber. He roared up and tackled the creep, hurtling them both into the spray-painted wall. Decrepit plaster and lathe crumbled over them, dust roiling the air and into Mockler's eyes and he punched out blind, praying to connect.

Something hard broke over his skull and he flattened. A hissing sound spit into his ear and it took a moment for the sparks to clear before he realized it was Gantry.

"Stay the fuck out of it, copper. This shite will poison you."

Mockler shot to his feet and that's when he felt the heat wash over him. A fire raged to life all around him. Rising up from the floor in a distinct pattern, the pentagram blazed high with tall flames that blackened the ceiling. The whiff of sulphur returned, stronger than before and as he waved the smoke away, Mockler caught sight of the human skull in the flames. The hollow eyes seemed to mock him now.

Gantry was gone. Poof, just up and vanished and Mockler scrambled for the door as the entire tinderbox flat flared hot with fire.

Twenty minutes later, he sat on the bumper of an ambulance and relented to the prodding of the paramedic. His shirt was soaked through with sweat but he shivered like a little kid running for his towel after a cold swim. His gut was pushing at him to get away. *This is spooky shit and you don't want to mess with it.* Gantry's words still rang in his ear, something about poison and nightmares. Mockler had learned the hard way to trust his gut. Its first instincts were often the right ones.

Not this time. Gritting his molars together, he resolved to see this through. To get his hands on the murderer named John

Gantry, no matter what sort of spooky shit he had to endure. He asked the paramedic for a tissue but no matter how hard he blew his nose, he could not get shed of the stench of sulphur burning his nostrils.

18

BRISTOL STREET WAS quiet and serene when Ray Mockler pulled into his driveway. It always was.

Getting his bag from the backseat, he stopped to give the street a once-over. The houses were an odd lot of Victorians and mid-century bungalows with narrow lots and a few trees. It wasn't the prettiest street in town but he liked the way the streetlight dappled through the leaves of the elm tree in his yard.

For a man raised in an overcrowded and smelly apartment building, he cherished the house he owned now with its narrow front lawn and peeling green trim that needed painting. He and Christina had taken the plunge three years ago, when the house came on the market. From the outside, it was perfect. Even with the battered gable trim that needed replacing and the crumbling parging around the base, it was still a dream home and he loved everything about it.

At least from the exterior. Pushing open the side door and

coming into the landing, the familiar crush of dread rolled over him like a wave of heat from an oven. How long had it been like this, he wondered, this almost unnatural gloom that came every time he stepped over the threshold and into the house. After the misery and frustration he waded through at work on a daily basis, home should be a refuge from all of that. A place of safety and comfort that welcomed him in like a traveller in a storm.

It hadn't been like that in a long time.

Two steps up brought him into the kitchen and he looked over the mess. Dishes and glassware cluttered across the counter, two pots left on the stove. He dropped his bag onto a chair and took the lid off the bigger pot and looked inside. Whatever it had been was now baked into crusty mess.

"Christina?"

No answer. Not that he'd expected one. She would either be in front of the TV or in her studio. The only real question was, how bad was she tonight? Catastrophic or just mildly tragic?

Pulling off the tie, he shrugged out of his jacket and hung both over the back of a chair. A soft chatter filtered in from the other room and he knew she was still up.

Christina was curled up under a blanket on the sofa, her eyes glazed over as they reflected the light from the television.

"Hey," Mockler said, standing in the doorway. "How was your day?"

The same boring question. He needed to cut that entire phrase from his lexicon and think of something new. A different opening that might get her talking.

"Great." Her eyes didn't move from the television screen.

She pulled her legs in to give him room as he sunk into the sofa. Her bare feet poked out from under the blanket and he could see the red scrape mark on the back of her Achilles tendon, worn raw from a new pair of shoes.

"That looks like it hurts." He touched her ankle. "You want a band-aid?"

She flinched and pulled her feet under the blanket. "Don't."

A bottle of wine stood on the coffee table, an inexpensive Spanish red that she liked. The glass beside it was empty.

"What happened to dinner?" he asked.

"Please." Her head lifted slightly from the cushion, half tilting in his direction before settling down again, as if the effort exhausted her. "You know what happened."

He did and should have known better than to ask. Christina had gotten overwhelmed, as she often did, trying to coordinate it all so everything was ready at the same time. Frustrated, she had simply abandoned the whole thing. He could almost picture the cursing and the slamming of a pot, followed by tears and then fetching the bottle and retreating to the sofa.

She hadn't always been like this. Christina used to love to cook, couldn't wait to get home to try her hand at something new. What had happened? Mockler took up the bottle and splashed some into the glass and knocked it back. Staring at the television screen, he said nothing.

It wasn't just Christina. He had changed too. In the past, he would have killed the TV, made her sit up to look at him and they would have talked it through. Neither was a stranger to the frustrations of work or the toll it takes, the way it feeds on one's energy and leaves them drained. In the past, they would have let it all out until the gloom passed over their heads like a thunderstorm moving on.

Now he sat silent as the grave and let himself be hypnotized by the mindless images on the screen. His fiancee lay no more than three inches away from him but they didn't touch.

He poured more of the wine. How much of it could he blame on his job? It came home with him sometimes. No matter how hard he tried to leave it parked outside their front door, the misery of the job slithered inside like a rat finding a crack in the foundation. He scolded himself for doing that. He needed to take advantage of the counselling provided by the force. There he could unpack all of the nasty shit and come home clean. Or, if not clean, at least not so stained with it all.

Christina rose into a sitting position, her toes brushing his leg as her feet swung to the floor. She sighed. "I'm going to bed."

Seeing her hair cascade over her shoulder, he reached out and touched her arm. "Anything happen today? We could talk. If you want."

"Nothing happened. Maybe that's the problem." She didn't flinch at his touch but her arm slipped away all the same. Her words drawled slightly and he looked to see how much wine was left in the bottle but the glass was too dark to tell.

She took the glass he had poured and downed half of it and settled the glass down again. "Goodnight."

He watched her drift from the room and listened to her footfalls on the stairs. Scavenging up the remote, he killed the TV and the room went dark. He took the bottle and the glass to the kitchen and looked at the disaster littered across the counter. It would wait until morning, he decided and went to check the studio before turning in. Hitting the light switch, he saw that nothing had been moved, nothing changed. The easel stood empty. She hadn't painted a thing in months. He turned off the light and went upstairs.

Sometimes he blamed himself, other times he blamed her. Christina had always been prone to dark moods but in the past, the dark spells would last a day or two. In the early days of their relationship, he made the mistake of thinking he could cure her mood with jokes or gifts or surprise outings. She appreciated the gesture but said there was nothing to do when the moods struck. She simply needed to let it unfurl and it would pass of its own accord and their world would tilt back to normal.

That wasn't the case now. The dark mood came on over the winter and settled in to stay. Therapy wasn't helping and the couples-counselling they had tried was a bust. Christina had all but given up, medicating the problem with red wine and camp-outs on the sofa.

He draped his tie over the chair in the bedroom and flung his damp shirt into the hamper. Christina came out of the bathroom and shimmied out of her clothes, leaving them on the floor where they dropped. He stirred instantly, fanning hot at the sight of her. That's how it was for him. It could be the furthest thing from his mind but one look at her and it was there. A sudden heat and a longing that wrenched deep into his chest.

Coming up from behind, he folded her in his arms and put his lips to the back of her neck.

"I'm tired," she said, slipping away.

He pulled her back in. "I need you."

"I'm not in the mood."

"How long has it been?" He hated having to beg. "Two weeks?"

"Who's counting?"

He lowered her onto the bed. "I am."

She relented with a sigh. He smothered her body with his own and felt slightly lightheaded once he finally got his hands on her skin and dug his mouth into her long neck. He pushed her legs apart and leaned up to kiss her mouth, already feeling like he would explode but Christina turned her face to the side, her eyes looking out the window. Her face was as blank as it had been while staring at the television screen, disconnected and lifeless. Her hair fell over eyes and an image flashed through his mind. The eyes of a dead woman in a crime scene photo, glassy and unseeing and not dissimilar to his fiancee's eyes at this moment. He winced and rolled onto his back.

She looked at him. "What's wrong?"

"Nothing."

"Are you done" she asked.

"Yeah. I'm done."

Christina turned onto her side, pulled the sheet up and switched off her bedside lamp.

He lay there in the dark, still hard and his heart still thumping and he tried to flush the image from his mind. Of all the things to pop into his head, why that? It was a war of attrition, really. It was only a matter of time before the wreckage he witnessed infected everything. He forced his inner eye to conjure something else. A beach, the lights over the harbour, a Christmas tree hung with decorations. Flipping through mental snapshots but the dead eyes lingered. He stopped the scrolling images and backed up. Something had snagged.

The young woman with dark hair. The one he'd knocked into the water. Billie. A boy's name for a pretty girl.

He tried to shoo that from his mind too. It felt wrong to be thinking about Billie Culpepper while his erection throbbed unrelentingly and his girlfriend lay next to him. The dead woman's eyes flashed back. The white paint of the pentagram underneath her head. A second image popped, the photograph of the dead English woman found murdered in the same fashion. Gantry's late wife and his Jane Doe could almost be sisters. Same hair, same build and roughly the same age.

His eyes shot open as it hit him. Billie Culpepper looked a

hell of a lot like the two women John Gantry had murdered. That explained why he was stalking Billie. The sick son of a bitch was grooming her.

19

CLINICALLY DEAD.

That's what Gantry had said. The reason why this ability had awakened in her after being dormant for so long. How could she have had this her whole life and not known about it until now?

Unless she had blocked it out somehow. Or it was quashed from the outside. Did aunt Maggie know? Was that why her aunt was so religious, dragging Billie to mass every Sunday and confession every second Friday until the time when Billie had put her foot down at the age of thirteen and refused to go anymore? Was Maggie capable of that?

As unsettling as the idea was, it gelled the more she chewed on it. With a click, another piece of the puzzle locked into place. Her troubled history with attention spans and learning disabilities. The ADD, the OCD and a raft of other labels she had been subjected to as aunt Maggie sought treatment for her foggy spells and poor performance at school. None of those diagnoses had stuck, none of their corresponding therapies had helped. Had this latent ability to sense the dead been the real problem all along, forever misdiagnosed by a rational world that refused to believe in such things?

Underscoring all of it was the shadow of a mother she barely remembered. Poor Mary Agnes Culpepper, the town crazy woman. The woman abducted from her home twenty years ago and presumed dead. More than that though, Mary Agnes Culpepper was also the town's only psychic. Billie had few tangible memories of her mother but she remembered the cards. How her mother used to make her run the tarot and how Billie hated it.

Did she come by this gift honestly? Bred in the bone and brought forth in the flesh? Did Mary Agnes have this same gift and if she did, had it driven her out of her mind?

Noting the time on the clock, Billie reached for her phone and dialled the house on Long Point.

"Oh hi honey," Aunt Maggie replied after hearing Billie's voice on the line. "How are you feeling? Have the headaches gone?"

"Yeah. Much better. Are you busy?"

"Watching the neighbourhood boy cut the lawn. He always does such a poor job."

"Liam?" Billie said. "He always does a nice job."

"Not Liam. He lives in Guelph now. Liam's younger brother, Wyatt." Maggie clicked her teeth. "Not a straight line anywhere.

Anyhow. It's nice to get a call out of the blue. What can I do for you?"

"Uhm. Well." Billie choked. She hadn't thought this through before picking up the phone. What exactly was she going to say? *Say, aunt Maggie, did I see dead people when I was a kid?* "Uh, I was thinking about mom."

"Oh?" The warmth in her aunt's tone cooled by a degree.

"Do you know what was wrong with her? I mean, she had some form of mental illness, right? Do you know what it was?"

Silence hummed down the line. Then Maggie replied "No. Your mother hated doctors. Refused to see them. Honey, is everything all right?"

"I'm fine. Just been thinking about stuff."

"Why all this interest in your mother? What brought it on?"

"I dunno. I was wondering if it was hereditary, ya know?" Billie chewed her lip for a moment. "Was she always like that? Even as a kid?"

"Mary was different," Maggie said slowly. "Even when we were little. God, was she a nightmare when she hit her teens. But it grew worse as an adult."

"Did she have foggy spells back then? Like mine?"

"What are you getting at? Has something happened?"

"No," Billie fibbed. "It's just, sometimes I worry that I'll get it too. What she had."

More silence filled the line and it went on too long. Billie sat up. "Maggie? Are you still there?"

"Yes. I'm here," Maggie sighed. "Billie, there's always been a history of mental illness in our family. That's not what they called it back then, of course. I remember aunts who had it. God, how they were treated. It scared the heck out of me when I saw Mary Agnes heading down that same road."

Billie heard the crack in Maggie's voice as all of this ancient history was dredged up from its muddy sediment. She shouldn't have called.

Her aunt cleared her throat and went on. "Your mother's foggy spells used to frighten me when we were kids. It was like she became a different person. She used to talk to people that weren't there. Our father tried to beat it out of her."

"He did?" Billie had never known the man.

"He was a hard man. Violent. And something about Mary always set him off. Her woolgathering, her imaginary friends. I think he was trying to knock it out of her."

"God. That's awful."

"It was," Maggie agreed. "Every family has its secrets, honey. Ours seemed to have more than its share."

Another snap of the puzzle. "Who were these imaginary friends mom used to see?"

"Oh, I don't remember. They all had names. Or specific things, like what they were wearing. She'd tell me they were right there in the room with us. It used to scare the hay out of me when she did that."

"Is that why you took me to so many doctors?" Billie asked.

"Did you think I'd get it too."

Another long pause. "I thought that, if you did have it, it could be treated. Before it became a problem. God, I tried so many different therapies. Do you remember all of those? Some were a bit kooky."

Billie remembered. Exercises that Maggie would put her through, to focus her mind or keep her in the present instead of drifting off into a fog as she was wont to do. "I remember the fights we had."

"So do I," Maggie sighed. "It was hard. But it was necessary. I thought I would lose you."

"What do you mean?"

"After the incident," Maggie said, her voice catching. "When I brought you home after Mary disappeared. You were practically catatonic. Didn't speak a word for almost three weeks. You came back, slowly, but you'd get those awful spells where you would just go blank. Or you'd talk to someone who wasn't there. Like your mother did when she was a child. It scared me."

"I don't remember that."

"I was scared that the illness in our family, the kind your mother and our aunts had, would take you too. So I did what I could. Took you to doctors. And church."

It was Billie's turn to go silent. Was this how her ability was suppressed? Maggie had tried to treat it clinically with doctors and therapy. Spiritually, with church-going. Maggie had quashed it early on.

"Aunt Maggie," she ventured, "did you ever wonder if mom really did see people that weren't there?"

"What do you mean? Like spirits or something."

"Yeah."

"No," her aunt retorted, firmly and without hesitation. A conviction of iron behind it. "Never."

"I wish I remembered more about her."

"Honey, what's this all about? Did something happen?"

Exhaustion crept over Billie's shoulders. The exertion needed to stay on the phone seemed too much. "No. I've just been in a weird mood since the hospital. Reflective, you know?"

"Of course. It happens, after a scare like that. Why don't you come home for a bit? Get out of that awful city."

"Maybe," Billie said. "Listen, I should go. I'll talk to you later, okay?"

"Sure. Please try and come down."

Billie said she would try and told her aunt that she loved her and hung up the phone. She stood motionless for a moment, the phone still in her hand as she tried to fit it all together. The trauma of her mother's death, the catatonic state and Maggie's efforts to cure her of the family 'illness'. Somehow it had all contributed to suppressing her ability to see the dead. An ability passed down on her mother's side, like a history of near-sightedness or scoliosis.

It had driven her mother insane. Was that to be her fate too?

She looked up. Even with the sunlight streaming through the windows, the apartment looked grim. Too quiet. Most of the time, Billie liked living alone but not now. She dialled another number. She needed to talk to Jen.

When a man's voice answered Jen's cell, she thought she had hit the wrong number. It was Adam, Jen's beau. He told her that Jen didn't want to talk right now.

"Is she all right?" Billie asked. "How's the lump on her head?"

"She's fine," adam answered. "Well, physically. She's pretty torn up about the fire. She won't get out of bed."

"She does that sometimes. When it's really bad. Are you taking care of her?"

"Yes." He sounded annoyed.

"Maybe I should come by. I can usually get her out of a funk."

"That's not a good idea, Billie. I'll tell her you called, okay?"

Why was he being so short with her? A horrid thought bubbled up. "Adam, does she blame me for what happened? The fire?"

"I dunno, Billie. Just give her some space right now."

Jen did blame her. It hurt but what stung more was the fact that she couldn't tell Jen what really happened. Billie felt her cheeks burn. "Okay. Make sure she eats something, Adam."

He hung up without saying goodbye.

The clock ticked on in the kitchen and the apartment

remained too still and too empty. She needed to talk to someone but Tammy was never good in a crisis unless it was her own. Kaitlin had nothing but attitude for her lately, so she was out. Her circle of friends had never been big but it seemed cruelly small now. How had she let that happen?

There had to be someone.

Among the clutter on the table lay the plain-looking business card. She picked it up and read the imprint. How crazy would it be to call Mockler? She didn't understand what it was about him but she liked talking to the police detective. He had a quiet but accepting air about him that made him easy to be around. Like he would listen without judgement, no matter what she said. She looked at his name printed on the white cardstock and then laid it back onto the table. A silly notion, easily dismissed.

The phone rang, rattling along the tabletop as it vibrated. She picked it up, hoping it was Jen, calling back to talk it through.

"Billie?" A man's voice said when she answered it. "It's Ray. Detective Mockler. Can I buy you a cup of coffee? I need to talk to you about something."

Billie pulled the phone away and looked at it. She had just been thinking about him and here he was. Maybe she was psychic after all.

20

"YOU'RE IN DANGER."

The first words out of his mouth. No greeting, no idle chitchat. Just boom, bad news. Detective Mockler sighed as if he'd been holding his breath.

Billie crinkled her nose. She had taken this all wrong, thinking it was a social call but it clearly wasn't that and she felt foolish for thinking otherwise. She had actually fussed over what to wear before heading out the door. Why, she scolded herself silently, had she assumed this was anything more than business for him? Stupid girl.

Mockler had suggested meeting somewhere close like Mulberry's but Billie begged off that idea. Too busy, too great a chance of running into ghosts there. Anywhere busy or public was a bad idea so she suggested meeting in Gage Park, near the bandshell. It would be quiet and more than likely deserted of people, both living and dead. He agreed, then asked how she took her coffee.

There was an urgency to his voice that she mistook for something else. Dashing into the bedroom, she had fussed over what to wear and deplored her reflection in the mirror. She hadn't left the house in more than a day but there was no time to shower. She found the skirt Jen had given her from the shop, decided that it didn't look absolutely terrible and checked the hallway before leaving. The mess of salt over the threshold had scattered but the hallway appeared empty. Unlocking her bike, she sensed that she was being watched and looked up to see the half-boy in a third floor window. Pressed up against the glass, his narrow little eyes following her.

Walking her bike across the wide lawn of the park, she spotted Mockler in the shade of the tall elm trees to the left of the bandshell. She waved hello and he hit her with the bad news.

"Nice to see you too," she replied, leaning her bike against the tree trunk.

"Sorry. Hi." He handed her a tall of cup of coffee. "You look nice."

A grin bloomed over her face and would not recede no matter how hard she tried to stifle it. He motioned for her to sit. Laid across the bench was a folder weighed down by another coffee cup. He slid it out of the way as she sat and Billie wondered what was in it.

Mockler smiled back at her. He seemed thrown off after his

poor greeting. He nodded at her skirt. "Did your friend make that?"

That took her by surprise. He recognized one of Jen's designs? "Yeah. Cute, huh? How'd you know?"

"I saw inside the shop the night of the fire. How is she, by the way?"

"Not great. Still in shock, I guess." Billie straightened the hem of the skirt. She didn't want to think about Jen right now. "So. What's all this about being in danger?"

He sought out her eyes and held them. "I think Gantry wants to kill you."

"Oh," she said. He seemed dead serious and Billie paused to mull it over. Then, trying to keep things light, she said "I didn't get that vibe from him."

"Don't laugh it off, Billie. I think he means to hurt you."

From deep in her belly, a tiny zap of electricity crackled at hearing him say her name. Her brain scoffed but the frisson in her gut argued otherwise. "Okay. Why do you think that?"

Mockler hushed his voice, the way one does in church. "The women that he murdered were eerily similar in appearance. And they look like you."

Her eyes went immediately to the folder under his untouched coffee. "You're serious?"

"I am."

"Okay. Let's see 'em." She held out her hand. He leaned back, about to protest but she waved her hand impatiently. "You brought pictures. Hand them over."

He slid the folder out and balanced the cup back on the spar of bench seat but kept the plain file folder closed. "You could just take my word for it. These aren't pleasant."

"Your word is no good with me," she said with a playful tilt of her shoulders. Where did this easy banter come from, she wondered. This wasn't like her. Don't over-think it, just run with it.

"You think I'm lying?"

"No. I just need to know you better before I can take you at your word."

"Fair enough." He opened the folder and removed two large photographs and laid them side by side on the bench between them.

She had expected to see crime scene photos. Gory, blood and guts stuff but neither image showed that. Instead, Billie looked down at head-and-shoulder shots of two dead women. Their eyes were closed and something about the sag at their cheeks suggested neither subject was quite right. Their hair, dark on both women, was wet and draped thick across a stainless steel table. Whatever state these poor women had been found in, it was clear from their appearance that they had been cleaned up before the photos were snapped.

"I don't see it," she said.

"Look again."

Maybe she didn't want to see it but the closer she examined

the two faces, the more of herself she recognized. It was chilling; looking at a picture of herself already dead. The face in the nearest photo had a split upper lip. Her dull teeth protruding through the slit flesh.

Billie leaned back, pulling her eyes from the awful images and settled her gaze on the bandshell with its pretty aquamarine shade. Mockler gathered up the pictures and slid them back into the folder.

"Do you see it now?" he asked.

"Sort of. A coincidence?"

"Not with this guy."

"Which is the woman you found?"

Opening the folder again, he held up one of the pictures. "This is her. The other one is Ellen Gantry. His late wife."

She tried to suppress a shudder. Seeing the image a second time, the dead woman looked even more like a grim reflection.

"I'm worried about you." He leaned in, propped his elbows on his knees and looked at her.

"I appreciate that." She honestly did. "But I just don't think it's true. I mean, if that's what he was going to do, he's had plenty of opportunity."

"It's not that straightforward. He's not some impulse killer. He's a schemer. I think he's grooming you first, the way he did these other two women. He pulls them into his bizarro world with his voodoo schtick, then wham."

She considered telling Mockler what Gantry had said about

the dead woman, how it had been an exorcism gone wrong. It would sound insane, uttering it aloud like that. And why did she feel the need to defend Gantry? For all she knew, Mockler was right and the English weirdo really was a psychopath.

"Have you seen him again?"

Yes, she thought. Right in my apartment, not two seconds after you dropped me home. "No."

He seemed relieved upon hearing that. "I'm worried about you," he said a second time. "This guy is dangerous and he seems fixated on you. I think you should get out of town for a while. Is there somewhere you can go? A friend or relative?"

"My aunt's place. I can go there in a pinch if I need to." She sipped her coffee. It was lukewarm. "But I honestly don't think I'm in danger." At least not from him, she left out. The violent spirits of the dead, yes, but not Gantry.

"Your aunt," he nodded. "The one who took you in?"

"Yeah." She turned sharply to him. "How did you know?"

His smile was sheepish. "I ran your name. Looking for something that would tell me why Gantry picked you. Then I read what happened to your mom."

As always, Billie stiffened up at the mention of it. Her history usually elicited two responses; smothering pity or a stony silence. The net effect of either was always the same, the conversation flat-lined. Which reaction would Mockler have?

His eyes stayed on hers. "That's awfully young to have gone through something like that. Is that where you get the tough exterior?"

"Tough? I don't have a tough anything." The response threw her off.

"Maybe tough is the wrong word. Wary? Watching everything around you, putting up a wall. If someone wants to get through, they have to earn it."

Billie turned to see if he was talking to someone else. The park remained deserted. "I don't do that."

He had finally brought the coffee to his lips when he laughed at her reply. A tiny spit-take. He wiped it away. "I can't be the first person to tell you that."

"You are," she said. "And I don't think I believe you." Doubt crept in. Aunt Maggie used to always tell her she needed to warm up to people. If she wanted to make friends, that is.

"You don't have to believe me. But I'm right. It's just how people deal with trauma at a young age. They either toughen up or shut down. Develop a tic or stutter or something. You don't stutter. Unless I missed it."

She almost bristled at that. His smug conclusion. And yet there was a tiny zap behind it. "You a psychology minor?"

"Just what I've observed," he shrugged. "Anecdotal evidence only. Nothing empirical."

"You're a funny guy, detective," she said.

"I am?"

"Yeah. In a weird way."

"I can't tell a joke to save my life. I always get the punch line wrong."

"Being funny has nothing to do with telling jokes."

He nodded, mockingly serious. "So you're just laughing at me."

"Your arrogance is kinda laughable. Feels fake, like you're trying to come off as world-weary."

"No one's told me that either." He raised his cup in a goofy salute. "This is turning out to be a red letter day for uncomfortable truths. Cheers."

The paper cups made no sound as they tapped and she sipped hers while he put his back down. "It's bad luck," she said, remembering something she had been told once. "Not to drink after a toast."

"It is?" He snatched it up and sipped then tapped his cup against hers again. "Do it again. I don't need any bad luck."

The banter was too easy. She kept reminding herself that he was a cop. "Do you believe in bad luck?"

He tilted his head slightly, thinking it over. "No, not exactly. But I think you get back what you put out into the world."

"Like karma?"

"Close enough."

Out on the wide field of grass, lushly green from an unusually wet summer, a dog bounded past the bandshell to the stand of oaks and back to the lawn again. Apparently running wild, no dog-owner following after it with a plastic bag stuffed into a backpocket. They both watched the pooch nose the ground then sprint off to sniff some other patch of grass. It seemed to be in a hurry to smell everything and run everywhere, the way dogs get when they're cooped up in the house too long.

"So," she turned back to him when the dog disappeared into the trees again. "You dug up my awful past, huh?"

"It's not awful. Tragic yeah. You don't like talking about it, do you?"

Billie brushed a fly from her bare knee. "I don't bring it up. People get weird when they find out. Act differently, like I'm suddenly made of glass or something."

"I guess they would." He scratched his chin, stalling over something. "Can I ask you about it?"

"Sure." Please not the sympathy card.

"Did they ever find her?"

"No."

"Nothing? No remains or possessions?"

"Not even a stray shoe."

"The file's a bit spotty on the details. You know they suspected your father, right?" She nodded, he went on. "Do you think he did it?"

"The husband's the usual suspect, isn't he? I barely knew the man."

"He wasn't around?"

"He'd parachute in when I was little. Like day-tripping with a family he'd forget he had. He smelled like diesel fuel and Dial soap."

"Do you ever see him?"

"Nope," she said. "Not since the incident. Hardly saw him before that either but afterwards, no. He disappeared the same time she did."

Mockler stretched his legs out, crossing one ankle over the other. "There was one thing. The case file listed your mother's occupation as psychic. She had her own shop and stuff."

"She read tarot. What about it?"

"Dunno," he said. "Psychic stuff, tarot cards. That's up Gantry's alley. Just wondering if there was something there. Do you read tarot?"

"Me?" Not on your life, she thought. "Nah. Never been into that stuff."

"Nothing like that? Astrology or palm readings? Ouija boards?" When she shook her head, he turned his palms up. "So there's nothing there to bring his attention to you. The physical resemblance, his 'type', makes more sense then."

"I suppose. Wouldn't want to blow that precious theory of yours, would we?"

He smiled at the jab. "I thought my little theory was quite brilliant, thank you very much." The smile faded a little. "Are you okay talking about this stuff? Your mom?"

"Yeah." She was too. Which was unusual. Why was it okay now? "It's a relief to not have to fake anything."

"Fake what?"

"Faking to meet other people's reactions. The concern or pity or shock. It all happened so long ago, I don't feel anything anymore. But I feel the need to fake something, for the other person's benefit." She let out a laugh. "I fake being normal. It's a joke."

He grunted an approval. "Sometimes faking it is just easier."

"Oh? What do you fake?"

"You called me on it earlier. Acting world-weary. I fake being jaded. Or that I've seen it all and nothing phases me. But it's all bullshit."

"Then why do it?"

"Part of the job," he shrugged. "A defence, maybe. But it's not working anymore. I don't know if I'm cut out for this job anymore." He twitched as he said this, as if surprised at uttering aloud something he rarely acknowledged within himself. A stopper had been uncorked, stuff was bubbling out.

"I have to fake that it doesn't bother me at work. Then fake being normal after work so I don't bring the shit home with me. But I do anyway and I think it's slowly killing my fiancee and I don't have a clue what to do about it."

Like a hammer stroke on piano chords. Fiancée.

Her eyes shot down to his left hand but there was no ring there. Of course there was no ring, the ring comes after. He said 'fiancee', not wife. The butterflies lolling around inside her belly dropped dead as the warm, almost drunk feeling that enveloped her popped. She felt immediately foolish and exposed and wanted to leave. How stupid could she be? How could she have misinterpreted this easy banter as anything but plain old conversation?

The clammy sensation quashing her warm glow continued to plummet until she shivered.

"Hey," he said. "Are you all right?"

Billie didn't answer. Her mouth dropped open at the sight of the dead man rising up out of the earth behind Mockler.

21

THE DEAD MAN hung motionless, a few paces behind the detective, his horrid face looking down at the earth as if transfixed by something in the grass. His clothes were dark and old-fashioned, a strange tie coming loose under a wilted collar. He looked like an undertaker to Billie. She had never met an undertaker before, all she had to go on was a cartoon image of one. But this individual fit the bill.

Flesh so pale it looked blue against the dark clothes. His features were hard to see, muddied by what she thought was dirt or soot but then she saw the soot move. It was a mass of flies. Common bluebottles and everyday houseflies, wriggling out of his mangled ear and crawling over his face. They crawled and swarmed and settled again over his mouth and crawled over his eyes. Like the newshour image of a starving child in a faraway country, too weak to wave off the flies picking over its eyes. It made her cringe, like she could feel those filthy insects on her own flesh.

Mockler didn't see the dead man. Of course, she reminded herself. Only she could see him but something came over Mockler, as if he could feel its presence. He sunk down, shoulders drooping like a weight was lowering on him. His voice trailed off as if he'd forgotten what he was saying. It reminded her of her own foggy spells, the way it dampened everything around.

"What was I saying?" Mockler looked up sharply, as if caught falling asleep.

Billie kept her eyes on the undertaker man and spoke quietly to the detective. "We should go."

"Sure," Mockler said. He rubbed his eyes. "Jesus, I'm tired."

The dead man's head tilted, rotating slowly, almost mechanically, on its thin neck until its gaze locked on the man sitting on the bench. The flies swarmed up at the movement and resettled quickly, determined and single-minded. The only sign of life throbbed from its eyes but it was difficult to discern the emotion. Hatred or anger or hunger. Whatever it was, it blazed hot and steady at the detective sitting on the park bench.

Then it moved, its hand stretching out and Billie could almost hear the click of bone as it moved. It reached out for Mockler.

Billie shot up. "Let's go now."

The dead man turned its gaze on her and this time the eyes were crystal in their intent. Pure murder.

Mockler mumbled an answer but remained sluggish on the

bench. The undertaker man stretched his thin fingers out to the detective, brushing his hair in a disturbingly intimate way that made Billie sick to her stomach.

Mockler flinched, rubbing his temple as if overcome.

"What's wrong?"

"Just a headache," he grumbled. "They come on fast sometimes."

The dead man clicked his neck a few degrees to leer up at Billie and she could have sworn the fly-bedecked man was grinning.

"Let's just go, okay?" She took Mockler's arm and tried to haul him up but he was all dead weight.

"Gimme a second. I feel dizzy."

"You can walk it off."

"It's not a pulled muscle."

The undertaker man rotated his eyes back to the detective and reached out again. Its pale blue hand sunk into Mockler's side as if trying to pickpocket him.

Mockler instantly clutched his stomach. "Whoa. Too much coffee today."

She couldn't take the awful look of perverted glee in the dead man's eyes. Billie yanked Mockler's arm. "On your feet. Start walking, you'll feel better." She had no idea if that was true but she needed to get him away from the dark man.

"Okay, okay." He let himself be pulled away, marching across the grass. He glanced back at the bench. "What about your bike?"

"I'll come back for it. Are you parked in the lot?"

"Yeah. The blue Crown Vic."

She could see it, an unmarked police car that screamed 'unmarked police car'. "The grampa car?"

"Yes."

She was practically pulling him along now. Glancing over her shoulder, she spotted the fly stricken man. Following them.

"Wait." He stopped and looked back at the bench. "I forgot the folder."

"I'll get it, drop it off at the station." Just keep moving, damn it. "Maybe you should go home. Lie down or something."

"That's the last place I want to go. It's worse there."

Puzzling over that, she pulled him along to the driver's side door. "Maybe the station then. Or take a drive along the ridge. Get some air."

"Maybe." He fumbled the door open and dropped under the wheel looking green around the gills. "Hang on to that folder for me. I can't lose it. But don't look at it, okay. Please."

"Sure." She looked back. Undertaker man was just hitting the gravel too, lurching in faltering steps. "See ya."

His hand shot out and gripped hers. "I mean it, Billie. Don't look at it. You don't want that stuff in your head. Promise me."

The urgency of it was startling. "Okay. I promise."

She swung the door closed and listened to the engine turn over. The dark undertaker drifted up and bared his teeth at Billie like an angry dog. The teeth were grey and more flies crawled out when his mouth opened. His hand appeared, one accusatory finger levelled right at her like some scolding school teacher.

Then he melted into the car and appeared through the glass of the windshield, hunkered down in the passenger bucket like he was Mockler's phantom cop partner.

The long car backed out and rolled away through the parking lot and Billie felt her jaw drop. The dead man on the passenger side swivelled his head around to look at her, a mass of flies already boiling up against the rear window.

~

The dead man with the flies dripping from his ears wanted nothing to do with her. Unlike the others Billie had encountered, this one had no tragic tale to moan at her, no burning grievance that needed avenging. If anything, it had warned her away. It was Mockler it wanted. Following him home like some stray puppy. It had physically hurt him. Worse still was the look of glee in its narrow eyes as it inflicted pain on him. Why? What did it want and why had it latched onto Mockler?

The questions scrambled around as she slipped the key into the crusty lock of her door. The buzzing questions scattered when she saw the threshold of her front entrance.

The heavy line of salt she had laid down had been disturbed. Claw marks raked through it, the crystaline salt burned black in places. Like something had tried to claw away at it only to have its hand burned. The half-boy. He must have tried to scratch his way in. Testing boundaries. The charcoaled strands meant that he must have gotten scorched in the process. Good, she thought and slammed the door shut again.

Sweeping the apartment for the creepy amputee-boy was routine by now. With that established, she tossed the folder on the coffee table and flopped onto the couch. Her next thought wasn't about the undertaker man nor Mockler. It had to do with the state of her home and the mess piled everywhere. She had become a shut-in. One of those agoraphobic people who lock themselves inside. The only thing missing was an overabundance of cats.

Clean tomorrow, she resolved by way of procrastination. Back to Mockler and that disturbing thing trailing after him. What did it want with the detective? What was it capable of? Did it follow him home? Was that why Mockler didn't want to go home when she suggested it? The undertaker man was tormenting him. Mockler had intimidated that he was morose, depressed even. The job getting to him. Was it just the dead man?

He had also mentioned his fiancee. Hinting that all was not well there.

The thought of it still stung. Fiancee. What had she been thinking? Getting all moony over this guy she barely knew. Like he was different somehow. Why? Because he listened to her?

Because he seemed genuinely interested in what she had to say? That he didn't require constant ego-stroking and coddling attention like all the other men she had encountered in her life? How could she have developed feelings for someone so quickly? A cop no less. One who was planning to get married.

It was as humiliating as it was confounding. She blamed the near-death incident and subsequent ability to see the dead. It had fried her brains, making it impossible to think clearly. And if it had knocked her brains atumble, then it made sense that it had tilted the equilibrium inside her heart too. An organ not to be trusted now, not after leading her so far astray.

Jesus, she griped under her breath. How did I get here?

Pushing it all away, Billie clicked on the TV and immersed herself in its passive glow. The news report from the local Hamilton station. Gunshots off Beach Road, a charity event at Dundurn Castle. Sixty percent chance of rain overnight. The stream of information became a meaningless drone no matter how hard she concentrated on it and forced herself *not* to think about the police detective. He crept back in like water seeping into a leaky boat, impossible to plug up.

The folder lay on the table in front of her. Photographs of dead women hidden inside. He needed it back. Fine. She'd drop it off at the station tomorrow. She wouldn't ask if he was in, just leave the folder with the person at the front desk. Calling him would be an absolutely stupid thing to do.

Billie dug up her phone and dialled the number on the card.

He picked up after the first ring, stating his surname by way of greeting.

"Hi. It's Billie. I just wanted to see if you're okay."

"Sorry I had to bail on you like that" he said. "I don't know what came over me."

"Does that happen to you a lot? Those headaches that come out of nowhere?"

"Sometimes."

"Have you ever seen a doctor about it?"

"I did," he said. "He said it was stress. Told me get more sleep, more exercise."

"Oh." The doctor was wrong. She could feel it humming down the line over the phone. A sickly sense of dread and gloom that surrounded him. The undertaker man infesting Mockler's life. Did her abilities extend that far, that she could sense the presence of the dead over a phone line?

"Did you call just to check up on me?" An uptick of hope hitched his voice.

"You seemed surprised."

"It's nice. Thank you."

He seemed genuinely grateful and it baffled her. Why had she called? This wasn't helping. "I have your photos too. I was going to just drop them at the station but I thought that might get you in trouble."

"It would. Hang on to them. I'll pick them up."

An idea flitted across her eyes. A silly idea. "Are you

downtown? I'll be running errands on the bike later. I could drop it off."

"Well. Do you know where Bristol is?"

"Yup. You home now?"

"In an hour," he said, giving her the street number. "Are you sure? You don't have to, you know."

"I know. See ya then."

She clicked off, letting the phone drop onto the sofa cushion. Was that a completely daft thing to do? Of course it was.

Too late now. She put her feet up on the table, flattening the folder she would return, and wondered what his house looked like.

22

THE HOUSE WAS nice. An old redbrick with green trim that was peeling. There was a rose bush under the front window that needed to be tied back, the long branches bending forward under the weight of the blooms. Fallen petals dotted the grass, the colour bleaching out from them.

She rang the bell and waited under the porch light for a long moment. When the door opened, Mockler stepped out onto the veranda looking no better than he had at the park.

"Thanks," he said as he took the folder from her. "I appreciate this. You didn't look at them again, did you?"

"Nope. I promised." Billie looked over his shoulder to the open door but she didn't make out much beyond the front hall. "You look tired."

"Long day." Mockler nodded at the open door. "You want to come in? I got a pitcher of iced tea in the fridge."

"I can't stay." She wondered what his home looked like but

no force on earth could have made her step inside that house. Evil rolled out the open door like a wall of heat coming off a blast furnace.

She had wanted to know if the horrific man with the flies had followed Mockler home. Turning her bike into his driveway, she hadn't sensed anything and her hope lifted a little, thinking that the detective had gotten shed of the dead man. When the door opened, a sickening feeling washed over her. Her heart dropped instantly as a mournful gloom poisoned her thoughts. It was like a death had occurred, the grief of it.

How could he stand it, living in that house? She'd go crazy. He looked halfway there, his eyes sullen and shoulders drooped.

There was also the small detail of the fiancee. Billie wondered what she was like. She was probably beautiful and charming and funny and would wonder why a street urchin was standing on her front porch.

"I'll get out of your hair," she said. "Try and get some sleep, huh."

"Have you given any thought to getting out of town?"

"I'm thinking about it." She lingered and she wanted to run at the same time. This push and pull made her seasick. Wanting to talk to him but feeling repulsed by the darkness rumbling out of the open door.

He took a step forward, in no rush to let the conversation end. "If you do, give me a call and let me know where you are."

"You want to keep tabs on me?"

"Where does your aunt live?"

"Place called Long Point. Near Port Dover. You know it?"

"I've heard of it," he said. "Never been."

"It's a beautiful spot. Beach town, very laid back, very peaceful. You'd like it."

"I could use some peaceful."

She smiled. "You can come visit me. Bring your swim trunks."

Jesus, stop it already. She was flirting with him right on his porch but she couldn't stop. It just came spilling out. Get out of here, she scolded. Before his fiancee shows up because then you are going to feel like a real shitheel.

A housefly buzzed around her face and settled on her arm. She brushed it away, bristling at its touch. Flies revolted her. She associated them with filth and rot and disgusting things. It buzzed around them. Mockler took a swat at it.

"Damn flies," he said. "There's a lot of them around here."

"Ray?" called a voice from inside the house. A woman's voice.

Billie made for the steps. "I should go. See ya."

She took up her bike from where she had leaned it against the fence and hustled away. The damn fly kept zipping past her ear, more than one now. Glancing back, she dreaded seeing the woman step out onto the porch but she hadn't. Mockler stood alone on the stoop. He waved.

She had meant to wave back but movement in the second

story window caught her eye. The curtain pushed aside and a face leered up behind the dusty glass. The hollowed-out face of the undertaker man glared at her. His jaw opened and a countless horde of flies swarmed out and buzzed against the window pane.

~

Where was Gantry when she needed him? She had no way of contacting him; no phone number or address or even an email. Mockler was in trouble and she didn't know what to do about it and the only person who could possibly help was AWOL. There was Marta Ostensky but Billie doubted that the psychic would be any mood to help after she had led a ghost into her home.

Coasting through a stop sign, she pedalled the bike for downtown and cursed aloud. "Damn it, Gantry. Where are you?"

Her phone chirped in her pocket. Rolling to a stop, she pulled it out to find a text message.

Green door, end of Chatham street
Gantry

Billie blinked at the message. She hadn't given him her phone number but she supposed he could have found it easily enough. At least she could reach him now. She texted him back.

What address?

The text bounced back, undeliverable. Jesus, she griped. Even the dude's messages were spooky. She pushed off the curb and headed west toward the other end of town.

TIM McGREGOR

Chatham Street was little more than an access road that serviced the loading bays of old warehouses. Tumbleweed territory with few street lights and almost no traffic this time of night. A squat raccoon waddled across the road and scurried on as she approached.

Cruising slowly down the strip, Billie saw grey doors and beige doors but no green. Was Gantry pulling her leg? Steering around an oily puddle, she spotted a figure up ahead. Standing alone outside a looming warehouse, smoking a cigarette. She picked up the pace but the closer she came, she could see the heavy form of the lone smoker. Too big and bulky to be Gantry.

The heavy man looked up when he heard her tires on the pavement. Lit under a single bulb behind him was a green painted door. Music thrummed from the windows above.

Locking her bike to the chain link fence, she marched for the entrance but the big man stopped her. "Private party," he said.

"I need to find someone inside."

"Sorry."

Doormen, she murmured. "I'm not crashing the party. I just need to find the guy. He texted me to come here."

"Izzat right?" Disdain dripped from every syllable. "Who?"

"John Gantry," she said.

"That asshole is in here? Shit." The big man dialled his phone and marched inside. The door swung slowly back into place and she darted forward, slipping inside before it clicked shut.

A club of some kind. Dark and moody, humid from all the people elbowing into one another. Music thumped the air but she couldn't see a stage nor a DJ. The patrons were an odd mix. No hipsters or nerdsters, no one close to her own age. Older and well dressed with a baffling mix of tongues. Her ears picked out French and Spanish, a little German. Lots of Italian and what she thought was Russian. Men with gold chains and too much product in their hair. The women with bursting cleavage and gaudy jewelry. Eurotrash.

Most of the patrons towered over her. How was she going to find Gantry among all these sleazesters? She checked her phone but there were no new messages. A hand brushed her behind and she turned sharply but all she saw were shoulders and big hair.

Someone tapped her shoulder.

Spinning about, she expected to see Gantry but instead she was beset by a woman with dark hair and decolletage that plunged all the way to her navel. The woman leaned in, speaking with a hot whiskey breath. "Are you Gantry's little friend?"

"Not by a long shot."

The woman curled her finger in a come-hither motion. When Billie hesitated, the woman took her hand and slid through the crowd toward the back of the vast space. Billie collided into shoulders and elbows until the bodies cleared and the woman spun her around like they were dance partners. She mocked a kiss and waved Billie on before melting back into the crush of bodies.

The music wasn't so blaring here in wallflower territory and above the din she heard Gantry's laugh.

He sat hunkered over a table lit by a tall candle. Four other men seated around him, grim-faced and silent. Gantry was the only one laughing. She drifted closer and clocked the mess on the table. Cards and a gun and rounds of bullets spilt about. Something wet was speckled over the loose cards and as she closed in, she saw that it was blood. The cards looked all wrong too and she realized they were tarot, rather than the standard playing deck.

Gantry flung a card onto the table and guffawed like an ape. The grim man to his left spoke harshly, responding in a language Billie couldn't place.

Gantry spit onto the floor and bellowed at the man. "That's because you're a lying sack of shite, mate." The man grumbled again, his eyes burning hatred but Gantry laughed and turned to the equally grim fellow on his other side. "Do you believe this nonsense? What do you expect from a fucking thief?"

All four of the other men looked ready to kill. Gantry flapped his hand, flicking more blood on the table and took up his drink. "Piss off. Come back when you have a real offer."

The men exchanged glances. The one with the knife snapped it closed and they all stood and walked away.

Billie gave the men a wide berth and came around to the table. "Gantry?"

"Hello Billie." He grinned up at her, his eyes sparkling.

"Hand me that cloth, would you?"

She shook a cloth napkin out from under the mess of cards and held it out to him. A bullet rolled to the floor. "Are you bleeding?"

"Just a scratch." His left hand was bleeding but it was difficult to see how bad the cut was. He wrapped the cloth over it. "What do you want?

"Every time I see you, you're bleeding. What happened?"

"Tossers. Trying to swindle a swindler. Ha!" He fumbled a cigarette from a pack on the table and lit it. His good hand was shaky.

Billie took a seat, perching lightly on it. "How did you text me?

"With a phone. Pour us some of that, yeah?"

There was a bottle on the table with no label or maker's mark. Dark liquid inside. "I think you've had enough."

"Don't be a fucking pilgrim." He snatched up the bottle and splashed some into two glasses, spilling the booze over the table as he did. He handed one to her. "Cheers."

She sniffed it. Whiskey. She took a sip, set it aside and took out her phone. "What's your number?"

"Put that away. I despise phone calls."

"How do I get in touch with you?"

"You don't. What do you want, Billie?"

She swirled the whiskey in the glass. "Have you ever known a ghost to haunt a specific person? Instead of a place or whatever, it goes after one person?"

"Sure. They're like leeches sometimes."

"Leeches?"

"Feeding off somebody. One person in particular." Gantry winced, tightening the cloth on his hand. "You know how ghosts work, yeah?"

Billie felt reluctant to answer, like it was a trick question. "No. Why would I?"

"Someone's been skipping their homework," he tisked. "You need to catch up, sweetheart."

"I don't want this, remember?"

He leaned forward, the smoke billowing around him. "The dead feed off the living. Well, most do. As far as I can figure out anyway. They feed off the energy of people. Emotions, mostly. The stronger the emotions or the drama, the more they feed. They're cold, you see. And you and me, we're like little campfires for them to warm their hands over."

He smoothed down his tie but it didn't help. "Take a look out there. How many dead people do you see?"

She looked at the crowd around them. The Eurotrash set, drinking and sweating and yelling over the music. "I don't see any."

"Open your eyes."

She looked again and the dead emerged like magic. Crushed in with the crowd, skulking through the press of flesh. None of them took notice of her, their focus on the people around them.

"There's lots."

"They're drawn to people," Gantry said. "Drawn to their emotions. Happy, sad, angry or horny. They suck all that stuff up. They're drawn to wherever people are. It's rare you find one rattling around some deserted house. That's why you found refuge in the park that night. There were no people there, so there were no dead arseholes either."

She had intuited as much herself. That's why she met Mockler there, instead of a crowded coffee house like he suggested. "But they latch onto specific people too?"

"Some of them, yeah. The nasty ones."

"Why?"

He shrugged. "Some people swim in drama all the time. They work in situations where emotions run hot. Certain jobs attract that. Cops or firemen or paramedics. They're around trauma all the time. Sometimes they bring the dead home with them."

Cop. Billie flinched at the word. A homicide detective would be around death all the time. Unnatural death. And the grief of the families, the anger or fear of the suspects. It must happen all the time.

"Occupational hazard, I suppose," Gantry went on. "That's why I've avoided getting a proper job myself."

"Is it harmful?" she sputtered. "If the dead latch on to one person?"

"Very. The more one of them hangs around, the more it feeds. Makes people sick. Or depressed. Wears 'em down. They start ailing or they get cancer." Gantry dropped his cigarette to the floor and crushed it under his shoe. "Sometimes it becomes a bit of a nasty cycle. The more it feeds on the poor bastard in question, the stronger it grows. The more it can manipulate the physical world. The more it can torment the person, ratchet up the drama so it can feed more."

She thought of Mockler standing on his porch. The defeated look he carried, like pressure bearing down on him. His reluctance to go home when she suggested it. That it wasn't a place to find refuge. "How do you get rid of them?"

He shrugged. "Damned if I know. Some will leave if you bark at them. Others though, especially the stronger ones, the well-fed ones? They might need a stronger push."

"Like what? The salt thing?"

"See, this is where your homework comes in. You have to figure that part out. There's no one-size-fits-all. You have to find what works for you." Gantry lit up again, his features lost in the fog of smoke. "So. Who's the poor son of a bitch who's being haunted?"

Billie chewed her lip, reluctant to drop a name. "Just someone I know."

"You flinched when I said 'copper'. Who is it, Billie?"

"Mockler," she said with a here-goes-nothing sigh. "Something's latched onto him. A nasty one. I watched it reach into his chest and hurt him."

"You're having me on."

"It followed him home. I think it's slowly killing him. I need to know how to get rid of it."

The Englishman's laugh was as cruel as acid. "You gotta be fucking kidding me? That stupid bastard. Serves him right."

"Don't be cruel, Gantry. He needs help. I need help."

"Do you think I'm gonna help that prick? I hope the spook fucking eats him alive." He waved his cigarette at her. "Stay away from him, Billie. Toodley-doo."

"You're being petty," she said.

"Petty's my middle name, luv. Now shove off. I'm working."

A scream rose up from the crowd behind her, harsh and guttural. She turned to see a man charging through the tangle of bodies, brandishing something over his head. It was a sword, the blade long and curved. Shrieking the whole way, the man charged in running and swung the weapon down hard on Gantry.

The chair was empty, Gantry had vanished. The heavy sword cleaved through the leather and wooden frame underneath. White stuffing blew through the air and the crazed man struggled to pull the sword free.

Billie dove into the crowd and elbowed her way quickly back to the entrance and burst out the green door.

23

THIS IS HOW crazy people live. The shut-ins and the twitchy paranoids who believe the government is tracking their every move. This is how it starts.

Billie looked over the mess piling over the counter, the stack of dishes in the sink. Despite having every window open, the air inside the apartment was as flat as day-old soda and was beginning to smell. She hadn't left the house in almost two days. Too many ghosts out there. The cupboards were bare now, as was the refrigerator. Last night, she had ordered a pizza but that was down to one crusty slice in the fridge. She hadn't even bathed in the last two days.

Do crazy people know they're going crazy at the time?

The image of the dead man haunting detective Mockler would not go away. Yes, she had taken to referring to him as detective Mockler in a bid to distance herself. It wasn't really working. The mental snapshot of the flies crawling over that thing's face drifted back in her dreams, snapping her awake and leaving her terrified.

The dead were everywhere and the only defence she had was to barricade herself inside and keep them out. Crab-boy continued to stalk the hallway and scratch at her door. The dead lingered on every street corner. Some stood out on the street, silently observing her windows for movement. Looking to see if Billie could come out to play.

No, Bille cannot come out. So go the fuck away. See? She was already talking to herself.

So this was the plan. Hide away from the world, or at least the dead world, which seemed to be everywhere now that her eyes were open to it. Most of them had these shocked expressions on their faces, as if they didn't understand how they ended up here. Fine. They can have the world. She would pull up the drawbridge and hold up in her squat little flat like an outlaw making a last stand in a bad movie.

Yeah, as far as plans went, it sucked hard. Planning had never been her strong suite so she remained kind of baffled about what else to do. She had no precedent to go by, no handbook to reference. This wasn't her problem, these dead people who got stuck here and were too stubborn or shocked to move toward the bright light. If there even was a bright light. She had yet to see one. So everyone can just look after themselves, thank you very much. Sybil Culpepper could barely manage her own small life. She certainly couldn't be expected to fix anyone else's. Tough titty, as Tammy would say.

Even detective Mockler would have to get along without her. The creepy ghost who looked like a mute undertaker was his problem, not hers. She was never leaving this apartment again.

Billie leaned back and let out a sigh, almost laughing at these paper convictions. Vows made of smoke, a resolve that held the consistency of jelly. There was nothing she could nail to the wall and she gaped at her capacity to lie even to herself. The look of pain on Mockler's face as the dead man tormented him rarely left her mind. The thought of him trapped in his own home with that awful thing was too much.

And yet, what was she to do? Tell Mockler? Like he would believe her. So what did that leave? Getting rid of the ghost herself. She tried that once and it blew up in her face. She had no idea how to deal with these things, let alone eject one from a house like a landlord handing out eviction notices. She had nothing to back it up with, no consequences or follow-through.

She had spent the last few hours searching online for information about ghosts but it was a tiresome slog. There were a few common themes however. Burning sage to cleanse a dwelling or placing salt over thresholds. Sometimes iron was the key.

So what did she have? The one common element in her encounters with the dead was their need to vent their personal tale of woe. Some wanted revenge and others wanted to share their grief or sorrow. The common thread was the need to talk, to be heard, to be acknowledged. Which, if she thought about it, was what everyone wanted. Wasn't it? Even in death, these lost souls needed to be heard.

Billie was not one to give advice. Where some seemed to have an infinite supply of wisdom or ability to fix problems, she had none. But she could listen. Hear the person out. Whenever Jen was fuming over a fight with Adam or Tammy needed to vent about the idiots she worked with, Billie found that simply hearing the person out helped the aggrieved party better than any advice she could offer. And it always arced the same way. A blast of anger or despair followed by a long-winded story with many sidebars until the spewer flushed it all out. The spewer would slump back with the satisfaction of having let it go. More often than not, the person would come to a solution all on their own when given the chance to talk it all out.

Maybe the dead were no different? The Undertaker Man had a story to tell like all the others. She would hear him out first, then tell him to leave. Her mistake last time was trying to banish the ghost first from Jen's shop. This time would be different. She would hear the dead man out, no matter how long it took. After he leaves, she would burn the sage and salt the doorway.

With that settled, there was only one small detail left to sort out. Getting into Mockler's house when both he and the fiancee weren't home.

24

SHE HAD A plan. It just wasn't a very good one.

Coasting along Bristol Street, Billie made a reconnaissance pass by Mockler's house. The cracked driveway was empty. His car was gone but she had no idea if the girlfriend had a car too. Turning the bike around at the end of the block, she doubled back and swung into the driveway.

The house loomed before her, framed against dark-bellied clouds passing overhead. Rain was on its way. Two windows on the second story felt like eyes, watching her lean the bike against the juniper trees.

Slung over her back was a heavy courier bag with the things she would need. A sack of sea salt and three smudge sticks of dried sage she had bought at an occult boutique just around the corner from Mockler's house. The shop owner was helpful and friendly, tossing in a bundle of sweetgrass for free. Alongside these supplies was a small bottle of holy water. Ducking into Our

Lady of Souls church on the way over, she had tried to be discreet while plunging the plastic bottle into the marble basin near the entrance. Thankfully there was no priest around but an old woman had hissed at her for doing so, like she was a stray cat that had wandered into the church.

She had been surprised to see the dead inside the cathedral. She counted five of them, sitting quietly in the pews as if attending mass. All of them turned to look at Billie when she stepped inside. When the nearest one rose to his feet, she capped the bottle and fled. Riding away quickly, she wondered what the priest would say if he learned that the spirits of the dead had come to pray.

With the small arsenal tucked inside the bag, Billie went up the wooden steps of the front porch and stood before the door. She had no idea if the girlfriend was at home or if she was inside. She wished she knew the woman's name, then decided it was easier if she didn't know. She rang the doorbell and waited. This was the lame part of the plan. She had to make sure the house was empty. If the woman was home, she would just make an excuse about getting the address wrong and leave.

No one came to the door. She peered through the glass but the interior was dark. She rang the bell again, just to be sure. The house remained quiet.

First part accomplished, she now needed to get inside. This was where the plan became even lamer. On the off chance the door had been left unlocked, she tried the knob but the door didn't budge. Stepping back, she looked over the porch. Where would Mockler hide the emergency key? There was no welcome mat to check under but there were two flower pots flanking the front door. She lifted each one but no key was hidden under them. Standing tiptoed on the door sill, she ran her fingers over the ledge of the lintel but found only dust blackening her fingertips.

There was always the back door. Billie was about to descend the steps when a click sounded. The lock unlatched and the door creaked open.

An invitation, one that her gut advised her to refuse. She took a breath, stepped inside and immediately felt a wave of dread wash over her. Not just dread but a sadness, acute and sharp. Billie could actually feel her heart sink as she stood inside the front hallway. The air was humid with misery and pain. How could Mockler live in this? No wonder he didn't want to go home. Did he feel it as acutely as she did or was it amplified by her abilities?

"Hello?" she called out. "Anyone home?"

The house was quiet. She looked into the front living room before passing on into the kitchen. The furnishings were nice, the decorations eclectic but tasteful. A woman lived here for sure and Billie wondered what Mockler's girlfriend did for a living. The thought of his betrothed still stung. Was the detective a bit of a player? The kind that liked to keep a woman at home while he chased skirt on the job? Maybe this was simply her lot in life, to be the other woman. Never good enough for the real thing and condemned to sideline relationships with philandering—

She stopped cold. This sudden onslaught of doubt and self-loathing churning up inside her wasn't real. It was this house that was doing it. Or rather, the thing hidden inside the house. She'd have to be mindful of that, to keep the false misery from swallowing her up. She had work to do.

"Why don't you come out?" she said aloud. Not a bellow but calm and firm. She needed to show the ghost dwelling here that she wasn't afraid but she wasn't angry either. Friendly was pushing it. A parley.

"It's just you and me. And you know I can see you. Come out so we can talk."

Nothing. Billie dropped her bag onto the counter island and perched on one of the stools. She hoped this wouldn't take long, coaxing the dead spirit out into the open. How mortifying would it be if Mockler came home unexpectedly? Or worse still, his girlfriend.

She took out the sage sticks and bottle of holy water. A soft click sounded to her left and she turned but saw nothing. A few dishes left in the sink, a mug on the counter. A message on the refrigerator door, spelt out with cheerfully colourful magnets.

Get out

Short and to the point, she thought. A tacky parlour trick.

"I get it. You don't want me here." Be assertive but courteous. Don't scare it off but don't anger the damn thing either. "But I'm not leaving until you come out and talk to me. Tell me your name."

Quiet. The house ticked and creaked, the way old homes will. A hissing sound touched her ear and she traced it to the vent on the wall. At first she thought the furnace was running but the closer she came, the more it sounded like whispering. Kneeling down, she lowered her ear to the wrought iron grate. Like a bad phone connection, she could barely make out a voice in the hissing. One word, repeated over and over.

Bitch bitch bitch bitch...

Name calling. Compared to what she had seen the Undertaker do so far, it seemed petty. What was it up to, this small potato spookshow?

A rumble came from overhead, the sound of furniture scraping across wooden floors. Crossing back into the foyer, she stood at the bottom of the stairs and looked up. The banister thinned into darkness on the second floor. Lights off and curtains drawn. The air grew humid with each step she climbed and a bad smell filtered down over her. Reaching the landing, she felt seasick and unsteady.

It was close. The nausea and bad smell were telltale signs but more acute was the misery pushing her down. It was like suddenly stepping into a room full of mourners at a funeral, their collective grief dragging her down with it. She needed to guard against that. And yet the gloom and unrelenting sadness felt irresistible, like slipping into a warm bath.

The sound of running water issued from down the hall. The shower turning on in the bathroom. Billie stood her ground.

"Enough tricks. Just come out." A heartbeat or two, then she said "You don't have to be afraid."

A new noise came from the bathroom. A woman's voice, calling for help.

Billie felt a zap along her spine. Was the fiancee still here? Was she hurt? Indecision clouded everything and Billie felt her gut urging her to run again. She inched to the bathroom and looked inside. Steam rolled out from behind the drawn shower curtain, water dribbling from its mildewed hem onto the tiled floor.

Even a child knew how this plays out. Something nasty was hiding behind the curtain. As simple as that but impossible to resist, the way a 'wet paint' sign won't stop one from touching a freshly painted surface. She tiptoed in and reached for the curtain. The water shut off. She took a breath and drew the curtain back.

She had steeled her nerves for the sight of the grotesque wraith with the flies in his mouth but it wasn't him. It was a woman, not much older than herself, coiled up in the bathtub. Her slip was soaked and her hair plastered down her face. Her eyes were lost and unseeing when she spoke.

"Help me," she pleaded. "He won't let me leave."

"Who won't let you leave?" Billie asked. "Where is he?"

"Those awful bugs. They're everywhere."

The woman quaked. Her eyes were bald with terror, her lips quivering wet and blue. Billie wasn't sure if the woman even saw her or knew she was there. Was it possible for one ghost to imprison another?

"Why can't you just leave?" Billie kept her tone soft, not wanting to scare the woman further. "What does he want?"

The woman coiled tighter, the wet curls falling over her mouth. "He wants to hurt me. Like he did the others."

"What others? How does he hurt you?"

"Oh God. He's coming—"

The woman's eyes widened in panic and Billie followed her gaze. Something dark trickled up out of the bathtub drain. Bluebottle flies crawled out of the opening and scuttled across the porcelain in their staccato march. Two or three at a time then more and more until a dark mass vomited forth in a reverse pole from the drain. They buzzed angrily over the woman in a thick swarm until she vanished as if swallowed whole.

Billie threw the curtain back but the flies were already on her, the filthy insects creeping over her skin and buzzing into her ears. She scrambled for the hallway. Swinging the door closed, there was a glimpse of a face in the bathroom mirror before the door banged shut.

The sound of the insects was loud behind the bathroom door and when the first of them slithered out from the uneven gap under the door, Billie fled into another room.

The master. A big bed with decorative but useless pillows lay opposite the picture windows. The view looked out over the tree lined street and pretty houses. She wondered, almost idly, what direction it faced and whether it afforded a nice sunrise.

Get a grip, she told herself. This thing, this undertaker man, knew how to get under her skin. Did it know that flies disgusted her or was that a coincidence? She needed to push the fear away and show the ghost that it couldn't intimidate her (a bold-faced lie). She needed it to come out into the open and get it to talk. If, that is, she could stomach seeing the flies crawl in and out of the orifices of its face.

On the opposite wall was an old dressing table with a round mirror and stool. It looked decadent and out of place to Billie, something suited to Hollywood starlets rather than working people. But there was something wrong with the mirror. It reflected what was not there. In the mirror, she saw Mockler asleep in bed. Next to him a woman but her face was turned away from the mirror. All Billie could see was her long hair fanned over the pillow and her naked back. The fact that she slept naked was irksome. The room was dark.

The real bed remained empty and made, the fluffy pillows placed neatly over the spread. The mirror over the vanity stubbornly maintained its other night-time image of the occupants asleep in the darkened bedroom. The digital clock in the nightstand read 3:42 AM, in reverse.

Something shifted in the reflected image of the darkened bedroom. A shadow, darker than anything in the room, slid down the wall and over the bed, slipping under the blankets between the sleepers as if seeking warmth. The spread shifted and rolled and slowly tugged down until the woman lay exposed. The dark mass bubbled over her like smoke. It solidified and took on shape until the disturbing form of the undertaker man revealed itself. It pawed and pressed down on the woman, doing terrible things to her. Then it turned its awful head and looked right at Billie, meeting her eyes in the mirror.

"Get off her!" Billie screamed at the reflection. The real bed remained empty but in the mirror, the hideous man simply leered at Billie as he thudded at the woman, obscene and cruel. It was maddening. She wanted to smash the mirror but hesitated. She hadn't come to trash Mockler's home, just to get the unwanted phantom to leave.

The floor shook, vibrating under her feet. The mirror shifted, the dark figure and sleeping couple vanishing and the round mirror reflected the bed as it truly was, empty and made.

Pain flexed her stomach muscles. A bad smell wafted up and when something whispered in her ear, she jerked away as if electrocuted. The undertaker man loomed beside her, his mouth of blackened teeth open as if laughing but he made no sound. The only noise came from the flies launching out of his maw. His hand was outstretched from where he had touched her, his fingernails dark with grime.

It took everything she had to simply stand her ground. Her mouth was reluctant to work properly and she stammered. "Why are you hurting them?"

His only reply was to shamble forward.

"This is their house. You're not wanted here." She had meant to stand up to this monstrosity but the moment she stepped back, she knew she had lost.

Its jaw clamped up and down mechanically and its eyes were distilled malice. It kept coming and Billie ran but when she reached the stairs she felt a strong push and down she went. Tumbling hard and skidding along until she wedged herself between the wall and the railing. Everything hurt at once. She slid the rest of the way to the bottom step and limped for the kitchen. She wanted the holy water. She wanted anything that might fend off the thing. A baseball bat. A bazooka.

When it lumbered through the doorway, the dead man seemed impossibly tall, a giant stooping low under the lintel, cloaked in its armour of flies. Billie half-remembered what Gantry had said about it feeding off emotions. Her own terror was making it stronger but the knowledge was useless to her. Could she choke off her fear, like flipping a switch?

Snapping the cap off the bottle of water taken at the church, she flung it at the ghost, screaming out nonsense she remembered from a horror movie. A half-assed exorcism performed by someone who clearly had no idea what she was doing. To her surprise, the undertaker man sidestepped the spray of water. Some of the flies, caught in the flung water, dropped immediately to the floor. A few even smoldered as they hit the tile.

Another hard push, tumbling her over a kitchen chair and when Billie smacked against the cold floor, she knew it was all over. The houseflies dove after her, smothering her in a black cloud. The damned things crawled her flesh and buzzed her ears, their tiny appendages sticking to her as they found their way into her mouth and nostrils. Pecking at her clamped eyelids, squirming to get in. She wanted to scream but that would only let the vermin in.

She felt an intense chill as the thing pressed down on her, smothering her with its weight. Its voice, barely audible above the deafening buzz of the flies, whispered into her ear. It told Billie to get out. It said that those in this house belonged to him and she was the one not welcome. Stay, it told her, and I will eat you alive.

Her revulsion hit the tipping point and the scream came full bore. Something more than a scream came out of her, pushing across the room like a wave of energy. The flies retreated and the awful weight of the wretched thing fell away. Blind with panic, she scrambled to her feet. The flies remained but were scattered, not swarmed together as before, as if her shriek had blown them around the kitchen. Billie grabbed her bag and bolted for the door in full retreat.

The antique butlers table in the foyer lifted off the floor and flew at her, flung by an unseen hand. It knocked her hard into the wall and she slid to the floor. She scrambled forward, clawing for an escape as even more objects hurled themselves at her. The dangling light fixture fell, smashing to the floor before her and the heavy ottoman from the living room knocked her sideways. The walls cracked and old plaster rained down in dusty chunks.

Billie kicked and crawled and finally threw herself out the screen door, landing hard on the front porch. A car pulled into the driveway. The look on detective Mockler's face was almost comical.

25

"WHAT ARE YOU doing here?"

Billie lurched to her feet but the seasickness threw her off balance and she gripped the railing for support. Her stomach curdled at the thought of explaining herself.

Mockler shot up the porch steps two at a time and helped her up. "Easy. Here, sit down. Jesus, you're shaking."

"I'm sorry," she said, without knowing exactly what she was apologizing for. Her whole body was quaking. She didn't want to sit, didn't want to be anywhere near this awful house.

Mockler settled her onto the wicker bench. He touched her bare forearm, then her hand. "You're freezing." The humidity of the day was peaking and Mockler's brow was beaded with sweat. He pressed the back of his fingers against her forehead. "It's like you're going into shock."

"I just got a chill. I'm sorry." Again, this need to apologize. She lowered her gaze to the uneven floorboards.

"What happened?" His eyes clocked the open door then returned to hers. "Why are you here?"

Think fast. How could she explain this? She had waltzed inside his home like she owned the place. Then the house was destroyed by a vengeful spirit. "I was passing by. Thought I'd knock on your door, see if you were in."

"I see," he nodded. "And you just made yourself at home?"

"The door was open."

"It was?" He looked at the door again.

"Yeah." That part was true. "I knocked, stepped inside and called out."

Mockler straightened up and stepped onto the sill, examining the door knob, the lock. "I always lock it before I go."

"I heard someone inside. Knocking around upstairs. I kept calling out, thinking it was you but no one answered." The lies came a little too easily for her liking. White lies were one thing but this was different. And more lies were needed. How was she going to explain the fact that his house was trashed? Maybe that's what she kept apologizing for.

"Was it Christina?"

"No."

"Stay here." Mockler disappeared inside the house and Billie scrambled for some way to explain the cracked plaster and upended furniture. How bad would it be if she just collected her bike and got the hell out of here?

His voice called out from inside the house. "Hey. What is all this stuff?"

Billie steeled herself for what was to come and went back inside. Everything looked absolutely normal. No broken glass on the floor, no shattered plaster or exposed cracks in the wall. The furniture that had been hurled at her was back where it belonged. Like nothing had happened. She crept in further, around a corner and saw Mockler standing in the kitchen.

Her bag lay on the island countertop, its contents spilling out. The floor was wet, holy water puddled over the black and white tiles.

"Is this yours?" Mockler picked through the mess on the counter, holding up the smudge stick of bundled weeds. "What is it?"

"Sage," she said.

"Did you drop your water?" He reached down to fetch the discarded container. A completely normal water bottle.

"Sorry. I'm a klutz."

Reaching into the bag, he lifted out something for her to see. A large brass crucifix, the figure on the cross burnished with a dark patina. "What's this?"

"My aunt collects those." This was not a complete lie. Aunt Maggie did collect those and the one he held had been given to Billie as a housewarming present. It was meant to hang over the front entrance. To keep her safe, Maggie had said. Billie never put it up.

"I've always found these creepy. Handy if you run into a

vampire, I guess." He put the crucifix back. "So you heard someone. Then what?"

His tone altered, more business-like, and she wondered if this was how he spoke to people on the job. She didn't care for it. "I heard someone upstairs. I called out but no one answered. Then there was a bang, like something got knocked over. I got scared."

"Wait here." He went out of the room and she listened to his heavy stomping on the stairs. The ceiling of the old house creaked as he swept from room to room and then he stomped back down the steps again.

"Find anything?" she asked when he returned to the kitchen.

He shook his head. "No."

"Maybe a raccoon got inside," she suggested. "Or a squirrel."

"Maybe." He sounded unconvinced. His eyes darted back to her bag on the counter.

Billie crossed to the island and zipped up the bag. "I shouldn't have just walked into your house like that."

"Don't worry about it." He crossed to the back window and peered out at the backyard.

She hated herself for lying and hated how easily they flowed out of her. They always had though, to cover up her odd behaviour or her foggy spells. What else could she do? Would he believe her if she told him the truth?

The fine hair on her arm prickled and when she looked down, there was a fly. Another one of the degenerate insects touching her. She recoiled and flung it away. The pest buzzed around the room and Mockler took a swipe at it.

"These damn flies." He rolled up a newspaper to swat at it. "I don't know where they all come from."

"I hate flies," she said.

The bluebottle landed on the edge of the table, swiping its forelegs over its alien eyes. Mockler snuck up on it. "Same here. Sometimes I'll find a hundred of them buzzing against the window pane. It's disgusting." He smacked it but the fly escaped with that preternatural sense they had. Mockler frowned. "I looked under the porch, thinking something had crawled under there and died."

"And?"

He shrugged. "Nothing. I can't figure out why they keep coming in."

"What if it's something else. Like a toxic house thing. It happens with old houses."

Mockler sighed, as if he'd thought the same thing. "I really don't want to start tearing into the walls. God knows what I'll find."

"Maybe stay away for a while. Live somewhere else until it goes away."

He looked at her. "Isn't that the advice I gave you?"

"What's good for the goose." She hoisted the bag onto her shoulder. "I'll get out of your hair. Sorry about all this."

He followed her out and stood on the stoop while she climbed back onto her bike. "I still think you ought to go stay at your aunt's for a while."

"I'm thinking about it." She backtracked the pedal to kick off. All she had to do was coast away but she looked back at Mockler. It was killing her that she couldn't warn him about the danger. For a second time, her attempt at helping someone had blown up in her face. "See ya later, detective."

"Hang on," he said, coming down the steps. "What was it you wanted to see me about?"

She shrugged and then smiled. "I don't remember now." Billie waved and pushed off. At the periphery of her sight, something had moved in the second story window but she didn't look back to see what it was. The last thing she wanted to see was that obscene face.

Detective Mockler waved even though the girl was out of sight and then went back inside. He had been three blocks away doing a follow-up interview with a witness and decided to stop home to make a quick sandwich before heading back to precinct. Checking the door knob and the lock again, he found nothing amiss and shrugged it off.

He took out last night's chicken and a head of lettuce from the fridge and plunked them onto the counter when he noticed that Billie Culpepper had forgotten something. Turning the brass crucifix around in his hand, he examined it from different angles before sliding it onto the top of the refrigerator so he wouldn't have to look at the creepy thing.

26

"WHERE IS IT coming from?"

"I don't know," Mockler said. The same answer to the same question inside the last ten minutes.

Christina folded her arms, her shoulders squared stiff. "Well it has to be coming from somewhere."

The smell had come back during dinner, the same noxious odour that had tormented them since the winter of last year. Never consistent, never localized anywhere, the smell would waft up in one room then appear in another. A poisonous rank of sewer gas and sulphur and something left to rot, the smell would rise one day then disappear only to come back a few days later. They chased it like fools, passing from room to room, sniffing the air like bloodhounds trying to locate its source.

Mockler banged his skull off the frame as he crawled out from under the sink. The smell was strongest in the kitchen this time and he looked there, thinking there was a crack in the drain pipe. No crack, no leak. Rubbing the throbbing spot on the back of his head, he said "Nothing down here."

"I can still smell it," Christina said. Her jaw was set, one hand over her nose. "I can't live like this anymore."

"It's just a bad smell." He took a breath. Her knack for blowing small things into melodrama infuriated him. He needed to remind himself to brush it off.

"Don't dismiss everything. God, I can't even think when it gets like this."

His spine groaned as he got to his feet. "Where's it coming from now?"

Christina tested the air and then pointed to the basement door. "It's over there again."

It was like a bad game of Marco Polo, the smell popping up in different places while they chased after it with their hands outstretched and groping. He opened the basement door and pounded down the wooden stairs, taking his frustration out on each worn step. Breathing in the foul air, he stumbled around nose first, trying to track it down. It made him lightheaded it was so noxious.

"Check the stack again." Christina sat halfway down the steps, covering her nose. "Maybe you missed something."

Mockler crossed to the unfinished part of the cellar where the furnace and water heater stood draped in cobwebs. The spiders had a field day down here, their webs constantly dappled with dead flies. The fly problem, he knew, was tied to the mystery smell that plagued them. If he could fix the smell, the flies would go away.

"There's nothing here," he said, shining the flashlight up and down the thick pipe.

"You're useless. My father could fix anything."

"Bully for him," he shot back. This particular needling made him bristle. The comparison, followed quickly by the feeling of being judged. A nasty fight was building up and if he wasn't careful, it would get ugly. But he wasn't in a careful mood and the truth of the matter was that he almost wanted the fight.

"I don't smell it anymore." He crossed back into the centre of the room and clicked off the flashlight. The smell had moved on again, waiting to poison them in some other part of the house.

Christina rubbed the bridge of her nose. "I can't live in this house anymore. I never felt right about it in the first place."

She was right but he held his tongue. He was the one who had wanted the house more, its old construction and wonky charm appealing to something deep inside him. And it had been affordable. Christina was the one who thought they were taking on too much, moving too fast. What did either of them know about owning a home? It was only later that he realized she had meant that they were moving too fast as a couple. Unprepared to take on the commitment of living together, let alone sharing the burden of owning a house. He had pushed her into it, dismissing her doubts as groundless jitters and cold feet.

He followed her back upstairs. Their uneaten dinner remained on the table where they had abandoned it after the stink turned on them. The fish had been overcooked and the vegetables mushy but he had said nothing, grateful that the meal had simply been finished. Now it just taunted him, his stomach turning oily from the stench in the house.

There was a snap and when he turned, he saw her pop something into her mouth which she chased down with wine. The prescription bottle was crammed back into her bag before he could see what it was. He said nothing, too tired and too irked to raise that particular twist in their life. Christina had a soft spot for self-medicating. The warning signs were everywhere but, like enabling spouses the world over, he waited for her to somehow pull herself out of this 'bad spell'.

"I'm going to take a shower," she said, taking the wine with her.

He looked at the uncleared table and the disaster in the kitchen. "Sure. You do that. This mess will just clean itself, I suppose."

"Don't keep score, Ray. It's petty."

He cleared the table, pushing down the embers flaring up in his chest as he listened to the steps creak under her feet. He hated when he groused like that, petty and whining in his own ears. It just came out so easily, this snipping back and forth. Shot fired, shot returned. This was how they communicated now, this sniping across the bow. It was that or him talking her down from the ledge of her depressive turns.

How had it come to this? By degrees, the decay of their communication like a piece of space junk gradually falling to earth. Slowly and without notice, until it was too late and then everything was burning white hot as it all crashed back to earth--

The scream from upstairs cut his thoughts short. Blood-curdling and urgent. He bolted for the stairwell, bounding up two at a time. Christina straddled the doorway of their bedroom and the hall, pointing at something inside the room.

"What the hell is that?" she bellowed. "Did you do that?"

Mockler skidded to a stop. Their bedroom looked untouched save for one small detail on the wall above their bed. A cross hung there from a nail, suspended upside down.

"Is that your idea of a joke?" She shoved a palm against his chest. "What the hell is wrong with you?"

He blinked as if his eyes were playing tricks on him. It was the crucifix Billie had left behind. How the hell had it gotten up here?

"Is this some comment on us?" Christina fumed. "Or me? Ha ha, Christina's the devil? Very funny."

He crossed to the bed and pulled the brass object down from the wall. He turned it over in his hand, looking for something that would explain its strange appearance. "Christina, I didn't put this here."

"Please, the joke's over." She took the object from him. "If you didn't do it, then who did? Where did it come from?"

That question he could answer but he balked. Explaining

Billie Culpepper's presence in the house might seem odd, especially after this. "I don't know where it came from."

She folded her arms. "So what are you saying? Someone broke in, hung this up here in our bedroom and snuck out?"

"I don't know." He thought of all the times he'd heard that answer from suspects, shrugging off serious allegations with the flimsiest of excuses. I dunno. A child dodging an interrogation from a parent.

She stomped into the bathroom and closed the door, her voice carrying from the other side. "Then figure it out, detective."

The crucifix was tossed into the trunk of his car, rattling against a spare flashlight and coil of Bungee cords. At least it was out of the house. Mockler closed the trunk and went back inside to deal with the kitchen. Christina came down later, her wet hair dampening the collar of her bathrobe. Retrieving the bottle of red, she retired to her studio that overlooked the backyard. A sunroom they had refitted into a space for her to continue painting.

Their exchange was kept short but civil. No mention of the inverted cross found over their bed. Christina said she wanted to work the rest of the night and told him not to wait up. The kiss goodnight was curt and perfunctory. A formality.

The wine, an almost full bottle of Shiraz that he knew would be gone by morning, bothered him but her return to the studio was hopeful. Christina was a talented painter who, like most artistic people, didn't have enough time in the day to devote to her work. But the work had suffered as Christina's depression took hold. She shunned the studio, preferring to spend her nights zonked before the television or out with girlfriends. She said she couldn't paint when she felt so lousy and for a while, Mockler thought she would never go back to it. So, despite the row they'd had, her desire to work was a good sign. A small step in her path out of the black fog that had taken hold of her.

Fetching a beer from the refrigerator and his book from the living room, he retreated to the front porch. The wicker bench creaked under his weight and he propped his heels onto the railing. Moths fluttered around the yellow porch light but thankfully no flies appeared. Ten minutes in, he yawned and closed the book. He looked at the cover. The Sun Also Rises. He'd been reading it for weeks, part of his ongoing effort to become well-read but the truth was that fiction bored him. He struggled to simply get through a book, let alone understand it. Hemingway seemed like a good fit, something he could sink his teeth into but even this he found a chore. The writing was simple and direct but the story seemed to be going nowhere. Endless rounds of drinks in little cafes, fishing trips, dance halls. Was there some hidden meaning here that went straight over his head? Settling the book on the bench beside him, he leaned back and listened to the crickets in the yard.

He turned off the porch light after the second beer and locked the door. The back studio was dark, Christina having gone to bed. Stepping inside the sunroom, he flicked on the light. Christina hated showing work in progress but he was curious to what she was up to. Her big easel stood dead centre in the room, a cloth draped carefully over the frame to cover it without letting the fabric touch the paint. He lifted up one corner of the coverlet.

The canvas was blank. Not a drop of pigment nor thin sketch lines from a pencil. Nothing.

Mockler blinked at it, wondering what it meant. What had she been doing in here all night? Letting the cover drop, he scanned the room. A paint-spattered table to his left, her materials neatly arranged and ready to use. A bookshelf on the opposite side held oversize art books, a stereo and jars of gesso and linseed oil. Wooden frames were stacked under the windows, ready to be fitted with canvas. Everything looked the same. Untouched.

The sketchpad. The big one Christina used to rough out her ideas before opening any paint, it sat on the wooden chair, the only thing out of place. He picked it up and flipped the cover over. A gruesome face stared back at him. Hollowed out eyes and a yawning mouth, it looked like something from a nightmare. Even more unsettling were the insects dribbling from the open mouth. Flies, a black swarm of them, crawling over the subject's features.

He turned the page over. The same horrid face appeared, with only a slight variation in the rendering. He flipped this paper over the spiral ring only to find the same awful image on the next page. And the one after that and the one after that. A dozen pages filled with the same gruesome face. On the thirteenth page, there was no drawing but words scratched hard into the paper.

Woe to the women who stitch magic bands on all wrists.

Mockler folded the cover back and threw the sketchpad back onto the chair where it slid off the seat and flopped to the floor like a dead bird.

27

HALF-BOY HAD found a way inside. Scratching at the salt barrier until his hands were burnt black, he cleared away enough of the granules to drag his carcass over the threshold and now he was inside the apartment. Knocking over dishes and rattling cupboards, scurrying from sight whenever Billie looked his way. She no longer cared.

The television flickered silently, tuned to some claptrap with the volume muted. Billie hadn't moved from the couch in hours, staring mindlessly at the screen while the legless ghost scampered through the squalor of her flat. Something in the bathroom clattered to the floor and then a sharp knock issued from the bedroom. Billie remained numb to it, reaching for the wine glass to numb herself further.

Roomies, she concluded. That's what they would be now; she and the creepy boy without legs. Sharing the cramped apartment. Her new boyfriend. Oh don't mind him, she could tell her friends when they came over. Her new man prefers to scuttle around in the dark and drip blood everywhere. It's his thing.

It's what she deserved for having such crazy thoughts about Mockler. He's engaged. Verboten, off limits. She wasn't that kind of person. She simply wanted to help him but that, like so many things she'd attempted, backfired spectacularly. Now he probably thinks she's crazy. Her help was proving to be hazardous to others. First Jen and now the detective. Why bother?

A dish clattered to the floor and something dark shuffled near the doorway. The half-boy dragged himself out into the open in his peculiar legless trot and squatted there, looking at her.

"Go away," she said.

He scuttled in closer, watching her with the dark eyes of a timid woodmouse.

Billie ignored him. She was getting good at ignoring things, people especially. The bar had phoned twice, asking if she was coming into work. Her friends had texted her, asking where she was and if she was all right. She ignored them all. Everything was fine here at Fortress Culpepper. She was keeping herself prisoner inside the tower, a Rapunzel without the locks.

The half-boy slithered forward, pulling himself along on his hands. He rapped his knuckles on the floor to get her attention.

She refused to look at him. "What do you want from me?"

His arm came up and he pointed at the door.

A sharp thud against the front door ejected Billie from the

sofa, leaving her stomach behind. The half-boy scurried away and the knocking on the door became urgent. Ghosts don't knock, people do. But who at this hour?

Tiptoeing to the entrance, she hoped whoever it was would give up and go away. The peep hole revealed her friends, refracted in its fish-eye optics.

"Open up, Billie" Tammy demanded, prominent in the range of vision. "I can see your shadow under the door."

Relief blew through her lungs at the sight of familiar faces but it was tainted with apprehension. Billie turned back the bolt and let her visitors inside. "What are you guys doing here?"

"Oh we just thought we'd swing by to see if your cat was eating your mummified corpse," Tammy huffed, barging her way in. "No biggie."

Hot on Tammy's heels came Jen, who smiled sheepishly as she swept in, and then Kaitlin. That surprised Billie. Kaitlin had never been to her flat before. "I'm still kicking," she said.

Tammy looked the room over; the mess of bottles and take-out cartons on the coffee table. Dirty clothes draped over chairs. "I like what you've done with the place," she sneered.

"Love and squalor," Billie shot back. She wasn't in the mood for being upbraided and wished her trio of friends would just leave. "Anybody want some wine?"

Kaitlin slid an empty pizza box from the green armchair and perched herself on the very end of it, as if afraid to touch anything. "What kind is it?"

"The cheap kind."

"My favourite." Tammy clasped her hands with mock gusto. "Let's have a drink."

Jen rearranged a pillow on the sofa and sat down, back straight and knees together. She'd yet to say anything or even look Billie in the eye. She fetched the remote from the clutter and killed the TV.

"I'll get some glasses." Billie retreated into the kitchen with a lead weight dragging in her guts. Tammy's bravado was false and the other two looked like they were on their way to a funeral. What were they up to, some kind of half-assed intervention? Glancing at her reflection in the darkened kitchen window, Billie shriveled. Her hair was a mess and there were dark circles under her eyes, like she hadn't slept in days. She hadn't, really.

Sweeping back into the living room with the glasses, she poured a round of plonk and avoided her friend's weirdly earnest eyes. "So, what's the big emergency?"

"You are." Kaitlin sniffed the glass. "You haven't returned any of our texts."

Billie leaned up against the old hi-fi cabinet. A big floor unit in burled walnut that she had found curbside. It didn't work but it was the nicest piece of furniture she owned. "I've been busy."

"Barricading yourself in?" asked Jen. Her face remained neutral.

"Nope," Billie shrugged. She refused to let the ladies get under her skin. "I've just had a lot going on."

Kaitlin looked over the mess. "Like what? Hoarding?"

"It's a new look."

"It has a squalid charm." Kaitlin raised her glass in a mock salute.

"Let's play nice," Tammy interjected, taking the role of referee. "It's a rescue operation, Billie. Like that time you broke up with whats-his-name. Brian?"

"Ryan."

"Whatever. We came to save you from yourself and drag you out of your Fortress of Solitude."

Billie sipped her glass. "Thanks. But it's not necessary."

"Come on," Tammy said. "Out with it. What happened? Did you meet somebody?"

Of course they would think that. It just had to be a guy, right? She wanted them to leave.

Jen smoothed the hem of her dress. "We just want to know what's going on, Billie. That's all."

"How's the shop?"

"Coming along," Jen said. Her cheeriness felt forced. "The repairs should be done soon. I hope to re-open in a week or so."

The guilt of it stung like salt in a papercut. Billie took a breath and looked her oldest friend in the eye. "I'm sorry about what happened, Jen. I honestly am."

"It's okay. Not your fault."

"Yes, it was my fault. I wanted to help but instead I messed up. As usual. And ruined everything you worked so hard for. I'm sorry."

"I know." Jen's eyes were wet but she was fighting it down. "I know you wanted to help."

Tammy studied the two of them, observing every tic and creak of body language. "Is that what this about? The fire?"

Billie drank her wine, letting the question just hang there like a bad smell.

Taking her silence as an affirmative, Tammy got to her feet. "Problem solved. Why don't you change out of those stanky clothes and we'll go out."

"No thanks," Billie said.

"Ugh." Tammy rolled her eyes heavenward. "You're gonna make us work for it, aren't you?"

"I'm not asking you to do anything, Tammy." A little too much edge to her voice. Billie set her glass down and tried again. "I appreciate the effort. The concern, I really do. But there's nothing to do. I just need to figure this out."

"Figure what out?" said Jen. A matching edge was undercutting her tone now. "You're not yourself."

"Losing three days in a coma will do that to you." It was a cheap shot and she immediately regretted it.

The three of them looked down at their drinks. Jen broke the silence. "You're still recovering from that?"

"I guess. I don't know."

"Then what?" Tammy never did well with impatience. "Whatever it is, you can tell us, Bee. No one's gonna judge you."

But they would. All three would judge her certifiably insane if she told them the truth. Still, the idea floated on the surface and a giddiness flushed over at the prospect of telling them everything. It was like that feeling she got looking down from a rooftop; an irrational urge to jump.

The clock ticked on in the kitchen, stretching the silence beyond comfort. Tammy sighed and leaned against the wall. "Jesus, Bee. If you can't trust us, who can you trust?"

The giddiness was irresistible. "Have you ever seen a ghost?"

"What?"

"I see them," Billie said quietly. "I see them all the time."

Tammy laughed. "You're hilarious."

Billie said nothing. Jen leaned in, a gentle crease in her brow. "Billie, what are you talking about?"

In for a penny, in for a pound. Aunt Maggie's saying. Billie took a breath and let it all out. "After I woke up in the hospital, I started seeing things. Weird things. I thought I was hallucinating. But I'm not. They're real. Dead people. They're everywhere. And they won't leave me alone."

She watched them react. Tammy guffawed, dismissing it like she did everything. Jen squirmed in her seat, physically uncomfortable. Kaitlin became very still, her eyes on the floor. Billie shrugged and said "You asked."

"You see ghosts?" Jen squinted at her, as if trying to see through smoke.

"Yup."

"You know how crazy that sounds, right?"

"You don't have to believe me."

Kaitlin raised her eyes. "So these ghosts, they're just, like, wandering around everywhere?"

"Yes," said Billie. "There's one right behind you."

Kaitlin shot out of her chair. There was nothing there. "Stop it."

Something dark scuttled away, leaving a trail of blood on the floor that only Billie could see. She dipped her head, wondering why she had even bothered. Did she expect them to believe her? No. She had simply wanted to shut down this bullshit intervention.

Tammy wasn't laughing. "You need to pull yourself outta this, Bee. This," she gestured at the state of the place and at Billie herself, "this isn't helping. Clean yourself up. Get out of this apartment. Go back to work."

Billie scowled. Tammy prided herself on her practicality, her knack for cutting through the bullshit to hack at the truth. Under normal circumstances, it was an asset, but these circumstances were less than normal and Billie resented being dismissed. "You think this is just a funk, Tammy? You think I'm, what, depressed?"

"Clearly. Look at you. Look at this place. You're a cliche, you're so fucking depressed." Tammy set her glass down. "Get outta your own head for a while. Get some fresh air. Stop drinking."

"Everything is so simple for you, isn't it? Do this. Do that. 'Get better'. Jesus, you sound like a man."

"Easy," Jen interrupted. Always the peace-maker, a role learnt from having two sisters and one that played out within her circle of friends. "We just want to help, Billie. How do we do that?"

"You can start by believing me." It was asking too much and she knew it but she was tired of hiding it, tired of pretending that the world hadn't turned completely upside down and batshit crazy.

None the women spoke and the silence flattened the mood like a poorly told joke.

Billie looked up. "Maybe you guys should go. Thanks for the visit."

Tammy was already on her feet. Jen was stuck in the middle as usual, pulled between the pole of two people. Unsure of what to do.

Kaitlin chimed in, trying to mediate. "We could help you clean up, if nothing else."

Billie watched as Kaitlin, with her perfect nails and precious manners, did something she had never seen her do. Kaitlin gathered up the empty take-out cartons with their crusty food remains, piling them into a stack to be taken away. Disturbed from their feeding, insects took to the air. "This stuff," she said, "is attracting flies."

A handful of them at first, then it seemed to be hundreds.

Buzzing and circling the table as Kaitlin tidied up. Simple houseflies, feeding on the food left out to spoil, as flies will do.

Something cold sluiced down the back of Billie's neck at the sickening buzz of the flies. An unnaturally thick swarm of the vile things.

The glass fell from her hand. "You have to go."

"Hold on." Jen held up a hand, calling for a time-out. "We want to understand what—"

"Not now," Billie hissed, shooing her friends toward the door. They shuffled so slowly. "Just go. Please."

Tammy didn't need to be told twice. Kaitlin brushed her hands and sauntered away, shaking her head.

The dark man with the flies in his mouth had found her. Had he followed her home or simply tracked her down? Did it matter? He was here and if she didn't get the ladies out, he might hurt one of them. Or follow them home to infest their lives like an unholy plague.

Jen lingered, oblivious to how her need for keeping the peace was putting her in danger. "Don't leave it like this, Billie."

More of the flies pelted themselves at the window, the racket of their wings impossibly loud. Billie shoved Jen toward the door. "Get out!"

Jen wavered, the hurt on her face was crystal. This, Billie realized, was the worst position to put her in but the alternative was unthinkable. Tammy, bless her pragmatic heart, snatched Jen's wrist and tugged her away.

"Billie, for God's sakes—"

The three of them staggered over the broken barrier of salt on the threshold and out into the hallway. Jen glanced back once and Billie winced at the look on her face as she slammed the door shut on her oldest friend.

She held the door for a moment, as if the trio might bust it down. Then she turned around.

The man with the flies in his mouth was there.

28

"WHERE IS THIS asshole?"

"Chill," said the man across the room. Crypto Death Machine slumped back in the great wingback chair like some debauched king. His ghoulish face paint was cracking. "He'll be here."

The man with the paunch did not chill and he did not stop pacing the floor. "I don't know, Crypt. This guy sounds like a bullshit artist to me."

"Better hope he doesn't hear you say that, Marty. I hear he can be vindictive."

"Ooh, I'm real scared," Marty spat, a tad overly emphatic. Marty was a band manager, had been for the last seventeen years. Drug busts, overdoses, psychotic fans, these he could handle. Even a dead prostitute once, down in Tijuana in the late nineties but this? This spookshow, underworld supernatural shit was a first and, frankly, he could do without it. Managing Crypto Death Machine and his unnatural appetites was enough. "Twenty bucks says this dipshit ain't gonna show. John Gantry. Oooh, big spook."

"I wouldn't do that," said the bodyguard standing at the door. Big, with a bull neck and a tattoo running up the back of his bald head.

"Do what?" Marty snapped.

"Say his name."

Marty whipped around to the doorman. "Oh yeah? Why not?"

"Bad luck," replied the doorman in a flat tone, as if any fool knew this.

"What the fuck is he, Voldemort?" Marty continued to pace. "Jesus Christ!"

"I'm just relaying what I heard." The doorman looked at the king slumped in the tall chair. "You heard that too, right Crypto?"

"That's what they say." Crypto Death Machine swung his leg off the arm of the chair, letting his heavy boot thud to the floor. His driver's licence, which had been rescinded after a DUI in '05, stated the name Stanley Gottferb, but no one called him Stanley any more. His face was hidden under lurid greasepaint, giving him the visage of a diabolic jester. Thousands more knew him as Crypto Death Machine, mysterious titan of the death metal scene. Hero to a hardcore fanbase of mostly white, all male suburban kids who daydreamed in vivid Technicolour about violent revenge fantasies.

Crypto (formerly Stanley) held an abiding obsession with the occult and the paranormal, something he used to cultivate his persona of diabolical and perverted mystery. Accompanying these obsessions was the collecting and curating of well known but rare occult objects. This was the intent behind the hard-to-arrange meeting with the man known as John Gantry.

He kicked a bottle with his boot, rolling it across the floor to Marty, his long suffering manager. "Any word?"

Marty scrolled through the phone in his hand. "Nope."

The doorman clicked his radio handset, spoke quietly to his counterpart outside the building and listened to the squawk-box response. "No sign of him," he reported to his employer.

Marty checked the time. "Mister spookshow was supposed to be here thirty minutes ago. Let's get outta here. He ain't gonna show."

"Have the Rover brought around," Crypto said to the doorman. "Keep it running. We'll give him a few more minutes."

"It's a fucking scam," Marty said. "This asshole is all rep and no show."

Crypto Death Machine shifted in his throne, growing annoyed at his manager's whining tone. And then, just like that, all the lights went out.

"What the fuck?" came Marty's voice from the void. The darkness was total.

The doorman's voice rumbled from the other end of the darkened room. "A fuse musta blown."

"I like the dark," said Crypto.

"Fuck Gantry," leaked Marty. "Let's just blow."

A small flame erupted in the dark. There was a crackling sound and then the flame went out and all that remained was the glowing end of a lit cigarette. Red then orange in the darkness. A voice. "All right, mates?"

"What the fuck?" Marty again, shriller than usual.

The voice behind the cigarette drawled out in a heavy accent. "You talking trash about me, Marty?"

"Oh fuck…"

The overhead lights fired on and everyone in the room squinted against the harsh light.

John Gantry nabbed a chair, swung it backwards and flopped down. "Right. Let's get on with it."

Crypto sat up but maintained his mask of practised indifference. "Do you always make a grand entrance, Gantry?"

"I do have a reputation to uphold." Gantry shot a look at the band manager. "Right, Marty?"

Marty mumbled something under his breath but kept his distance.

"Do you have it?" Crypto asked.

"Yeah." Gantry nodded to a black bag at his feet. It was big with a tortoise shell handle, like an old doctor's bag. "You prepared to pay for it?"

"If it's real, I am." The musician's eyes lit up with a dark sparkle. "Let's see it."

Gantry gave the bag a hard kick, sliding it across the floor to the man in the wingback chair. No one made a move to fetch it.

"Bring it here," Crypto ordered his manager.

Marty didn't move. "How do we know it ain't rigged?"

Gantry took a drag on his cigarette and grinned from ear to ear. "Life's full of risks, innit?"

"It's moving," said the doorman.

The cracked leather folds of the bag swelled and shifted, as if something inside was moving around. Marty took a step back. "See?"

Crypto snapped his fingers and the doorman retrieved the bag and set it at his employer's feet. "What's inside, Gantry? A rattlesnake?"

"Just the item in question. If you don't want it, I can find plenty of other buyers."

The sparkle in the musician's eye deepened. He reached down and undid the metal clasp.

Marty jerked forward. "Whoa, boss. You don't know what's in there."

"Don't spoil my fun, Marty." Crypto beamed with a sort of glee. "Will it hurt? Let's see." Crypto reached inside. He winced, then dug his hand in further and lifted something out. A package wrapped in oily cloth.

Crypto set the leather bag back onto the floor and propped the package on his knees and began to unfold the cloth. A boy at his own birthday party. "Ahh," he cooed, lifting up his prize. A handgun. A standard military issue Browning 1911. Old, the gunmetal aged into a dull patina.

Marty pursed his lips. "How do we know it's real?"

"Oh it's real." Crypto cradled the weapon in his hands like it was made of eggshell. "I can feel it."

Gantry draped his arms over the back of his chair. "It's engraved. On the side of the handgrip."

Crypto turned the piece over and examined the metal run under the trigger guard. An inscription bored into the metal. *To Reverend Jones, with love.*

"Still," Marty cautioned. "How do we know this is the piece he used to blow his brains out?"

"It's the same one found in his lap," Gantry said. "The original evidence bag is inside the satchel. The police inventory too. It's real."

Crypto studied the gun, captivated by its look and feel. "It's beautiful."

"Check the magazine." Gantry straightened his tie but it still looked rumpled. "Marty, can you offer a mate a drink?"

The doorman crossed to the bar on the far side of the room, glancing up at the wide saloon mirror that hung over the length of it. Setting two rock glasses on a tray, he poured two fingers in each and brought the tray around.

Gantry took one. "Ta."

Crypto waved his away, too entranced in his prize to think of anything else. Marty, miffed that there was not a third glass on the tray, took the remaining glass.

Gantry never let his eyes off the death metal star. Rumour had it that Crypto Death Machine was writing a rock opera about the late Reverend Jones and his little cult down in Guyana. Gantry had no idea if this was true and he didn't care. Crypto was a collector of macabre artifacts and he was willing to pay. More importantly though, Crypto Death Machine, prat though he was, had influence. Power. Legions of fans across two continents were eager to do whatever their idol asked of them.

"So," Gantry said. "We have a deal, yeah?"

Crypto waved a hand at his manager. "Pay him."

Marty's face darkened but he stepped behind his employer's tall chair and came back with a black satchel that looked identical to the one Gantry had. He placed it before the Englishman and stepped away quickly.

Gantry twisted the clasp open and looked inside and then closed the bag again.

"It's all there," Marty said, offended.

"Deal's changed." Gantry dropped the cigarette to the floor and stepped on it.

Crypto tore his eyes from the pistol and levelled them at the other man. He remained silent.

Marty fumed. "That's the price we agreed upon. Every dollar. Take it or leave it."

"Situations change, Marty old man. Your money's no good. I want something else."

Crypto leaned forward. "What do you want?"

"A debt. A boon. A favour." Gantry shook out another cigarette from the pack. "Not now, not tomorrow. But sometime. And when I call it in, you do as I say. Immediately and without question."

Crypto's eyes narrowed, as if souring on the deal. Marty laughed loudly, like he couldn't believe his ears. "You want a favour? So we walk out of here with the piece and the money? Done."

The doorman, of all people, interjected. "That hardly seems fair."

"No one asked you!" Marty barked. He turned back to Gantry. "He has a point though. Crypto doesn't like to owe anyone anything. Whatever favour you need, he may not be able to make it happen."

"Oh, he will."

Crypto spoke up. "You sound awfully sure of yourself, Mister Gantry. What's to stop me from taking the piece and my money and never answering your call?"

"That's your perogative. But you'd regret it."

"How's that?" Marty scoffed.

"There's a little lock on the gun there. Don't bother looking for it, you can't see it. The thing is, Crypto, the gun your holding is bound to a lot of angry souls. How many people drank the Kool-Aid back in Jonestown? Nine hundred or so. That's a lot of ghosts."

Gantry flipped open his Zippo and lit the cigarette. No rush, watching the other men react. "So, if you renege on our deal, all I have to do is turn that little lock and the gates flood open. Nine hundred pissed off souls come screaming out, looking for a little payback. Think you can handle that, Crypto?"

The silence was taught and the manager's brow took on a sheen of sweat. This is where the reputation came into play. An article of faith among the players. Do you believe?

Crypto Death Machine folded the gun back into its oily rag and placed the package into the satchel at his feet. Then he snapped the clasps shut. "Agreed."

Marty was about to stutter out a protest but a glance from Crypto shut it down.

Gantry got to his feet. "Super. I'll be in touch." He turned to go but then stopped. Reaching down into the black bag near his chair, he withdrew a bundle of bills and stuffed it into his back pocket. "Walking around money. See ya."

The big man guarding the entrance swung the door open and John Gantry walked out of the room. When the door clicked home, Marty turned to his employer. "You honestly believe that shit?"

"Course not," Crypto said, but there was a tiny crack in his voice as he said it.

Curbside, the lights over the club entrance were dark as John Gantry stepped into the night air. He looked around for a cab but the street was empty. He put a finger to his ear and wiggled it. The ringing in his ear had been a low buzz inside the club but stepping out into the night was like someone had dialled the volume way up. It was splitting his brain like an ice pick through his eardrum.

Something was wrong. Really wrong.

"Shite," he spat and walked faster toward the lights on Barton Avenue.

A man stepped out of an alleyway after the Englishman had passed, watching Gantry walk away. He dialled his phone, put it to his ear and waited. When someone on the other end picked up, he said "Hey. It's me. Guess who I just saw?"

29

THE THING HOVERED in her living room, glowering at Billie with its sightless hollow eyes. The flies boiling the air around him grew in number by the second until the dark figure appeared cloaked in the pests and the awful nattering sound of their wings became thunderous.

It had tracked her down and now its filth was infesting her very home. She screamed at it to get out, to forbid it from entering her home but the undertaker man didn't react. He simply watched her while the flies crawled in and out of his empty eye sockets.

The cold terror in Billie's heart bobbed to the surface. Outrage and indignation ran hot. She threw a book at it. The flies scattered at its impact but the dark figure didn't react. She had half-expected the paperback to sail right through the entity and hit the wall behind it but that didn't happen. The book simply vanished, as if swallowed up by a black hole.

Could no one in the building hear the racket she was making? The people in the flat downstairs had no problem banging the ceiling if her music was too loud. How could they not hear her screams?

The dark mass of insects boiled through the air, crawling over the ceiling and the walls. She felt them land on her skin and in her hair. Then something snatched her wrist and she screamed again.

It was the half-boy. His thin hand locked around her wrist, as solid as rock but cold on her flesh, and he tugged her away. Pulling her towards the open door. Billie blinked stupidly at the legless creature until she realized that the ghost was trying to pull her away from the danger.

Billie ran. Staggering out into the hallway, she tried to shake off the nasty flies tangled in her hair. She bolted for the stairwell door and looked back.

The flies swarmed out of her door en masse as the undertaker man emerged. The half-boy galloped along on his hands, dragging his bloodied stumps after him but his gait was slow and no match for the winged insects. The swarm enveloped him and in a heartbeat the undertaker was hovering over the diminutive phantom. It snatched up the half-boy in its long hands and the little ghost screamed and clawed the floor trying to get away from the monstrous thing. The screams were terrible and the amputee's eyes dished wide with terror. The undertaker opened his mouth wide and there was a hideous click, like bone dislocating, and its jaw dropped wider and the crab-boy shrieked as he was swallowed up. The undertaker gulped the ghost down with its outlandish jaw in slow, jerking motions like a garden snake swallowing a mouse.

Billie hammered down the stairs and crashed out the doors. Sprinting fast with the piteous cries of the half-boy still ringing in her ears.

~

Ray Mockler shuddered violently and opened his eyes. An absolute cold had chilled him out of a dead sleep, as if he had gone to bed on a humid June night only to wake up mid-February with the windows open. Along with the chill came a gurgling nausea so noxious that he thought he was going to be sick.

The bed stirred and he rolled partway over to see if his shivering had woken Christina. The sickening feeling spiked hard at what he saw.

A man was in their bed, pressing down on his fiancee. Dark clothes, his face hidden behind inky hair. He seemed more shadow than human. His hands were pawing at her. The fingernails were purpled and there was grime permanently etched into the knuckles. Christina lay prone and apparently helpless, smothered by the assailant.

He wanted to kill the son of a bitch. Bash the side of his head in with his fist and throw him to the floor and stomp the bastard until his ribs caved in. For once, he wished he had brought his sidearm home, so he could empty the clip into this man who had violated their home and was clawing his woman. But Mockler couldn't move. His limbs seized up. Even his eyelids didn't obey, forcing him to watch.

That's when he knew it was a nightmare. Not unlike the other dreams he was prey to but those were about work. The misery and the deaths and the mindless, heartless ways that people end one another's lives. Christina never appeared in those nightmares. This was new, this horrific vision in his own bed. This assailant, who seemed somehow less than human. Other.

Christina's head flopped to one side, turning to face him, her eyes open but they were blank and without emotion. Her lips parted, as if to speak and something dark crept out. A common housefly.

He jerked awake, every muscle coiling in a spasm that left his limbs aching. The air felt hot and the sheets were damp with sweat. He lashed out a hand for Christina but the bed was empty. She wasn't there.

"Christina?"

He sat up and something moved in the mirror over her dressing table. It didn't make sense. In the reflection, he saw himself in bed but still asleep. Christina was there. And slithering on top of her was the dark assailant. Doing things to her.

Turning his head, he saw that the real bed was empty, the sheets wrinkled, and when he looked back to the mirror, the image had vanished. He saw only his own reflection, pale and terrified.

"Christina!"

Silence. He stumbled to the bathroom on creaky legs but she wasn't there. He went downstairs, gripping the railing to keep from falling, and checked the living room and the kitchen. Both empty. A glow of light from the hall where the studio was.

Christina stood before the easel. She was naked but she hadn't gone to bed that way. The big sketchpad was propped on the easel and her arm muscles flexed hard as she worked a piece of charcoal against the page.

"What are you doing?" he said. "Why are you up?"

She didn't respond. Her hand worked harder, stabbing and slashing at the page like she was working out a vendetta against the fine paper.

"Chris. Stop." He circled around and saw the look in her eyes. Glazed and wet, seeing nothing but the paper. She was sleepwalking. Or sleep-sketching. His brain too muddled to think straight. She was still asleep, caught in the grip of some somnabulist spell.

"Easy," he cooed as he took hold of her wrist and slowed her hand. Speaking gently, he told her to stop and let go of the shard of charcoal. She fought him at first but her movements slowed until the dark chalk fell from her fingers and she staggered suddenly. He caught her before she collapsed and led her gently from the room.

He gambled one quick glance back at the easel before killing the light, even though he already knew what she had been rendering in her sleep. The ghastly face that she had sketched before stared back at him. Despite not having seen the face of her attacker in his nightmare, he knew in his bones that it was the same man. If it was a man at all.

By the time they reached the bedroom, Christina was falling back to sleep quickly and he had to propel her limp form back into the bed. Covering her with the sheet, he stepped back and for a second time he felt his blood run cold.

The crucifix was back. Hung upside down on the wall above the bed. The same one he had tossed into the trunk of his car.

At that point, detective Raymond Mockler became scared.

The bleating ringtone of his cell snapped him out of it. Calls this late meant only one thing. Work. A body had been found and he was needed at the scene. Sighing heavily, he snatched up his phone from the nightstand.

"Mockler," he hissed.

"Ray? It's Gille. Sorry to wake you, man."

"That's all right." He turned away from the bed, trying not to look at the inverted cross but the thing drew his eyes like a sun. "What's going on?"

"This might be nothing but I know you'd kill me if I didn't let you know. We got a call from an informant. He just spotted your boy. Down on Sherman."

"Who?"

"Gantry."

Mockler became still. "When was this?"

"Half an hour ago."

"Stay put. I'm on my way."

30

MERCIFULLY, THE CHURCH was unlocked. Billie slipped inside and when the massive oak door clicked shut behind her, she felt safe. Whether the shadow thing that had invaded her home would follow her onto consecrated ground was still open to debate. Nothing about this made any sense, none of this ghost business seemed to follow any kind of logic.

The interior of the church was dark, the lights in the nave turned low. Alongside the south wall glowed dozens of tiny votive candles lit before a statue of the Virgin. The familiar smell of burning wax and wood polish filled her nose, almost comfortingly.

One lonely congregant occupied a pew up near the transept. His feet were propped on the back of the pew before him. He didn't move, catnapping inside the church. Something about it offended her, the disrespect, but at least he wouldn't bother her.

Better still, there were no dead people skulking about inside the church. Maybe it was too late for them, she wondered, imagining them tucking themselves back into their coffins after a long day of haunting.

Slipping silently into a pew, she turned back to look at the big church doors, wondering if the undertaker man had followed her here. Could it pass through those oak doors or was it waiting for her outside? There was a term for hiding in a church, wasn't there? A claim one could make where the church was honoured to protect you, even from the law. A frame from an old movie came to mind; a deformed bell-ringer barricading himself inside a cathedral. What was the word?

"Sanctuary," she said aloud. The word echoed up into the vaulted ceiling overhead.

The man upfront stirred, woken from his nap by her outburst. Billie scowled, hoping the stewbum wouldn't turn around and see her. She was in no mood for some lonely parishioner in his 'coming-to-Jesus' moment.

There was a click and then a plume of smoke billowed into the air, bubbling up into the chancel. Billie's jaw dropped at the audacity. Not only was he napping, the man was having a cigarette.

"All right, luv?"

Of course it was him, Billie sighed. Who else would it be? "What are you doing here, Gantry?"

"Rescuing you, apparently." Gantry let his feet drop and he rose up, sauntering down the aisle to the back row.

"What the hell is wrong with you?" she sputtered. "We're in a church for God's sakes."

"That's funny. Scooch over." He dropped into the pew next to her. "I like churches. Listen. Do you hear that?"

"Hear what?"

"Exactly," he said. "Absolute quiet. Peaceful too, if the Jesus people stay away. Good spot to kip."

Gantry opened his mouth and blather just seemed to fall out. Half of it made no sense to her. There couldn't be any coincidence to his being here. She turned to him. "How did you find me?"

He stuck a finger in his ear and wriggled it like there was water trapped inside. "You damn near blew my eardrum out from screaming so loud. What happened?"

She was going to ask how he could have possibly heard her but whatever answer he gave would just be another riddle. "I was attacked," she said.

"By what?"

"I'm not sure. I thought it was one of the dead but I don't know. It's different."

Gantry watched her slink down in the pew. He took hold of her elbow, examining the purple bruises on her forearm. "Did it do this?"

"Yes."

"Strong one. Where'd you find it?"

Billie pulled her arm back. "It's the one haunting Mockler. I went to his house, tried to get rid of it. I failed."

"Jesus, Billie. Didn't I tell you to forget that one?" He looked up at the ceiling above them. A fresco of the afterlife, dimply cherubs and haloed saints. "What happened?"

"It sort of kicked my ass. Then it followed me home."

"What did it look like?"

She related what she was able to put into words. The dead man's appearance, how she reminded him of an undertaker from some other era. About the hollowed out eyes and the mass of flies that swarmed around him like a cloak. How it had thrown her into the walls and how the flies seemed to do its bidding.

Gantry dropped his cigarette and stomped it. "Christ."

"I saw it eat another ghost," she added.

"Pardon?"

"The one that attacked you. The boy with no legs. This thing just opened its jaw and swallowed him whole. It was awful."

Gantry's face darkened as he massaged the bridge of his nose. "It's not a ghost."

"Then what is it?"

"Hard to describe," he said. "It's a shadow entity. But it was never human to begin with. It's like a black hole of negativity."

"Then why does it look like a man?"

"This thing, it swallows up energy. Other ghosts, particularly the nasty ones. Sometimes they can take on the memory or soul of someone powerful. It's a shadow that thinks it was once human."

Staring up at the large cross hung in the altar, Billie tried to sort out what Gantry was saying. It sounded ludicrous but her gut nudged her the other way. The spirits of the dead that she had encountered so far were disturbing and unsettling but there was something recognizable about them. Emotion. She could feel their anger or outrage or utter despair. With the undertaker, there was nothing even close to emotion. She groped for a word that would describe what the undertaker felt like. Evil. It was imprecise but it was the closest she could get.

"So what do I do?" she said finally. "How do I get it to go away?"

"You don't. It's not one of the dead. It was never human so it doesn't respond that way. You stay the fuck away from it, yeah?"

Billie slid further down the bench, her head resting against the hard pew. "I can't deal with this anymore, Gantry. This 'gift' is ruining my life."

"Please don't tell me your gift is really a curse, okay? That's a wee trite. Even for you."

"What does that mean? Even for me?"

"You're a bit of a sad case, aren't you? Mopey-wopey, feeling sorry for yourself. Where does it get you?"

"You're an asshole," she said.

"That's better. I'm just saying be careful. Pity can be a slippery slope." Gantry looked back up at the vaults overhead. "Yes, this sucks. This ability you have is a terrible thing and life would be so much more simple if you never had it. There. I've said it out loud. Feel better?"

She didn't respond.

"But you have accept it and crack on," he continued. "I know it's a freaky and it's terrifying but you'll adapt. You're stronger than they are. They should fear you. Do you know that?"

"No." She tried not to sound petulant but failed. "What about the shadow thing? Am I stronger than that?"

"Hell no. You're up shit creek there."

"Terrific."

"You were meant for something special," he said. "I'm not sure what that is but you have the potential to be a powerful medium. More."

"Well there's the problem, genius. I don't want to be. Who would?"

Gantry shrugged. "Point taken."

"You want me to become that, don't you?" She looked looked down. Her shoes were scuffed. "Why are you doing this?"

"Just trying to help," he grinned.

"Don't bullshit me, okay? What are you after?"

His grin fell away and he sat up, about to say something but then stopped and lit another cigarette. "Something bad is coming. And I'm gonna need some help when it gets here."

"What? What is coming?"

"I'm still trying to sort that out. It's hard to explain. But it's big and it's nasty." He ran his hand through his hair but it did nothing to straighten the mess. "Maybe I'm wrong about this. I hope I am. But if I'm not, well, we're all up a creek then."

"Well, thanks. That clears up everything."

"Anytime, luv." He sat up quickly. "Let's get out of here."

"I'm not going anywhere."

"Why not?"

"Because," Billie said. "That thing is out there."

"Oh come on," he scoffed. "No way he followed you here."

"It's already here. Looking for a way in."

John Gantry startled, whipping his head around as if he could see the thing. Billie felt a tiny smidgen of satisfaction for having spooked him for a change.

~

"How long ago?" Mockler said, clambering out of his vehicle.

The other man wheezed as he stepped out of the shadows to meet him. "Twenty minutes ago."

The street was quiet and underlit by a few blown streetlights. Mockler looked east then west down the strip but there was nothing. Not even a stray cat. "You sure it was him?"

The other man was an informant known in the detective units as Tapeworm. A stick of a man who ate constantly yet never gained a pound, as if the namesake parasite was in his guts, eating his dinner before he did. He had phoned in the sighting of

John Gantry. This happened from time to time but Tapeworm travelled in strange circles. He was also reliable, so his tip was taken seriously. Mockler had blown three red lights racing uptown to meet him.

"It was him," said the informant.

"Where did you lose him?"

"Right here," nodded the Tapeworm. "I was hanging back, saw him turn up this street. Running too, like he was in a hurry. When I caught up, he was gone."

Mockler studied the street. "How long? From the time he disappeared until you got to this spot?"

"Not long."

"How long?"

The man looked at his shoes. "Two minutes. Maybe."

"Okay." Mockler was already marching away at a smart clip. "Thanks."

"Yo, Mockingbird." Tapeworm rubbed his finger and thumb together in a charade for payout. "How about a thank you?"

The detective was already running. "Call the office. And clear out of here!"

The strip he ran down, like so many parts of the city, was a jumble of style and eras. Victorian row houses buttressed against squat concrete bunkers. A hundred shadowy doors or breezeways for a wanted man to vanish into. And the man he was after was a master at vanishing.

Mockler slowed to a stop and looked back the way he had

come. Something tugged at his peripheral vision and he rotated a quarter turn. A church loomed up before him. Limestone blocks sullied by a century of soot and washed-out stained glass. Nothing out of the ordinary. So why were his eyes drawn to it.

There was no way Gantry would have slipped inside a church. Was there?

The sudden and immediate boom changed his mind. A heavy thud that he felt in his feet. Then shattering glass, followed by a scream. A woman's voice. The massive doors blew open as if thrust apart by an explosion.

31

A GALE FORCE wind tore through the church. The candles winked out at the feet of the Virgin, tumbling to the floor. The pages of an open hymnal tore away, billowing and dancing in the air. Billie closed her eyes against the grit stinging her face.

"Duck!" Gantry hollered.

She felt herself yanked down hard between the pews, her elbow rattling smartly against the upright kneeler. Something shattered behind her and to the left came a thud so heavy that she felt it through the floor. It sounded as if the building was collapsing around them.

Gantry was huddled for cover beside her as the lights popped and flared in a sickening strobe. "Do something!" she barked at him.

"Like what?"

The curtain over the altar tore away and flapped through the air like a vulture let loose indoors.

Billie hugged the floor. "You're the supernatural guy! Do something!"

Gantry scowled at her. Peeking up over the pew, he cupped his hands around his mouth and hollered. "Oy! Piss off!"

The wind blew harder. Gantry ducked. Billie shook her head. "That's the best you can do?"

"This is your territory, Billie, not mine. I say we rabbit."

"What?"

"Run."

The wind died instantly and without warning. Loose pages from a torn Bible fluttered back to earth and along the far wall where the candles had fallen, something had started to burn.

Billie rose up slowly, eyes darting everywhere for signs of the entity but the bulbs had blown and the church was dark. Street light filtered in through the stained glass, mottling everything in reds and blues.

"Nasty bastard, isn't he?" Gantry said, already fumbling out another smoke. His eye caught something. "Christ, now what?"

The nave of the church was littered with debris and loose paper but something else had changed. There was a coffin propped up at the transept, surrounded by wilting lilacs, as if readied for a funeral service. An open casket but Billie couldn't see inside from where she stood.

"Leave it," Gantry warned but Billie was already moving toward it. She had to see. The smell of the lilacs was strong but too sweet, as if past their date. The little petals of pale purple fell to the ground as she approached.

"I have to see," she whispered.

"Leave it!" he hissed.

She could see the folds of the casket liner and the hands of the deceased clasped one over the other. Holding her breath, she saw the chest and arms and finally the face. How does one prepare for the worst? She had expected to see herself lying there, dead and ready for the grave. Or even Gantry, with coins over his eyes to trap his soul inside. But it was neither.

Laid out inside the casket was a woman. Dark hair, same age as herself, the features sagging from the pull of death but some hint of recognition therein. The curve of the nose, the shape of the lips. It took three more steps before Billie realized it was her mother.

She had never witnessed this tableau, her mother's remains laid out in a casket within a church. There had been no service, no visitation, no proper mourning. She just wasn't there anymore.

The woman in the casket sat up. Slow and creaking, the eyes still closed. A dry whimper leaked from Billie's throat.

"Get away from it," Gantry's voice rumbled behind her. "It's just screwing with your head, Billie."

Her mother rotated her head to face Billie and then opened her eyes. The pupils were milky with cataracts, as if burned out from what they had witnessed beyond the veil.

Billie wanted to speak but her mouth didn't work, her lips

stuttering over the first syllable. Mama. Such a simple word. The first word.

In contrast, her mother's mouth opened and Billie felt her knees falter when the flies came vomiting out.

She heard Gantry curse as he rushed past her and kicked the casket over. It toppled backward, her mother along with it, and thudded to the ground. The lilacs tumbled and the petals scattered everywhere. Gantry was barking like a lunatic, cursing out a blue streak of every obscenity he could muster.

The lights blinked back on. The casket was gone and the white noise had vanished. A single lilac petal had landed on Billie's knee. She brushed it away.

"Time to go," Gantry said, taking her arm.

Staggering to the doors, Billie looked back over her shoulder at the chancel but the casket was still gone. Gantry pulled her along but stopped abruptly as the church door blew open.

Detective Mockler had his firearm drawn and positioned in both hands, the barrel levelled straight at Gantry's face.

"Get your hands off her," he said.

32

MOCKLER SNARLED WHEN he spoke, his teeth bared. "Get on the ground."

"Christ," Gantry spat. "Not now."

Billie felt her jaw hang open. Like witnessing an accident, everything slowed down as each man glared at the other across the church pews. "Mockler. Put the gun down."

"Billie, are you all right?" Mockler didn't take his eyes off the other man. "Are you hurt?"

"I'm fine. Please. Just put the gun away."

Mockler took two paces, closing the distance between himself and the murder suspect. "Get on the ground, Gantry. Or I swear to God, I will blow your head off."

"Who're you trying to fool, Mockler? The girl?" Gantry kept smiling. "You're not cut out for this tough guy shit and we both know it."

"Wiggle a finger," Mockler hissed. "It's all I need to call it self defence and paint this church with your brains."

Gantry nodded at Billie. "You got a witness here, ace."

"She'll be in shock. Her statement unreliable. But you'll still be dead."

This time Gantry stepped closer. "Look at me, mate. That gun is awfully heavy. Pull it up."

Billie felt a crackle against her skin, as if the air had suddenly charged with electricity and she watched the gun tremble in Mockler's hand. She didn't know what Gantry was doing but there was power behind his words. Voodoo or hypnosis or mind control, she had no idea but she felt the power in it. And so did Mockler.

"Pull the gun away," Gantry said softly. "And then put the barrel in your mouth."

"Stop it!" She marched between the two men, directly in the line of fire.

Mockler turned the gun away. "Billie, get out of the way!"

"No." Billie hissed. "No one's shooting anyone. And no one's getting arrested."

"Have you lost your mind?" Mockler snapped, the trigger piece hot in his hand. "He's a murderer. Get out of the way."

The leer on Gantry's face fell by a shade. "Billie, clear off. Before you get hurt."

Billie scrambled for some way to defuse the whole mess. Sweat was beading over the detective's face and his hands seemed to tremble. "Mockler, listen to me. He didn't do it."

"He's lying to you. It's what he does."

"I can't explain it right now, but he didn't kill those women. Mockler, please. Put the gun down."

Something in her voice broke through the adrenalin juicing Mockler's brain. All he wanted to do was help her but not like this. How did this all get turned around so badly? The gun dipped toward the floor but then, behind Billie, he caught sight of the leer on John Gantry's ugly face. He snatched Billie hard by the arm and pulled her away quickly and kept her at arm's length. Her struggling would spoil his aim but he had a full magazine in the clip, all of which he was more than happy to unload on the murderous Englishman.

The leer on Gantry's face brightened. "You don't like guns much, do you Mockler? Not since that incident with the kid."

"Shut up." Mockler gritted his teeth, keeping his hand steady as Billie struggled to get out of his grip.

"That piece looks heavy. It looks all wrong on you, mate. Ten quid says it won't fire."

Billie cursed at them both to stop. Gantry was working some angle. Something in his voice was off, a heavy tone that buzzed the air, trying his voodoo trick again. Mockler, on the other hand, seemed possessed. The look in his eyes was frightening. She heard him growl. And then he pulled the trigger.

The firearm didn't go off. Misfire, as Gantry had predicted. Mockler tried again but the trigger piece locked up.

Gantry didn't waste the moment. He was fast and he fought

dirty and Mockler stumbled back, falling to one knee under a flurry of fists and boots and thumbs to the eyes.

Billie tried to pull Gantry off but he too seemed possessed, single-minded in his assault on the police detective. She was shrugged off and then she heard a rumbling growl as Mockler roared back. Snatching fistfuls of jacket and hair, Mockler pivoted and swung, hurling the Brit into the pews. Gantry crashed into the wooden benches and flopped to the floor.

The two men crashed and tumbled through the nave. A light overhead popped, plunging the nave into partial darkness and Billie lost sight of the combatants. But she could hear them curse and roar at each other.

"Stay down, Gantry!" Mockler's voice bellowed. "Or I'll snap your fucking neck!"

Another crash and thud, then Gantry hissed back. "See you in Hell, mate. Save me the window seat."

More scuffling and crashing from the far side of the chancel then Billie heard something heavy thunder against the floor.

"Mockler?" She groped her way in the dark. "Gantry?"

One of them rose up from behind the altar. Mockler, woozy and unbalanced. Of Gantry, there was no sign save for the jacket clutched in the detective's hands.

"Shit." Mockler spat blood from his mouth and flopped into a pew like a spent boxer.

~

"You sure you're okay?"he asked.

"I'm not the one with the bloodied lip," Billie said. She held a handful of paper towels she had found in the kitchenette in the church basement. There was a refrigerator but no ice in the freezer so she dampened the towels with cold water and ran back up. Mockler stood outside the front doors, pacing the stoop. "Sit down. Take this."

Mockler eased down onto the steps and touched the wad of wet paper to his swollen lip. Wincing, he looked at the blood staining the paper towel and then gingerly re-applied it to his face.

Billie sat down next to him, her eyes falling on his bloodied knuckles. "Your hand's a mess too. I'll get more towels for it."

"Stay put." He worked his jaw, testing the pain. "What the hell were you thinking, Billie?"

Billie blew the bangs from her eyes. How could she explain this? "I don't have proof or anything," she sighed. "I just know that he didn't kill those two women. He was trying to help them."

He turned, ready to refute it but the effort made him wince and he said nothing. He leaned to the other side and spit on the church steps. Bloodied foam dribbled down the concrete. Mockler took the towel away, folded the wet paper to apply a clean patch to his lip.

She watched his hands. "Your shaking."

"Adrenalin will do that to you." His words were garbled by the swelling lip. He looked at her. "I thought we were friends."

She flinched. Was it the bitterness in his tone or the word 'friends'? It stung and it soothed at the same time and it was maddeningly confusing.

"What does he want with you?" he asked. When she didn't answer, he shook his head. "Whatever he's selling you, don't buy it."

He lowered the towel and the limp paper quivered in his hand. He tossed it away and bunched his hand into a fist but the trembling would not go away.

"Does that happen a lot?" she asked. "The trembling in your hand?"

"When I'm tired. I haven't been sleeping much."

She could guess at the reason why but asked anyway. "How come?"

He shrugged. "Dunno. Just stuff going at home."

I'll bet, she thought. "You can talk about it. I mean, if you want to."

Mockler looked up at the dark street. "It's nothing. Forget it."

Typical. Like he had it all under control and there was no need to discuss it further. Why do men do that? "Can I ask you something?"

"Of course."

"The stuff at home. Is any of it weird? Odd things? Creepy stuff you can't explain? Nightmares?"

His face fell flat as he looked at her, as if he'd been caught out in a lie. "What are you talking about?"

"I think you're in danger."

"From what?"

Don't do it. He'll think your crazy and walk away as fast he can.

"A ghost," she said.

The air went flat. The trembling in the detective's hand stopped.

"I can see them. One of them attached itself to you. It's in your house. That's why you can't sleep. It's hurting you."

She waited for a response. Anything at all but Mockler was stone. She went on. "That's why I was at your house the other day. I tried to get rid of it. It didn't work. I'm sorry."

If anything, the silence became louder.

When he finally spoke, he sounded spent and defeated. "Jesus, Billie. You're as crazy as he is."

"I know how it sounds. But you have to believe me. This thing wants to hurt you."

Mockler got to his feet with a groan, knees popping, and he went down the stairs. "See ya around, Billie."

"Mockler, please. Don't walk away."

He stopped and looked back at her. "Hey. If you ever need anything, rip up my card."

Billie propped her elbows atop her knees and let her head drop, listening to his footfalls fade away.

33

A LIGHT DRIZZLE began to fall as Billie walked home. It steamed as it hit the sidewalk and she lifted her face to it, letting the rain rinse the few tears that had welled up.

You stupid girl, she mumbled. Drained from exhaustion, it took a force of will to simply plant one foot before the other and plod home. She felt brittle and hollowed out and hated herself for feeling any of it. It felt like she had been dumped and that was just plain ridiculous. What was he to her? Nothing. She barely knew him. He was engaged. He was a cop. There was no common ground. He had a crooked nose—

The crazy loop inside her head was already spinning out of control. She picked up the pace, hoping to outrun the cyclical torment she was prey to. Just get home, sort it out then.

The dead had other plans.

They came out of the rain, from the alleys and up out of manholes and crawling down fire escapes. Like sharks circling a wounded fish. Fragile and spent, Billie had let her guard down and the dead picked up the scent and came shambling forward. Dead men with twisted limbs or gaping holes in their heads, dead women with knives still stuck in their backs or blood dribbling from their wrists. Worst of all were the children, watching her with big, hungry eyes, these street urchins that had been cruelly used up and thrown away like trash into the rain gutter.

The spookshow in all its horrid glory, came out to greet her. All eager for their pound of flesh.

They trailed behind her and shambled alongside. Some reached out to touch her and her flesh prickled at their clammy hands. Others blocked her path, forcing her to go around or detour in the wrong direction. She told them to go away, to leave her alone, but they wouldn't listen. Their anger and their bitterness came at her like stones thrown at a rabid dog.

Look at what they did to me

I didn't deserve this

Someone has to pay

Pelted by laments and regrets and resentments, Billie turned numb. She wanted nothing to do with these lost souls. They had their chance and their misery held no claim on her. Their cloying neediness was suffocating.

She stopped in her tracks and the dead closed in around her like a mob. Their cold hands touched her flesh and pulled her hair and when one leaned in for a kiss, she could take no more.

Her pent up anger unleashed as she screamed at them to leave her alone. To go away. To stop touching her.

The first to drop away were the broken little children. Others backed away, some ran. The greediest and the neediest of the lost souls pressed in until Billie let loose in a banshee wail.

"You can all go to Hell!" she shrieked at them.

Some fell, others shuffled away. A woman in petticoats, flared hot and became corporeal as she ran into the street. Her face flashed visible in the headlights of the oncoming car and it swerved to miss her, the tires screeching as the brakes locked. A dull heavy thud echoed when it hit the lamppost, the front end crumpling in on itself.

The driver stumbled out, shaking his head and looking around for the ghastly woman who had ran into traffic. The only person on the entire street was Billie and she walked away quickly, leaving the driver confounded as he took in the damage to his grill.

The apartment felt wrong when she got back. Barren and too stuffy from the humidity. Her friends had walked away and now Mockler too and no one was coming back. Even the legless half-boy was gone and she almost missed the creepy little urchin. The only one coming back would be the shadow man that had devoured the little ghost.

She did not want to be here when the flies returned.

Quickly throwing clothes into a backpack, she locked the door behind her and scurried down to the second floor where she rapped her knuckles on the door of apartment three.

Bruce squinted his eyes at her as he swung the door open. "Billie. You wouldn't happen to have a can of beans, would ya?"

"Uh, no," she said, taken aback.

"I was gonna fix a mess of pork and beans but I didn't have no pork, so I figured it'd just be beans. Turns out I ain't got that either."

"You can raid my cupboards if you want. You know where the spare key is."

He scratched his belly through the threadbare cotton of his undershirt. "What can I do you for?"

Big smile here. "Can I borrow a car? For, like, a couple days."

Bruce kept scratching, like he needed to mull it over. "Which one?"

"Anyone. It doesn't matter."

"Take the Alpha." He dropped a set of keys into her hand. "You going to your aunt's?"

"Yeah. I just need to get out of town."

"No speedy stuff with that car. You gotta baby the old girl."

"Done. Thanks, Bruce."

"And don't ride the clutch."

"I don't," she said, miffed.

"Yes you do."

Getting out of the city was a breeze but an accident on the 403 had curdled traffic and she worried the old Alpha Romeo might overheat, stranding her on the highway. Her cell was charged but Bruce didn't even have a phone so she wouldn't be able to call him if there was car trouble. Getting it towed back to the city would break her bank.

Her worries were for naught. The Alpha rumbled along like a faithful workhorse and by late afternoon she was turning onto the causeway that led into Long Point. The creeping vines on the trees and the smell of the lake coming through the open window had her muscles unclenching and her heart slowing. Comfort around the bend.

Aunt Maggie was asleep in the deck chair as she came up the front steps. Billie set the backpack down softly to avoid startling her. Asleep, her aunt looked peaceful but she also looked old. Frail even. Growing up, aunt Maggie had always been strong and tireless. Her hands were hard and calloused, her arms freakishly strong for such a small woman. It simply hadn't occurred to Billie that the woman's strength would be something that would fade. That her aunt and mostly companion throughout childhood would ever be anything than the eternal rock that Billie could tether herself to.

Settling onto the opposite chair, she placed a gentle hand on her aunt's arm. "Hey," she cooed.

Her aunt opened her eyes and smiled, as if she'd been expecting her niece all along. "Well, hello there. I nodded off, didn't I?"

"That's good," Billie said. "You never used to nap."

"I'm taking more and more of them these days. Run down, I suppose."

Billie brushed a hair from her aunt's eyes, testing her brow at the same time. "Are you feeling okay?"

"I'm fine." Maggie swung her legs off the chair. "How long are you staying?"

"Dunno. Couple days maybe."

"Are you hungry?"

"Don't get up." Billie patted the woman's arm. "I'm going to bring my stuff in and get something cold to drink."

"I don't have any lemonade made but there's concentrate in the freezer."

"I'll make it. You sit." Billie hoisted up the backpack. "You want some?"

"Please."

~

The chicken turned out a little charred. Billie never could get used to her aunt's barbecue. The hot spots were never consistent. They ate it anyway and caught up on gossip in town. When the dishes were cleared, Billie had a nostalgic hankering for ice cream and suggested they take a walk. The Udderlee Kool offered heaping cones served up by polite but bored teenagers working summer jobs.

They settled onto the picnic table outside with mint chip and salted caramel in paper cups with little plastic spoons. Billie looked up at the horizon burning pink in the sunset. "The spiders are bad this summer," she said.

"It's all the rain we've had," Maggie said. "More mosquitoes means more spiders. I've had the boy next door sweep the house twice already. He doesn't do a good job of it, though."

"I can do that while I'm here."

Maggie watched the kids playing in the arcade, barefoot and still in their damp bathing suits. "Are you going to tell me the reason for the surprise visit? Or should I guess?"

"Just needed some quiet. That's all."

"It's not a boy, is it?"

"No." Billie looked into the paper cup, the ice cream melting fast in the heat. A white lie because it was partly about a boy but she wasn't willing to bring that subject up. Even though nothing had happened, Maggie would scold her for it anyway. "Did you know my dad very well?"

Maggie eyes flashed up, the spoon halfway to her mouth. "What brought that on?"

"We never talk about it."

"Why would we?" Maggie countered, as if the matter had been settled long ago.

Billie stirred the ice cream. She should have ordered the kiddie size. "What do you think happened?"

"The same thing everyone does," the woman sighed. "He took Mary Agnes away."

The same vague statement Billie had heard her whole life. The rare occasion when the topic had been broached. "But what happened after that? I want to know what you think happened."

"Honey, what is it you want? Details? I don't have any."

"Just tell me what you think happened. Did he spirit her away to Alaska? Are they shacked up somewhere with Elvis? What?"

Her aunt dropped the spoon into the cup and pushed it away. "Your father was not a good man, Billie. He was violent, especially when he was drunk. The two of them fought all the time. More so after you were born. She told him to stay away, his ego couldn't take it.

"He got drunk that night and broke in and abducted Mary. Then he took her some place where she would never be found and he murdered her. Then he killed himself. The police believe he took her out into the marsh. If that's true, they'll never be found."

The bluntness of it stung but she had asked for it and had no right to wince at its sting now. Billie watched her aunt stoop over, exhausted by the recall but no tears came. Her aunt, Billie supposed, had mourned her sister enough.

"I'm sorry to dredge it up," she said quietly. "I know it's painful but... I need to know."

Maggie patted her hand. "And so you should. But why now? What's brought all this on now?"

"I don't know," she fibbed. "I feel stuck. In life, you know. Like I can't get anywhere. I feel like I can't move forward unless

I have answers to this."

Another mosquito swam before her face and Billie brushed it away. "I'm not making any sense. Let's get out of here before we're eaten alive."

She walked down to the beach when Maggie went to bed. The wind coming off the lake was strong enough to keep the mosquitoes away but the sand fleas would gnaw her ankles if she lingered too long. She just wanted to put her feet in the water. The coolness of it felt good lapping over her ankles.

Long Point was riddled with shipwrecks. In Maggie's house there was a poster in the hallway that showed the locations and names of the ships that had run afoul of the massive sand spit that jutted out into the lake. Since the Great Lakes had been sailed, there had been over four hundred shipwrecks in the waters around this long finger of sand. That was a lot of deaths and some of the dead lingered here over the site of their demise. It was only a matter of time before they found her.

The first ghost came up out of the water. There was another further down the beach and more out on the lake itself. Soon, everywhere she looked she saw the dead. Panic set in but she pushed it down and calmed her breathing until her heart cooled. She needed to learn how to close herself off to them. Gantry's words. Keeping herself calm, she observed them without interest or fear. Fireflies in the night.

A few of them raised their heads, the way dogs do when they

catch a new scent, but after a moment they dropped again and shambled along. It was working.

A stone's throw up the beach was a dead man in tattered breeches and torn slops. Wading through the water, he kicked at the waves like he had lost something in the surf. She was glad he didn't notice her. The look in his milky eyes was crazed and wild.

Unsure of how long she could keep herself closed off to this many of the dead, she waded up out of the water and walked back with her shoes in her hand. This was a test and she had passed but it was tiring, like keeping a muscle clenched.

Climbing into bed, she could hear the trill of a bird outside and wondered what kind of bird it was. She wished she could identify birds by their calls. It would be a good thing to know.

The awful vision of her mother in the coffin shot up as soon as she closed her eyes. She concentrated on the bird calling out in the night but the image of her mother's face wouldn't go away. When she opened her eyes, the idea came fully formed. Her mother was dead. She herself could see the dead, talk to them. If she went back to the old house, the one where she had hidden in the crawl space all those years ago, her mother might still be there.

She hadn't spoken to her mother in twenty one years. Tomorrow, that would change.

34

POOLE ONTARIO WAS a burnmark of a town thirty minutes
north on highway 59. Billie hadn't been back since she was a
teen and there was little that had changed. A former tobacco
community, the township had dried up in the late eighties during
a land dispute with the local Ojibway nation. The old
Woolworths had shuttered long ago and now the windows in half
of the storefronts were ugly with plywood.

Rumbling down the main drag, Billie could have joked about
it being a ghost town but it didn't seem very funny now. The tour
of downtown was over quickly and she turned the car around and
doubled back but no part of this town matched up with the few
memories she had of it. Turning south at the church, she ambled
along until the tires thudded over the old rail tracks and on to the
street where she used to live.

The houses were shabby and used up, the lawns overgrown
and decorated with dollar store trinkets. Vehicles sat moored on

cinderblocks, never to be repaired. Realtor signs withered on their posts, unseen and unheeded but the trees were pretty, massive willows that swayed lazily in the breeze.

Her gut began clenching as she recognized a few of the houses. She was getting close. Given the faded state of the homes so far, Billie could only imagine how bad her old house must be. Did anyone live there now, after what had happened there? For all she knew, it could have been bulldozed or burnt to the ground. Bad history, bad voodoo. A haunted house nobody wanted.

She pulled the car to the shoulder. There was no sidewalk, just a ditch and then the lawn and then her old house. It looked the same. The white clapboard and dark green trim had been repainted some time over the last twenty years. The windows on the first floor had been replaced but the second story still had the old wooden sashes with the three-holed vent. The yard was mowed and rosebushes drooped with blooms under the picture window.

The gravel driveway crunched underfoot as she approached the house. She stopped, unsure of what to do now. She had expected the house to be deserted. Who could live here, with its awful history? There was a chance the current owners knew nothing of what had happened. It was, she reminded herself, over twenty years ago.

Billie gnawed her lip for a moment, feeling self-conscious and out of place but she hadn't come just to gawk. Taking a deep breath, she opened herself up to anything that might be here. Her senses tuned to any signal that her mother's ghost might still be here.

Hi mom. Remember me?

Her throat constricted as she choked up but the tears would just get in the way, blurring out her ability to see anything. Pushing it down, she took another step up the driveway and immediately the hair on the back of her arms stood up. Something was here.

Noise bubbled up and then someone came darting out from behind the house. A little boy, no more than five, ran past the side door and slowed when he saw Billie standing in the driveway. His hair was almost white it was so fair and it swooped into his eyes.

Billie smiled. "Hi."

The boy gave the tiniest of waves before looking away.

"Do you live here?"

He kicked at the loose stones, glancing up at her. "Did you bring bananas?"

"Uhm, no." She almost checked her purse to see if there were some there. "Sorry. I didn't bring anything."

With the sun directly in her eyes, the boy shimmered in the glare and she wondered if the child was whom she had sensed a second ago. Another one of the dead. She stepped into the shade and the boy became solid.

"Mom said you gotta bring something if you're coming for

lunch," he said.

"Oh. Well, I didn't come for lunch. I just wanted to see your house."

"MOM!"

The sidedoor creaked open and a woman stepped out, shielding her eyes against the sun. Her hair was a deep brown, in contrast to the boy's fairness, and she was young. Younger even, Billie guessed, than herself. "Josh, honey? Who are you talking to?"

She smiled when she saw Billie standing there. "Hi," she said. "You looking for somebody?"

Billie shifted her weight to the other leg, feeling suddenly like a trespasser. "No. I was just looking at the house."

"She didn't come for lunch," said the boy.

"You live here?" Billie asked. Stupid question. Of course the woman lived here.

"Yeah," the woman said, taking her son's hand. "Been here about six years now. No, seven."

Billie flustered. "I didn't mean to intrude. I just wanted to see the house. I lived here when I was a kid."

"Really?" The woman brightened at the thought. "I'm sure its worse for wear from when you were here."

"No. The place looks great. Better than I remember." She took a step back toward the road. She didn't want to leave but it seemed silly to impose on these people. They seemed nice. "Anyway. I'll get outta your hair."

"What's your name?"

"Billie."

The woman lifted the boy up and planted him on her hip and then held out her hand. "I'm Amanda. Come inside. I was just going to feed him a snack."

"No bananas," the boy said.

Bracing herself for an onslaught of memories, Billie followed the woman through the side door into the kitchen but her expectations deflated quickly. Nothing looked familiar, no flood of hazy images came rushing at her. It was a different house now, with nothing to show that she had ever been here, let alone spent the first eight years of her life within it.

She had left no impact on the place. Neither had her mother.

Amanda set the boy down onto a chair at the kitchen table. "Where you from?"

"Hamilton," Billie said. She smiled at the boy as he reached for a plate of crackers and cubed cheese. "How old are you, Josh?"

The boy crammed the cheese into his mouth, oblivious to anything but the food. Amanda set three glasses of water down and pushed one toward Billie. "He's four and a half. And still forgetful of his manners." She ruffled the boy's hair. "Slow down, honey. Don't put too many in your mouth."

Billie's hopes for a wash of warm memories about her childhood home withered away. The kitchen had been redone recently, reconfigured as far as she could recall. The refrigerator had been on the other side of the sink, hadn't it? The update looked nice but seemed unfinished, like the contractor had left before the last coat of paint was done or the final hardware put on the cupboards.

"The place looks really great," Billie said. "Did you do the renovations?"

"My husband and I." Amanda nodded at the cupboards. "There's still the finishing to do. God knows if that will ever happen. Hey, do you want some coffee?"

"Don't make it on my account."

"I was just going to make some." Amanda rose and then nodded at her son. "Just watch he doesn't cram everything into his mouth."

As the woman busied herself at the counter and the boy littered the table with crumbs, Billie took a breath to calm herself and opened herself up to the house. It was becoming easier, this slight shift in feeling where she tuned up her radar, probing for something that was hidden from the everyday world. The house felt quiet, her senses falling flat on an ordinary abode. Then a trickle of something, like an electrical charge raising the fine hair on her arm.

There was something here. But was it her mother's spirit? Billie couldn't keep her heart from lifting at the notion. The presence she felt was dim and far away but it was warm. Unlike most of the clammy dead she came across, this presence was inviting and protective. Loving.

"So when did you live here?" Amanda slid back into her chair. "How old were you?"

"We lived here until I was eight. Just me and my mom."

"Is it weird? Seeing your old home?"

Billie paused on the thought. "I thought I'd remember it better but I don't."

Amanda swept the crumbs from the table. "Memory's a funny thing."

"So you and your husband bought the place a few years ago?"

"Yeah. We started fixing it up, room by room. We couldn't afford to do it all in one go." Amanda smiled at her boy. "Then Josh here came along and all our plans went out the window."

"Was the house in rough shape when you bought it?"

"It was a disaster. Trashed by renters, then it sat empty for years. The mold alone was something awful." Amanda smiled, brightening again. "But, it was cheap. And Mark promised we would make it our own."

Billie wrapped her fingers around the water glass, feeling its chill. She debated asking what was tipping off the end of her tongue. "Do you know the history of the place?"

"The neighbour up the street told us a woman had died here years ago. That explained why it had sat on the market for years."

"Doesn't that creep you out?"

"Nah," Amanda shrugged. "Don't get me wrong. I wanted to move the moment I found out but we stuck with it. It doesn't belong to the past, whatever it was. It's our home now." She held her palm up to her son. "And we love it. Right, buddy?"

Josh smacked her a high-five, knocking over his glass in the process. Water rolled across the table. Amanda dove for the dishcloth to mop it up before it dribbled into her son's lap but she was too late. Soaked, the boy giggled.

Billie moved the glasses out of the way for the woman to mop up, wondering if she should tell Amanda that it was her mother who had died in this house. Why bother? Why trouble this sweet family with that now? The young mother had it right, the house belonged to them, not the past.

"Time for some dry clothes, mister." Amanda moved the boy to the floor and patted his behind. "I'm gonna change him. Go have a look around."

"Are you sure?"

"Please." Amanda led Josh away by the hand. "Make yourself at home."

Whatever her childhood home had been, it was gone now. Amanda and her husband had done so much renovating that the house was foreign to her. There was a twinge of memory as she climbed the squeaky stairs and another at the first sight of the second floor hallway but it was vague and fleeting. Nothing to hold onto.

Her old bedroom held no shards of remembrance. It was a little boy's room now. One wall was painted blue and decorated with stars and spaceships. The bedspread mottled with

Transformers or some other robot thing. She could barely remember what her old room looked like.

The door to her mother's old bedroom was ajar. She pushed it open all the way, hoping for a flash of recognition or a sense of her mother's spirit. A desperate longing for her mother to be there, sitting on the bed. Waiting for her.

There was no one in the room. Amanda had made the master bedroom completely her own, uncluttered and tastefully done. Billie perched on the corner of the bed and didn't move.

It was confusing. There was still a nagging sense that someone, if not her mother, was here in the house. Was it possible that she simply didn't recognize her mom's presence after all this time?

Her mouth was dry. She swallowed. "Mom?"

The zing of cicadas in the yard filtered in through the open window.

"It's me," she whispered. "I wanted to see you. If you're here."

Billie let her shoulders droop. There was nothing here for her. Not any memories and not her mother's spirit. She couldn't even laugh at the cruelty of it. That the one ghost she wanted desperately to see was not here. And if she wasn't here at the site where something so terrible had happened, then her mother wasn't anywhere.

In heaven or in hell? Did either exist or was it just a fairy tale told to ease the dying and console the grieving?

Padding downstairs, she wanted to thank Amanda for her hospitality and leave quickly. There was no point in lingering.

The man in the kitchen startled her. He stood at the sink, looking out through the kitchen window. Watching Amanda and Josh in the backyard.

"Oh hi," she said. "You must be Mark."

The man jumped back as if he'd seen a ghost. Which was funny, Billie realized, because he was the one who was departed.

Her thoughts jumped to Amanda and the little boy outside. This was why the kitchen renovations remained unfinished. Mark had died. His was the presence she had felt within the house.

He backed up, a look of confusion washing over his face. "You can see me?" he said.

Billie nodded. "Yeah. I didn't mean to startle you."

He shrugged, as if to say 'that's life'. His gaze went back to the window.

"You're watching over them," she guessed.

"What else can I do?"

"Can I ask you something?" She waited until he looked at her again. "Have you ever seen anyone else here? Anyone like you?"

He shook his head. "No."

"Okay." She crossed to the back door and then stopped. "I am sorry. You have a really beautiful family."

"Yeah. They're pretty great, huh?"

Amanda was unravelling the garden hose while Josh ran with

a big Transformer in his hands. Billie stepped onto the grass. "I should go. Thanks for letting me see the place, Amanda. It meant a lot."

"No problem." Amanda set the hose down. "I hope you found what you were looking for."

"I did. Thanks."

Amanda smiled at her and Billie feared she was going to burst into tears. This woman, who had to be younger than she was, had lost her husband and the father of her little boy. How she managed to stand up, let alone smile and be kind to an absolute stranger was beyond Billie's reckoning.

Unprompted, Amanda leaned in for a quick hug. "Wait a minute. I think I have something of yours. Hang on."

Billie couldn't think of anything of hers that would have been left behind as she watched Amanda run back into the house. The woman appeared a minute later and placed something in Billie's palm.

"Mark found it in the duct work. It must have fallen through the grate."

Billie looked into her palm. It was a locket, pewter inlaid with turquoise. The chain slithered through her fingers. The jolt of recall was immediate and precise. She remembered this with acute callback.

"Maybe it belonged to you," Amanda said hopefully. "Or someone in your family."

"It was my mother's," Billie choked. "Is there anything

inside?"

"Open it."

Billie worked the clasp apart with her thumbnail and opened it like an oyster. No tiny pictures. "It's empty."

"Look again." Amanda raised the open locket in Billie's hand. "See it?"

It was hard to see at first. A strand of very fine hair, coiled up inside the bowl of one half of the locket.

"Looks like baby hair to me," Amanda said. "Yours?"

Billie felt her mouth fall. "Do you think?"

"Who else's would it be?" Amanda gave Billie's shoulder a squeeze. "I'm glad we could return it to you."

She thanked Amanda again and again and waved goodbye to Josh. Walking back to the road, she caught a glimpse of the husband at the window and she climbed into the car and drove away. Once she was out of sight of the old house, she pulled over before the tears blurring her eyes caused her to run right off the road.

35

THE HOUSE ON Ravenscliffe Avenue was big and old, built to ostentatious tastes in the last century. Gantry spat onto the azalea tree as he came up the wide steps and rang the doorbell. A heavy gong chimed twice inside the house. Shaking out a cigarette, he patted down his pockets for a moment before his face soured.

"Oh come on. Where is it?"

He must have left it at the bar so he waited there with the cigarette hanging out of his mouth, cursing whoever it was who had lifted his lighter. He was about to ring again when the door opened and girl in her teens looked up at him. She took a cautious step back, her nose curling. "Yes?"

"Hi kiddo. Run and get your dad for me, yeah?"

The girl squinted at him, then her face fell. "You know you're, like, bleeding, right?"

"Then you better hurry along before I bleed out all over your stoop, luv. Tell him uncle Johnny's here."

The door closed and Gantry went back to patting his pockets, refusing to believe he was stuck without fire. When the door opened again, a lean man with greying hair looked shocked at what washed up on his doorstep. "Gantry," the man hissed. "What the hell are you doing here?"

"Needed a band-aid."

"Go to the hospital for Christ's sakes!"

"Can't do that, chief. Too much paperwork. You gonna invite me in or let me die here?"

The man waved Gantry forward before stretching his neck out and sweeping the street to see if any of his neighbours had seen the dishevelled man at his door.

Gantry was ushered quickly into the study where he beelined to the massive hearth, rummaging the stone mantel for matches. "Bingo," he said, finding a box of long stemmed ones. "So how you been, Jimmy? Still playing the ponies?"

The grey-haired man, whose name was Jameson, shut the door behind him. "Have you lost your mind? You don't come to my house, where my family is."

"I figured you wouldn't deny an old mate a favour." Gantry stuck the match and lit up. His smile widened when he emphasized the word 'favour'.

Jameson's face fell by a degree, regret registering hard. He composed himself. "What happened to your head?"

"Took a nasty one. I doctored it up myself but it started bleeding again. You can patch it up for me, yeah?"

"Does this look like an emergency room to you?" Jameson seethed.

"You telling me a surgeon doesn't have a first-aid kit?" Gantry drifted across the Persian rug to the array of bottles on a walnut sideboard. He plucked out one from the others. "Where's the glasses?"

"In the cupboard below," Jameson snarled as he crossed to the massive desk and flung open one of the drawers. He removed a metal kit and placed it on the desk and then turned on the desk lamp. "Sit here. We'll make this quick."

Gantry brought two tumblers to the desk and flopped into the leather chair. He winced as the other man stripped away the square of gauze on his forehead. Blood trickled out from a nasty gash under the hairline. "Aren't you supposed to wash your hands or something?"

"No," spat Jameson. He dabbed the blood away and tilted Gantry's head toward the light. "What happened?"

"Perils of the job. Sometimes when you poke at things, they poke back." During the dust-up with Mockler in the church last night, Gantry felt something else lash out at him. He had looked up in time to see a nasty face and sweeping claw before something ripped the flesh over his left eye.

"I have to stitch this."

Gantry downed the drink and shook the empty tumbler. "Go ahead. I just need another one of these before you start."

"Make it a double. I can't freeze this before I sew it up."

Gantry kept the bottle within reach while the doctor cleaned the wound and set about stitching it closed. His knuckles turned white gripping the armrest and his molars nearly cracked from biting down. He cursed the man as a butcher and a veterinarian but remained still until the man said he was finished. Gantry fell back against the chair, his face greasy with sweat.

The doctor wiped his hands on a towel. "There. We're even, Gantry. No more."

"Don't be daft, Jimmy," Gantry laughed. He prodded the stitching, feeling the prickly ends of the knots.

"I mean it. Consider the debt paid. I can't have you showing up here, extorting me."

Gantry rose stiffly from the chair and crossed to the mantel for another long-stemmed match. "Jimbo, do I need to remind you of the shite you were swimming in before?"

The man's face darkened and looked away, busying himself with his kit. "So this is how it plays? You just keep turning the screws on me until I'm done?"

"Relax. This was an unusual circumstance. You won't hear from me until I need you. But when I do, you'll be doing triage."

Jameson lowered himself slowly into the leather chair behind the desk. "This threat you mentioned before. It's still coming?"

"Yeah. Just a question of when. Where's your phone?" The other man gestured at the telephone on the desk but Gantry shook his head. "I need your mobile."

Jameson produced his phone and slid it across the desk.

"Can't you use your own?"

"Lost mine." Gantry took the phone and dug something small out of his pocket and plugged it into the mobile.

Jameson leaned forward, trying to see what the Englishman was doing. "What is that?"

"Masks the number." Slips of paper fell from his pocket as he dug for one scrap with a phone number and dialled. When the call went unanswered, he thumbed in a simple text message. *Where are you?* Then he lowered the phone and waited for a response.

"Who are you calling?"

Gantry leaned back. "A girl. I seem to have misplaced her."

The other man's brow arched. "Another one? You have a habit of losing women."

"Don't get cute, Jameson. You're too fucking ugly for it." Gantry looked at the phone in his hand, impatient for a ping back. "She's a friend. But I don't know where she scampered to."

"She ran away? Imagine that."

Gantry mumbled something then plucked the device from the phone and tossed the mobile back to its owner. He got to his feet. "Don't suppose you could give me a lift somewhere?"

"Not a chance. Where's your car?"

"Lost that too." He crossed to the door. "Screw it. See ya, Jimmy."

Jameson shot up. "Whoa, not that way. Use the back door for

Christ's sakes."

Ten minutes later, Gantry stood outside of the building on Barton Street, looking up at the third floor windows. Billie's flat was dark. No one home.

"Christ."

Climbing up three flights left him winded and a little woozy after the patch job that butcher did to his forehead. No wonder the man didn't practise anymore. Gantry patted his pockets for his cigarettes but remembered that he was still without a light. He'd want one before walking into that place. If he was honest with himself, he didn't even want to be here.

The door was locked but he tapped it a certain way and something clicked and he pushed the door open. Locks were never problem for him, especially the cheap kind. His eyes went down to the mess of salt over the threshold. The girl had been doing her homework.

He passed through the living room, noting the mess left behind and continued on into the kitchen. He knew she wasn't here but hoped to find something that would tell him where she had rabbitted to.

The place was quiet. The little legless bastard that had attacked him before was long gone but he wasn't the one Gantry was leery of. The ghastly mess that had ripped a chunk out of his noggin back at the church was the thing that had spooked him. That was power. Whatever it was, ghost or demon or black hole of pure fucking evil, it wasn't here.

What the hell had Billie gotten herself mixed up in with that thing? The girl had guts and she had a natural ability unlike any others he had seen, so why had she gone out looking for trouble? Mockler's trouble to boot. Of all people, why that sad sack of shite?

He picked through the mess on the table and scanned the photos and notes stuck to the refrigerator door. He wasn't even sure what he was looking for. Some clue as to where she would have gone. There was a chance she may have run for the hills with that awful thing skulking about.

There was nothing here. He crossed back through the living room and stopped cold when he saw the back of the door. The paint was scorched black as if blasted with a blowtorch. Angular scrawled lines, forming a simple message:

the

whore

is

mine

36

"BILLIE?"

Maggie hauled the grocery bags to the counter and hurried back to close the screen door before the bugs got in. The house was quiet, the cat curled up asleep on the armchair under the picture window.

"Honey, you home?" She padded down the hall and looked in Billie's room but her niece wasn't there. Maggie frowned. Billie's car, or the one borrowed from her neighbour, was back in the driveway. Had the girl gone for a walk?

The cat stirred as she crossed to the window. The sky was overcast and the trees rippled from a heavy wind. Not exactly a beach day but she could hazard a good guess as to where her niece was. The cat in the chair stretched its legs and rolled over and went back to sleep.

Trudging through the sand was becoming difficult and Maggie huffed at the effort. Cresting a dune, she looked down at the lake. There was only one person on the beach, looking out at the water with her knees tucked up under her chin. No beach blanket or umbrella. Not even a swimsuit. Just her shoes on the sand next to her.

"The water's rough today," she said, coming alongside the girl. When Billie didn't respond, Maggie shrugged out of her light jacket, laid it on the damp sand and eased down onto it. "Looks like there's some nasty weather headed our way."

Billie stared out at the water with her arms wrapped around her knees and the fall of her hair hiding her face.

Maggie brushed the sand from her hands. "Did you go for a drive this morning?"

The girl nodded but didn't offer anything more. Maggie watched the waves roll in. "Where did you go?"

"Home."

Billie tucked her hair behind her ear and Maggie could see her eyes. They were red and puffy. Maggie reached into a pocket and came away with a wad of folded tissues that she kept eternally at the ready. She gave it to the girl. "The old house? Whatever possessed you to go there?"

Billie shrugged, dabbed a tissue against her eyes. "I guess I just wanted to see it."

"Last time I drove by it, it was in bad shape."

"It's nice now," Billie sniffed. "The family that bought it fixed it up."

"I see. So you just woke this morning wanting to see the old place?"

"I'm not sure what I was looking for. But it wasn't there."

The wind picked up and both of them turned their heads away from the kicking sand until it died down. Billie balled the damp tissue up in her fist. "Can I ask you something?"

"Anything."

"When did mom start to go off the deep end? How old was she?"

Maggie frowned, disliking the question. "Hard to say, really. Late twenties? Maybe earlier."

Billie twisted her lips into a smirk like she already knew the answer. "I'll be thirty in six months."

"I know. What would you like for your birthday?"

That wasn't what she was getting at. Billie took a breath. "Did you ever wonder about all that stuff with mom? If it was true? The tarot cards and the palm reading. Second sight? Even just a little?"

Maggie picked a twig out of the sand. "Your mom sometimes knew when things were going to happen. It was spooky."

That word again, Billie thought. "Like what?"

"Deaths in the family. She knew before anyone else did. I remember when our dad died. He'd been in the hospital. I was at Mary's house and she was chopping carrots. Then she just stopped and said that dad was dead. The hospital called thirty minutes later."

"And what about the ghosts? Seeing dead people?"

Maggie tried not to frown when she turned to her niece. "Do we have to talk about this?"

"I have it too," Billie confessed. "Seeing ghosts."

Maggie stiffened. She kept her gaze levelled on the clouds over the lake.

"I think that's what drove her crazy," Billie went on. "Seeing the dead. She couldn't deal with it."

"Don't say that."

Billie looked at her aunt. "You knew I had it too, didn't you? That's why you took me to all those doctors. Dragged me to church twice a week. I get it now, I do. You tried to protect me from it." She shrugged again. "It worked for a while. But it's here. I can't block it out and it's going to drive me insane the way it did to mom."

"Stop it."

"It drives them all crazy, doesn't it? All those aunts you told me about, the eccentric ones? They all went insane too, didn't they?"

The woman snatched her niece by the elbow. "Stop it, Billie. You don't have it! You had an accident, you're not thinking straight. That's all!"

"I tried to convince myself of that too. It doesn't work anymore." Billie shook the woman's hand off. "Do you think I want this? I'd give anything to have my old life back. It didn't matter that I had a dumb job or I was just drifting through life. This is worse."

Maggie rose to her feet and peeled her jacket from the damp sand. "You are not your mother, Billie. Don't believe that for a second."

A thousand hateful words stung through her brain but Billie kept her mouth shut and watched her aunt march away. She turned and looked back at the lake. The storm clouds were almost here.

~

Billie snatched the clothes from the chair and stuffed them back into the bag. She hadn't a clue where she was going. Not back to the apartment but not here either. She just needed to be somewhere else.

Maggie appeared in the doorway. "You're not going?"

"I should get back," Billie said. The anger had drained off but she wasn't in the mood to reconcile just yet.

"I don't know how to help you with this," Maggie said.

"It's okay. Honest. I'll figure it out."

Maggie came further into the room. "It's not okay. Sit down."

Billie grumbled as she sat, twisting a stale tee-shirt in her hands. Waiting to be lectured or admonished.

"I've been thinking," Maggie said, folding her hands in her lap. "If this is real, then maybe it doesn't have to be a bad thing. Maybe it has more to do with how one chooses to use it."

"It's not good for anything. It's like having a disease."

"Why would God give this to you?" Maggie held up a finger, as if asking her to wait. "Don't roll your eyes at that. I'm trying to understand this. Why would He give you this ability if he didn't want you to use it? Maybe this is what you were meant to do."

"Or maybe God has a sick sense of humour," Billie countered. "What exactly am I supposed to do with it?"

"Help people."

Billie let her chin drop. "What people could I possibly help?"

"I don't know, honey. Maybe people who are grieving. Maybe the dead themselves."

"How? Point them to the bright light? There is no light, Maggie. There's just these phantoms with all their rage and despair and awful tragedies. I can't help them. And some of them are vindictive. They lash out."

Billie flung the rumpled garment at the chair. "I tried to help. Twice. I screwed up and made everything worse."

"How could you have made it worse?"

"There's this guy. I tried—" She clipped her words, not knowing how to explain it without sounding like a complete lunatic.

Her aunt perked up. "What guy? Like a boyfriend?"

"What? No," she said quickly. Recalling his last words salted the wound and she didn't know why this all got so confusing when it came to him. "He's a friend. I think he's in danger. Real danger."

"Then you have to help him."

"I did. But I made it worse." Billie fumed. Why couldn't she understand this? Because it's messed up beyond belief, she reminded herself. "And now he doesn't want anything to do with me."

"And he's still in danger?" When Billie nodded, Maggie held out her hands, as if the answer couldn't be any clearer. "Then you have to try again. Even if he doesn't want your help, you have to help him if you honestly think he's in danger."

Billie sank into the chair. "It's complicated."

"It couldn't be any simpler, honey. If you can help someone, then you have a duty to do so."

"I don't want this. It scares me."

Maggie looked out the window. The pane was cloudy with cobwebs and dotted with the dried husks of dead insects. "What's this man's name? Your friend?"

Billie clutched her stomach the moment his name tripped over her lips. A wall of nausea overwhelmed her instantly and she dropped to the floor, snatching up the flimsy wastebasket. One sharp dry heave and then it subsided. Accompanying the stomach churn was a vivid image of the man in question, his face contorted with pain. Hot tears ran down his cheeks like he was enduring something unimaginable.

Another twist to this freakshow that had become her life. When would it stop?

Coming to the rescue, Maggie cupped her palm over her

niece's brow. "What is it, honey? Are you sick?"

"It's him," she gasped. The police detective in question. "He's in trouble. Like right now. "

37

HE FELT SICK to his stomach.

He wished he could throw up. At least he would feel better afterward but whatever it was churning his guts was not making its way up. It hung low, turning his knees to shaky twigs.

Raymond Mockler looked at the drink in his hand. Could be the hooch, he wondered. The sensible thing to do would be to fling the rest of it down the sink but he wasn't in a sensible mood. He wanted to be numb. Comfortably numb, just like the song said. A few more of these and it would be like sinking into a warm tub, the world nothing more than a vague ripple in the water.

He also wished he had a match. And some gasoline. So he could burn every one of these paintings and sketches Christina had done of that awful face. She'd certainly been burning the midnight oil on this artistic phase she was going through. Picasso had his blue period. His fiancee was deep into what he termed her   scary-as-shit-nightmare-psychotic-episode   period. Sleepwalking to her studio every night and painting in this weird possessed state. He would find her down here, gently guide her back to bed and close the door. An hour later and she'd be gone again, shuffling back to the studio to paint.

It was unsettling, the look in her eye or the movement of her hand. She didn't speak or protest when he took the brush away and led her back to bed. In the morning, she'd claim to have no memory of it. Then she would sleep all day, snoring through the phone calls from her boss wondering where she was.

There was more than a good chance that this evil fucking face she kept painting was the source of his roiling stomach. Or it was the house itself because it wasn't just the studio that brought on the nausea. Every room in the house made him ill. So what did that mean? Asbestos in the piping? Toxic lead paint under all those other layers of pigment, leaching out to poison them both? Deadly mold leaking spores into the air to embed themselves in one's lung?

Maybe a match was needed for the whole damn property, not just the paintings. Wasn't that how they treated plague houses in the olden days? With cleansing fire? Because that's what this place felt like now. A plague house. Unclean and septic.

That, he mumbled to no one, was how most people died when shot. Well, the bad guys anyway. Sepsis. It wasn't the bullet that killed them but the damage afterwards. As the slug ripped through intestines and organs, it made a hell of a mess. Partially digested food or fecal matter leaches into the bloodstream, poisoning the victim. With the bad guys, they'd avoid hospitals altogether, getting some hack-doctor to patch it up. So the sepsis went untreated and the son of a bitch died a slow death. It was an awful way to die. He had seen firsthand evidence of that.

"Stay in school kids," he laughed. "Just say no."

Some small part of his brain was still rational. You're trashed, it told him. Go to bed.

Bed. That cold and pitiless void he shared with this woman who was no longer the woman he had known. She was an imposter, an alien. A pod person who resembled Christina but showed few signs of emotion. Invasion of the Depressed Nocturnal Artist. Great flick.

Another woman's face materialized before his mind's eye, her name rattling around his skull before he could push it away. He winced recalling her last words, feeling the sting of betrayal. Why did he feel that? Of all things, betrayal?

It was Gantry's fault. Again that slippery limey was to blame, luring another one into his weird schemes. Still, why did it sting? He barely knew the woman. Sure, they had gotten along and he had felt a strange ease around her but that didn't explain the sting. She was messed up, snookered by a charismatic lunatic. He had wanted to protect her, that's all. Simple as that.

Liar, the little voice returned. *It's more than that and you know it.*

Mockler leaned against the door jamb. It was confusing. He'd never been good at sorting out his own feelings. Not in the moment, anyway. Everything got mixed up when he thought about Billie. Churning up with his attraction to her and the ease he felt and the betrayal there was a tidal wave of guilt for even thinking about this. And the little voice was having a field day.

You're engaged, you cheating fuck. She's just a girl. Don't blow up your life for someone you barely know.

Pushing away from the jamb, he marched to the kitchen and flung the drink into the sink and ran the water until it was cold and splashed it over his face. It's just lust, he reasoned. That's all. Happens all the time. Forget her and carry on.

And Billie Culpepper was crazy. She had rattled on and on about what? A fucking ghost? That his home was haunted? She was as bad as Gantry. Worse.

But what if she's right? It would explain a lot of weird shit around here.

Mockler looked at the empty tumbler and regretted throwing it away. Another belt and maybe that nagging little voice would shut off.

The idea of it was ludicrous. Being haunted. Then the idea was repulsive. And then it flipped to feeling violated and churned into outrage. Then just plain rage.

"Show yourself!" he bellowed into the room, to the house itself. "I dare ya! Stop being a coward and face me!"

It felt good, the outburst of anger. Then he felt silly and self-conscious, yelling at something that wasn't there.

A figure drifted past the kitchen doorway. Christina, padding silently on bare feet to her studio.

He followed her. She was back at it, already slashing at a large swath of paper with a stick of charcoal. Without a stitch of clothing, her long frame lit by a row of candles all the way around the room.

How had she lit them all so fast? There had to be two dozen of the shallow tea candles. There was no way—

Christina's hand dropped to her side. The brittle charcoal broke in two as it hit the floor. When she turned around there was something wrong with her eyes.

And then she opened her mouth and all the flies came boiling out.

38

BY THE TIME she hit the highway, the sun had gone down and the needle on the fuel gauge was quivering over the quarter tank mark. Another delay she didn't need. She should have fuelled up in Port Rowan when she had the chance.

There was no way to get home any faster. The six was a provincial highway that cut through half a dozen towns on the way, forcing her to slow to a measly 40 kph every time. She tried Mockler's number for the fifth time. It rang without being picked up. That was unusual for most people. For a cop, it frightened her.

Calling the police was the obvious default but she hesitated, unsure of what to say. Just do it. She thumbed through the phone again but this time noticed an unread text message. When had it come through? Hitting it, the message was short.

Where the frig are you?

No name, no return number. Had to be Gantry. God only

knew what voodoo he screwed around with when contacting her. Why couldn't he just call like a normal person? Because it was his schtick, the man of mystery. The text was stale by two hours. She hit reply. Zilch, as usual.

Screw him. Not knowing the number for the Hamilton Police, she started dialling emergency when the phone rang. She thumbed the call and said hello.

"Where the hell'd you go?" groaned the voice. Gantry.

"Out of town," she gave back. "Where are you?"

"At a time like this? Jesus, girl. I would—"

There was no time for his bullshit. "Gantry, shut up and listen to me. Mockler's in trouble. I need you to go check on him."

"I seem to have the wrong number," he said.

"I'm serious. Go help him. I'm still an hour away."

"Are you daft? You want me to stroll up to his house and ask if he needs a hand?"

"You have to. That thing is hurting him. The undertaker. Please…"

"Why do you keep calling it that, the undertaker man?"

"Because that's what he looks like," Billie snarled. "Just go. Now."

"Right. I'll get on that forthwith."

It took all she had to keep from hurling the phone to the floor mats. "Do it! Just do this for me. Then I'll do what you want. Whatever the hell it is. Just help him."

"Billie, snap out of it. You should know better."

"You're a coward, Gantry. And a manipulator. And a fraud!"

"You're gonna have to try harder than that to hurt my feelings, luv." The click of a lighter sounded, the quick intake of breath. "Listen kiddo, don't risk your neck on him. All right? See ya around."

"Gantry, wait! I have to help him. How do I do that?"

"Bring an exorcist," Gantry chuffed. "Bring a dozen of them."

"Give me something. There has to be some way to stop that thing."

Silence buzzed down the line. Billie thought he had hung up.

"Learn its name," he said finally. Then, "Names have power."

"Name? You said it was a shadow-demon thingie. How could it have a name?"

"Not that thing, the Undertaker. His name. Whatever he is now, he used to be human before his ghost melted into the shadow entity. Learn the Undertaker's name. Use it against him."

Billie took the phone from her ear and looked at it. "How am I supposed to do that?"

"No clue, luv. But if you unearth his name, he might listen to you. That's all I got."

"Gantry—"

"Good luck," he said quietly. "You'll need it."

The phone buzzed when he hung up. Billie stared at the phone again, willing it to ring back. Again, there was no return

ID to call. She tossed it onto the passenger seat and stomped the gas pedal, a tiny prayer lifting off her lips for a gas station nearby.

~

Gantry hung up the phone and tossed it back to the woman he had borrowed it from. "Cheers."

"Bad news?" asked the woman. She sat on a heavy ottoman before an enormous stone hearth, her features rippling in the light of the flames.

"Nah," Gantry said but his eyes fell to the ornate design of the Persian rug at his feet and lingered there.

The woman tapped at her phone, her nails painted a deep red. "Billie Culpepper? Who's he?"

"She."

"Ah," the woman smirked. "Friend or foe?"

"That's still up for debate."

"For your sake I hope it's a friend, John. You seem to be running out of those." She set the phone aside, folded her hands together and looked at her guest. "So? Where were we?"

"You were taking me to the cleaners. You need to come down a little."

She smiled. "I can't do that, John. The price is set."

Resting on the low table between them was a book. It was thick and it was very old, the leather cover brittle and pockmarked with tiny holes made by tiny burrowing insects. The title on the cracked spine had faded to only two words; *Der Vermis.*

"Well, I have a cap on spending here," he said. "Come down and meet me. You said yourself you don't want it in the house anymore."

"We don't have to do this, do we? This silly haggling?"

Gantry stretched his legs out before him, crossing his ankles like he had all the time in the world. "Course we do. Especially if you're trying to pass that off as real."

"Don't insult me. We both know it's the real thing."

Gantry nodded at the mouldering grimoire. "Luv, if it was kosher, neither of us could stand be in the same room with it."

The woman straightened up and looked at Gantry. She was stunning, something she knew how to use. "Then why do you want it if it's not the real thing?"

Gantry put a hand to his ear, feeling off-balance. Normally he'd bask in the negotiation with a beautiful woman, the back and forth of easy flirtation but he felt off his game. A nagging thought needled at him. "I'm just the broker here, sweetheart. I'd sooner have nothing to do with the nasty thing."

"You're such a liar, Johnny." She smiled as she said this, an old and practised routine between the two of them. She prodded the fire with the poker. "I'll come down to four. Nothing more." When no reply came, she turned back. "John?"

His eyes shot up, returning to the here and now. "Yeah.

Sure."

"Well that was quick," she pouted. "Are you feeling okay?"

"No. Something's up."

"Oh." She rose to her feet, pulling the black shawl snug around her. "Can I get you anything?"

"Yeah. A bowl. And some moonlight."

The night air was a relief after the roasting heat of the drawing room. Gantry tugged at his shirt to get the material unglued from his sweaty back. The woman remained in the doorway, watching Gantry step out onto the stone veranda that overlooked the gardens. He held a clay bowl in his hand, the water spilling down the side as he went. He set it out down gently on the stone parapet and looked up at the night sky.

"Is that enough moon for what you need?" She hugged her elbows together as if cold.

A three-quarter moon shone down on them. "It'll do."

"Then hurry up," she said. "It's freezing out here."

Gantry glanced up at her, shivering in the terrace doorway. It was a humid summer night and yet the woman in the shawl quaked as if it was midwinter. "You can wait inside if you want."

"I want to see."

Gantry unfolded a pearl-handled pocket knife and sliced the blade into the pad of his thumb. Blood welled up in the split and he held it over the bowl until three drops fell and bloomed in the water. He stuck the cut thumb against his lips and studied the water in the bowl.

"Well?" the shivering woman asked.

"Shite." He took the bowl and flung the contents into the rosebushes. "I need to run."

"What is it?"

"Trouble. Don't ask me why I'm bothering though, because I don't have a bloody clue."

She withdrew inside and closed the door after him. "That doesn't sound like you."

"Getting soft in me old age." He looked at his thumb, the red tracing a line over the nail. "You got a plaster?"

"No," she said. Her eyes sparkled. She took his hand and pressed the cut to her own lips.

~

The side-view mirror swiped the hedges as she pulled into the driveway too fast. Mockler's car was parked on the cracked pavement but the windows of the house were dark. The engine ticked as it cooled and Billie pounded up the front steps. She banged on the door, calling Mockler's name.

The door opened at a slight push.

"Mockler!"

Her voice rattled down the foyer. No other sound from within. She swept through the living and dining rooms, through the kitchen and then hollered up the stairs. The place was empty.

She didn't need to search the house to know he wasn't here. She could feel his absence. She had no such sense for the girlfriend but she would have come running upon hearing someone break into her house. Where were they?

There was a sliver of relief in the fact that she didn't sense the Undertaker anywhere. He (or it, she wasn't sure how to render it) wasn't here. All three of them were gone and that was not a good sign.

She turned around, her attention drawn to the sunroom off the back of the house. The improvised studio. Mockler's girfriend was a painter, she remembered. Something about that irked her. Crossing to the entrance of the studio, she squinted in the gloomy light at the easel set up in the middle of the room. The framed canvas propped up against it, a work in progress.

She almost screamed when she saw the horrid face staring back at her.

39

THE SCREEN DOOR banged open as Billie ejected from the house into the backyard. Seeing that face again, she knew she was too late. Mockler was gone. She had failed him.

Nasty little nightmares bubbled through her mind about where he could be and what was being done to him. Stop. She got up off her knees and looked at the house.

Think. Find him.

She took a breath to clear her mind. Then she opened up, unfolding whatever part of her that could see the dead. Find him, she repeated to herself. There was some connection to him, one strong enough to reach her fifty miles away on the shores of Lake Erie. Surely she could pick up the scent now.

It was there but muffled, like a single voice in a crowd. A vague sense of him, like an echo. Filtering out the noise, she realized it wasn't muffled so much as overpowered. Something much stronger and more powerful was masking it. Something that stank of rot and death and evil. The undertaker.

She could almost see the trail he had left behind, like slime left by a snail, glittering wet in the light of the partial moon. It went from the house, across the parched lawn at her feet and continued on to where the yard ended at the fence. The boards were damp with rot and three of them had been snapped and pulled away.

Ducking through, Billie followed the trail through a thicket of raspberry weeds that scratched her arms. The brambles gave away as she stepped into a vacant lot. Bordered on all sides by thick weeds, the ground inside the lot was sandy and barren, as if toxic and unable to support any vegetation. Squared up inside the sandy lot were the ruins of a house, the brick foundation of a structure now long gone. A spire of brickwork on the north side suggested the remains of a chimney.

Clambering over the masonry, she dropped into the sandy grit of the former building. What looked at first to be a sinkhole turned out to be an entrance to whatever remained of the cellar. The trapdoor had been pulled open and, leaning in, she saw stairs going down. Dirt had been tracked into it, spilling down each step as they descended into darkness.

The smell wafting up from below was sickly. Without a doubt the shadow thing was down here but was Mockler here too? She could feel him down there in the dark, alone in the cold and damp. He was injured.

She did not want to go down there. No one would. Even the

dead would balk here.

The grit spilt over the steps made them slippery and each footfall announced her descent with a loud crunch. Her heart clanged inside her chest. It was dark but when her feet hit the landing she could make out small pinpricks of light in the gloom. As her eyes adjusted, tiny candles emerged around a vast space, their light bouncing off white tiles. The walls and floor were tiled in white porcelain, along with a mounted washbasin under the high window. Brown glass bottles lined a shelf to her left, on the opposite wall was a rusting metal contraption whose purpose escaped her. In the centre of the room stood a mortuary table of cast iron, the porcelain veneer chipped and stained. Underneath it lay the hydraulic lift and the flywheel that tilted the table to drain it of fluids.

Her nickname for the shadow had been correct after all. This place was his. Everything in it pulsed with his sickening power. Whomever he had been in life, he had dealt with death and its messy aftermath.

Okay, she said, twisting up her courage. Find Mockler, get out. Simple as that.

Shadows clung to the farthest corners of the mortuary room, too deep for the ambient light to dispel. Stifling the urge to whisper his name, Billie opened herself more to let her senses grope the dark for him. She found nothing but damp and mold and a little loose dirt.

A ping rippled down her sonar, movement or life or

something from the farthest span of wall. Her eyes picked out a thicker mass amid the darkness, shimmering like the surface of a lake in the night. Its span confused her, the depth. Not just one life but thousands of them and then she realized with revulsion that the mass was a swarm of flies, crawling and burrowing over each other in their stomach-churning multitudes.

Yet, underneath their hateful little lives beat the heart of another. The one she sought. Her gut flip-flopped when she understood that the flies were crawling over Mockler a thousand insects thick.

Billie ran for him, brushing the hateful things until they boiled up into the air and swarmed around her in a devilish cloud. Mockler was unconscious. His face was bruised and a split on his cheek was already festering. His hands were filthy with blood.

She called his name and smacked his cheek but he remained as limp as wet sand. The flies nattered her, buzzing her ear endlessly and crawling over her face.

She felt the vile things on her tongue and spat them out but more crawled in. Screaming, she dragged the man across the floor but the detective was big and she slipped and fell. Even if she got him to the stairs there was no way she could pull him up those steps.

The noxious stench grew stronger and she knew instantly what it meant. She didn't want to look but her eyes tilted up all on their own.

The undertaker man stood behind the embalming table. Watching her. He bent down and gripped the heavy flywheel. Cranking it hard, the table tipped until it was level. The undertaker man straightened up and lifted one hand. His fingers curled as he waved her forward.

He wanted Mockler on the slab. And he wanted her to put him there.

"He doesn't belong to you," she said.

The undertaker glowered. His hand went up and Billie felt a push. Mockler slipped from her hands and was pulled away, sliding across the floor to the mortuary table.

Something changed. The terror in her gut switched over into rage. She roared at the thing to stop. The air crackled around her as a wave of energy or heat swept across the room and Mockler fell from whatever grip he was held in. The undertaker staggered back under the force of it.

The look of surprise did not last long. He bared his foul teeth and Billie could already hear the flies swarming around her.

"Piss off!"

The voice startled them both. When she saw Gantry at the bottom of the stairs, she wanted to cry. The cavalry had arrived.

"Enough with the Beelzebub trick, huh?" The lighter flicked and Gantry lit a cigarette and then turned to the dark mass hovering near the table. He looked annoyed. "You're the shittiest excuse for a ghost I've ever seen."

The flies roiled angrily. The look in the undertaker's eyes

flared with hatred.

Billie felt her knees give out. She had no idea what Gantry was doing or how he was doing it, she was just grateful that he was here.

"All right, Billie?" Gantry asked.

"Mockler's hurt."

"Pull him out of there. We're leaving."

Billie scuttled in, snatched the unconscious man by the wrist and dragged him away. "You have to help me get him up the stairs."

"That big bastard?" Gantry sneered.

Something shifted behind him. A woman stepped from the shadows with a length of wood in her hands. It came down hard on Gantry's skull. The Englishman went down like a sack of dirt.

"Gantry!"

Christina stood over Gantry like a conquering hero, the make-shift club still in her hands. There was something wrong with her eyes.

The detective was yanked from her hands and pulled away into the darkness. Christina brought the club up high over her head with both hands, ready to bludgeon Gantry's skull.

Billie couldn't breathe. Caught between two evils with no lesser one to choose from, she shrieked at the woman. "Christina! Stop!"

Something rippled through the air. The strange light in the woman's eyes dimmed. Christina blinked, as if waking, and then terror spread over her face as she looked at Billie. Her lips quivered as she mouthed silent words. *Help me.*

"Put the board down," Billie pleaded. "Fight it."

The woman was crying and the wood quivered in her hands and then it was over. The unnatural glow flared up in her eyes and Christina was gone.

Billie felt something cold on her skin. The undertaker was breathing down her neck. She lashed out at the mass of flies hovering around her but there was nothing solid to connect with, nothing to clobber.

A thin hand emerged from the swarm and reached for her, the fingers snatching at her ankle. It looked wrong. Small and bony, like the arm of a child, it groped and clawed for something to hang onto. The grime-encrusted little fingernails looked familiar.

Billie clasped the hand tight, so small in her own, and pulled and pulled harder until the flies parted and it slid free like some obscene birth. The half-boy clung to her with a desperate grip, burrowing his face into her chest. Billie kicked out, propelling both of them away from the monstrous swarm.

The undertaker gnashed his teeth, as if in physical pain. The swarm thinned, flies scattering into the damp air until they regrouped and the whole awful mass swept forward.

The half-boy quaked, clinging to her like a barnacle. He glanced back once at the thing that had trapped him, then he tucked into her cheek. He whispered into her ear that there were more of them, trapped inside.

She could see them now, hands reaching out of the dark mass, desperate and pleading. More souls. She gripped the nearest one and tugged. A woman slid out, screaming the whole way, and flopped to the floor. The woman she had seen cowering in Mockler's bathtub.

More hands stretched out and she pulled another and another, souls tumbling out of the rip in the darkness and the undertaker man shrieking and wailing in an obscene howl and the insects scattering. The dead kept coming, clawing and scratching their own way out, one tumbling over the next until a hundred souls filled the old mortuary room.

The pests dispersed, confused and scattered, buzzing into the ceiling and the walls and the undertaker man withered and shrank until there were no more souls, just him squatting alone in a pool of darkness. His dark eyes locked onto hers and his expression shifted and then his hand reached out to her, as if he was just one more poor soul to be saved.

"Go to Hell," Billie said. She meant every word.

Her ears popped, as if plunged underwater and the world went silent. She saw the dead shamble silently around her and then all at once they looked up, as if a noise had called to them from the trapdoor above. The souls shuffled forward, climbing the steps to meet it.

She wanted to go too. Her ears registered absolute silence but she wanted to know what it was, this sound that was calling to them. She rolled onto her knees and got up slowly and she would have followed were it not for the tugging on her wrist.

The boy without legs clung to her arm to keep her from following the others and when she looked back it was too late. The assembled dead left without her. And then even the boy was gone.

40

THE SMACK TO her cheek stung. Billie blinked and Gantry's face swam into view.

"Up and at 'em, Lazarus," he said. "Time to go."

She sat up stiffly and shivered. The mortuary room was cold and dark. "Where is it?"

"Gone," Gantry said. "Along with the rest of them."

Everything seemed jumbled together in her head. "What happened?"

"Search me," he said. "Everything was quiet when I came to."

"Where's Mockler? And Christina?"

He nodded to something behind her. Billie rose and limped over to where Mockler lay on the floor. His cheek was bloodied but he was breathing.

Christina sat on the bottom step with her knees tucked to her chest. Her eyes looked blasted.

"Christina?" She approached the woman slowly. "Are you hurt?"

"She's out of it." Gantry came alongside her. "Shell-shocked."

She felt dizzy and took his arm to stay upright. "We need to call the police. Or an ambulance."

She dug out her phone but Gantry snatched it from her hand. "No cops."

"They need help. Give me the phone."

"And what are you gonna tell them, Billie? You had a rumble with a ghost? Dickhead's girlfriend here was possessed?"

She wanted the police and the ambulance and the fire trucks here, anyone who could help and make the world safe and normal again. She didn't want to admit he was right. "We can't just leave them here. They need a doctor."

"Cuts and bruises." Gantry stepped back and looked at the detective and the woman on the step. "We'll take them home."

"And that's it?"

He shrugged at her. "They'll wake up with a nasty hangover. That's all."

She knelt before Christina again. The woman's eyes were glazed and unseeing. "I don't think she's okay, Gantry. It's like she checked out."

"She has. Her mind has shut down. It'll wear off."

Billie studied the woman's face. It was downright spooky the way her eyes registered nothing. "Was she really possessed?"

"This bastard was strong. God knows how long he'd been feeding off the two of them." Gantry sneered at Mockler on the floor. "I almost feel sorry for the son of a bitch."

The damp rot seeped into her bones. "Let's get out of here."

Gantry bent low to examine Christina. "Let's get her up. See if she'll walk."

Billie eased the woman up to her feet. Christina complied, docile as a lamb.

Gantry looked down at his nemesis on the floor and then up at the stairs. "Christ. Look at this sod. He outweighs me by ten stone."

"Put your back into it," she said, mimicking his accent. "Luv."

"Maybe we can just, you know, leave him here?"

She fired a withering look at him before leading the woman up the stairs. Gantry flicked his cigarette into a corner and rolled up his shirtsleeves, cursing a blue streak into the stale air of the mortuary cellar.

~

Christina came quietly as Billie led her upstairs to the bedroom. She did a cursory once-over to make sure the woman wasn't injured and then eased Christina into bed. She lay quiet as Billie drew the covers up, her eyes staring at the opposite wall. Billie whispered to her to close her eyes and sleep.

Gantry was collapsed in a chair when she came down, red-faced and spent and still uttering obscenities. Detective Mockler lay halfway in the backdoor, sprawled across the threshold where Gantry had dropped him.

"Gantry!" Billie fumed at him. "You can't leave him like that."

"Screw that. He's good where is."

"We have to get him upstairs."

"Dream on, sister." Gantry rose unsteadily and teetered to the kitchen. "You wanna drink?"

"Water." She didn't realize how parched she was until now. She scooped her hands under Mockler's arms and hauled. "Up we go."

He weighed a ton, all dead weight. She blew hard just dragging him to the couch. No way was she getting him up onto it alone.

Gantry reeled back into the living room and handed her a bottle of water then flopped back into the chair and popped open the can of lager he'd found in the icebox. "Nice place. Guess the missus does the decorating."

"Help me get him on the couch."

"Talk to my union," he said. He motioned at the couch. "Sit down for Christ's sakes."

The cushions were soft and deep and the moment she collapsed into it, Billie knew it would be torture to get up again. She guzzled down half the water and stared up at the ceiling for a long time. Gantry's smoke polluted the air.

Neither party spoke. After a while, the detective on the floor began to snore.

"He needs to know," Billie said, prompted by nothing.

"Who?"

"Mockler," she replied. "I told him about the ghost. He needs to know the rest of it. Not just about the undertaker but about you too. Once he knows the truth, he'll stop chasing you."

Gantry laughed. "No."

"Why not?"

Lifting his head from the chair, he squared her with a look. "Do you think he'd believe you? Even if he knew the truth, he wouldn't accept it. Leave it. It's better this way."

The idea of Mockler being left in the dark appalled her. She stuck her neck out for him. She wasn't crazy. She needed him to know that.

"That's the way it goes, Billie. Go on and tell him the truth. See how the idiot takes it. He'd have you locked up faster than you can say police-brutality."

He watched her face fall flat. The girl was hurting, that was plain enough to see, and it only bit harder when her eyes fell to the man on the floor. He set the can down and pushed himself out of the chair. "All right," he said. "Let's get the bastard onto the couch."

It took two attempts but they hauled the detective onto the sofa. Mockler stirred once but didn't wake. Billie went to the kitchen to dampen a cloth and clean the blood from his face. Her pulse quickened and slowed, emotions warring with each other inside her as she dabbed the filth from his bent nose.

He'll never know, she thought. Kept from the truth, Mockler will wake up and still think she's a crazy woman who believes in ghosts. If he thought about her at all. She knew that she shouldn't be thinking these thoughts but she was tired of scolding herself. She indulged her heart while she dabbed the dirt from his face, wondering why it was that her thoughts always drifted back to this man. There was a familiarity she couldn't explain.

Billie folded the cloth. She wished he would wake up, even for a second, and see her but the detective remained dead to the world. She gathered a blanket and draped it over him.

When Gantry came back from the kitchen, he heard noise coming from the sunroom. He leaned against the door frame to find Billie inside the studio, pulling down sketches and paintings from the wall. "What are you doing?"

Billie tugged a sketch down and showed it to him. Another rendering of the horrid face of the undertaker man. "We can't leave these here."

"But she painted those."

"Neither of them need to see this again." She added the rendering to the pile she had made.

Gantry nodded. "What are you going to do with them?"

"Take them outside and burn them. See if you can find some barbecue fluid."

He reached into the pieces she had gathered and slid one out. "I'm keeping one."

"What for?"

He shrugged, rolling the paper into a tube. "Sentimental reasons."

~

After returning the Alpha Romeo to the garage, she walked Gantry up the alley to the street.

"You look tired," he said.

"I'm exhausted." Everything seemed to hurt at once and the three flights up to her flat loomed like Everest. "How do you feel about piggy-backing me up the stairs?"

"I've had my exercise for the week, thanks." He patted his pockets until he located the pack of cigarettes.

"You should quit," she said.

"Thanks. I hadn't thought of that." A truck rumbled past, the traffic warming up for the new day. He looked at her. "Will you be all right?"

She nodded her head. "How do I get ahold of you?"

"I'll be in touch."

"What if something happens?"

"Then you'll deal with it," he said. "I'll be out of town for awhile."

A twinge of panic rang out. As much as she disliked Gantry, she didn't like the idea of being completely cut off. "Where are you going?"

"Home. There's stuff I need to sort." He turned away. "I'll pop in when I get back."

Gantry walked to the end of the alleyway then turned back. "Will you take a bit of advice?"

"Depends what it is," she said.

"Steer clear of your detective friend. No funny business, yeah?"

"He's a friend, Gantry," she shrugged. "That's all."

He rolled his eyes. "Please. You're a tad obvious, ya know. Just watch out."

Billie folded her arms. She didn't want to give him the satisfaction of discussing it further.

Gantry smirked at her. "I guess I shouldn't be surprised. You two have known each other a long time."

"What are you talking about?" The Englishman's riddles were running her patience thin. "I've known him less than two weeks."

Gantry called back just as he turned the corner. "I didn't mean this lifetime."

What?

Billie ran to the corner and out onto the street. Gantry, of course, had vanished from sight.

41

THIRTY-TWO DOLLARS and seventy-three cents.

That was the balance printed on the slip of paper the ATM spit out. She was broke. What had she expected? She hadn't been to work in almost two weeks. Mario, the grumpy bar owner, had told her to heal up after the accident, promising she'd have a job when she was back to normal. Normal was something she'd never get back to but she needed to work and rode her bike down to the bar. Mario grumbled about re-working the schedule but she was rotated back into the line-up, taking a shift the next night.

Tuesday nights at the Gunner's Daughter weren't the busiest but she was grateful for the slower pace, wanting to ease back into it rather than get slammed by a packed house. The fatigue in her bones never left, worsened by the nightmares that jolted her awake. It was the same thing every night; the undertaker man waiting for her, his awful face popping from a shadow or around every corner. The broken sleep left her irritable, making her startle at any abrupt noise. The few regulars who were happy to see her back behind the bar were stymied by her scowling eyes and subdued nature.

She broke a glass when an ashen face leered at her through the window. One of the dead, looking into the bar like something had captured its interest there. Billie closed herself off to it and the phantom squinted, as if confused before drifting away. One side effect of being over-tired was losing the focus it took to keep her abilities closed off to the dead. She would weaken and get sloppy and then the lost souls would sniff her out like bloodhounds and demand to be heard. Sometimes all she needed to do was close herself and the dead would cast about in confusion as if she had vanished. The more tenacious ones would cling to her until she barked at them to leave her alone. The living souls around her would step away, suspecting she was disturbed.

It was a bit of a lose-lose scenario.

There was, however, one member of the deceased class that she didn't mind seeing. The legless ghost child that she still cruelly referred to as the half-boy. She had screamed the first time he re-appeared, scuttling out from under the sink. Once the fright had worn off, she had been initially saddened at his return. She had assumed that he had gone with the rest of the dead that night, pulled along by the same glow that had almost led her astray. Why hadn't he gone with the others? Had he missed his chance because of her? By staying behind to save her, she feared that he had sacrificed his own chances at the hereafter. Whatever that happened to be. Why had he done that? Why did he care if she had foolishly wanted to drift off to her own demise?

The second time Billie ran into him, she stayed calm, not wanting to spook him away again. She smiled at him, to show that she meant him no harm. Half-boy scuttled across the ceiling, curled up in a corner and watched her. Protective of his territory, he had even chased off another lost soul that had wandered into the building, drawn by Billie's beacon.

Now they acknowledged one another without conversation or alarm and the half-boy seemed content with the extent of their relationship. They shared the apartment like roommates who worked opposite shifts; he vanishing when the sun rose and she leaving for work just as he became active. If he could somehow scrounge up rent money, he'd be the ideal flatmate.

At work the following Thursday, she was surprised to see Jen and Tammy plant themselves at the bar. "Hey," she said, beaming.

"Hey Bee," Tammy said, nudging the man next to her for some elbow room. "Glad you're back to work. That guy they got to cover your shifts was a total drip."

"That's the owner. He hates customers." She looked at Jen, scrambling for something to say. She settled on simple honesty. "Hi. It's good to see you."

"Same here. We missed you." Jen smiled, then there was a pause, as if she'd lost her train of thought. "How's work?"

"It's all right. I'm just glad I still have a job. Where's Kaitlin?"

"With Kyle," Tammy said, rolling her eyes. "Picking out furniture or some shit."

Billie laughed and then the conversation withered. "What do you guys want? First round's on me."

"Margarita please," Tammy said. "A dirty one."

Billie served it up and pushed the glasses forward. The mood felt unsettled, as if the air needed clearing. "Listen, about my outburst the other night—"

"Ooh," Tammy perked up and cut her off. "Jen has some good news! Tell her."

The smile that broke over Jen's face was bright and contagious. "I'm re-launching the Doll House next week."

"That's great!" Billie had wanted to ask but didn't want to touch a nerve this early in the conversation. "The repairs are done?"

"Yeah. Wasn't as bad as we thought. Dad recruited some cousins to help us. Anyway, the re-opening party is next Monday. You'll be there, right?"

"Of course." A flush of gratitude bloomed on Billie's cheeks. Maybe life would settle back into some normalcy now. "I'll even work bar if you want."

"See?" Tammy rabbit-punched Jen's shoulder. "I told you

she'd offer."

Billie laughed. Normalcy, whatever that was, would be too tall an order to fill but hearing the laughter of friends was close enough for now. It felt good to be back.

~

All of the damage to the shop had occurred in the basement and, although the old wiring had been stripped out, nothing had been done to alter the charm of the shop floor. Jen swore that she could still smell smoke lingering in the place and went overboard with the incense.

As promised, Billie set up a makeshift bar for the re-opening party so Jen was free to greet everyone as they came in. She was happy to see Jen's dad, who was chatty as usual and, if he had any lingering doubts about the cause of the fire, he kept them to himself. Kaitlin arrived early with her boyfriend, Kyle, in tow.

Neither Jen nor Tammy made any reference to Billie's outburst about seeing dead people. They simply didn't bring it up and Billie was relieved to let the matter slip under the carpet for now. The only one who said anything was Kaitlin. Alone with Billie at the little bar, Kaitlin leaned in and whispered in a conspiratorial tone.

"For the record," Kaitlin said, "I think it's totally wicked. My great-grandma had the same thing. Nobody believed her either. It was her cross to bear, she used to say. You should really do something with this. Like charge people for it. Ooh, you could get your own TV show!"

Once the initial rush at the bar was over, Billie asked Kaitlin to take over for a minute. There was something she needed to do, she said, and slipped away to the basement door. She needed to know if the true cause of the fire was still lurking in the shadows of the cellar.

She had kept her senses closed off the entire day but descending the basement steps again, she opened herself up to the dead. Although constantly aware of the dead around her, opening up brought them into instant focus. It also made her visible to them. Twice so far she had opened up to find one literally breathing down her neck.

The basement, although creepy in its natural state, was quiet and still. There was no ghost here, charred or otherwise. Crossing to the far corner where the utilities were, she saw the reason why. The rusty hulk of the old boiler was gone, removed after the fire. It must have taken a lot of work to dismember and haul out that cast iron beast. In its place stood a much smaller and more efficient forced-air furnace.

The cindered ghost with its carbonized flesh must have left along with the old boiler it called home. She wondered if the poor soul had met its end inside the furnace, or if its mortal remains had been incinerated there in an attempt to hide evidence. Now she would never know.

There was, of course, a small chance that she herself had

gotten rid of it. It may have heeded her demands and moved on. Ultimately, she decided, it didn't matter. It was gone and Jen would be safe. That was all that mattered.

Closing the basement door behind her, she noticed that the bar was unattended. Kaitlin must have flitted off somewhere. A woman stood at there, patiently waiting for the barkeep to return. Billie ran back to her post.

"Sorry about that," Billie said, reaching for a clean glass. "What can I get you?"

When the woman turned to reply, the glass in Billie's hand slipped and smashed on the floor.

Christina leaned back in surprise and asked the clumsy bartender if she was all right.

42

"ARE YOU OKAY?" Christina asked.

Billie gaped at Mockler's fiancee. Three nights ago she had seen this woman possessed by something evil and here she was, standing before her looking radiant. What was Christina doing here? Does she know Jen? Had she been invited? Or was it just a fluke?

"Sorry about that." Billie straightened up, hoping her cheeks weren't too red. "Just clumsy tonight."

"Oh, I break wine glasses all the time," Christina said. "I've almost run out."

"What can I get you?" Billie had to force herself not to stare. The woman before her bore little resemblance to the haggard-looking wretch from the other night. Christina was tall and stunning, her dress draped perfectly over her frame. Her smile was wide and toothy and Billie forced herself to look away.

"Red, please," Christina said. "Two."

Billie poured, feeling the woman stare back at her. "Do you know Jen? The owner?"

"I'd bought something here a couple weeks ago," Christina said. "An invite showed up in the mail. I didn't even know there'd been a fire."

Billie pushed the glasses forward. "Yeah. I'm glad she's up and running again."

Christina tilted her head to one side, studying the bartender. "Have we met before?"

"I don't think so," Billie lied. Imagine trying to explain that one.

"You look familiar." Christina took up the glasses and stepped back into the crowd. "Oh well. Thanks."

Billie felt her hands shaking again. Of all the dumb luck. Panic set in when she realized Christina had ordered two drinks. She was here with someone. That meant Mockler was here. Even dumber luck.

She tracked Christina as the woman wove back through the crowded shop and hand one of the glasses to a man near the front window. It was him. Detective Ray Mockler was chatting with Jen.

Feeling her guts fall through the floor, she looked for an exit. Running into the girlfriend was weird enough, Billie was in no mood to go through some awkward greeting with him. Where was Tammy? Tammy could look after the bar while she ran out the back.

"Tammy!" she hissed, pulling the woman out of a conversation. "Watch the bar for me. I gotta run."

"Where are you going?" Tammy looked at her funny. "Hey, that guy was asking about you. The cop. Remember him?"

"Just take over for a bit. I need some air."

"Jeez. You look a little pale."

As usual, Tammy couldn't take a hint or even a direct order, blathering on and now it was too late. He had spotted her. Waving at her, the detective squeezed through the crowd on his way to the bar.

She suddenly felt very ill. "Oh God."

Mockler elbowed his way in, all smiles. "Hey Billie."

Hey Billie? What were they, old pals or something? Maybe he was tipsy. The ill feeling was not going away.

"I was hoping you'd be here," Mockler said.

"You were?"

The smile on his face dimmed to a lower wattage but didn't leave his face entirely. "Yeah. I was wondering how you were."

Okay, she assumed wrong. He was tipsy. She wished that she was.

"Hey, you're the cop, right?" Tammy butted in, as graceful as a rhino. "The one that body-slammed Billie into the drink?"

"Yup." He looked at the floor, guilty as charged.

"You remember Tammy," Billie said. Once the handshake was over, she glared at Tammy to get lost.

"Cheers, detective." Tammy sauntered away, batting her eyes

at her friend. "See ya, Billie."

As soon as Tammy was gone, Billie wished she'd come back. The silence was nigh awkward. "So. What are you doing here?"

"I saw the invite Christina got about the re-opening. Wanted to see it for myself."

"Oh."

"I figured I could check on you too. Two birds, one stone. Ya know?" He looked around the space, the crowd. "I'm glad your friend was able to re-open so soon."

"Me too." Billie shifted her weight to the other foot, wishing she had worn different shoes. Silence resumed and she scrambled for something to fill it with.

He looked back to her. "Have you seen your friend lately?"

"Jen?"

"Gantry," he said.

The air went out of the room. Gantry was the last thing she wanted to talk about. Or lie about. "I think he left the country."

"I see."

She watched his eyes narrow, trouble leaking into them. "What is it?"

"Hmm? Nothing."

"Come on," she said. Whatever it was, she could tell it was bothering him. "Did something happen?"

Mockler pursed his lips, as if he was trying to keep it bottled up. "I think he broke into my house."

Her back stiffened up. *He knows.* He knows what happened

that night. Play it cool. "Why do you think that?"

"He left me a note." He produced a slip of paper from his pocket and handed it to her. "I woke up on the couch one morning. This was in my hand."

Billie unfolded the paper and read the simple message scrawled there;

You owe me.

G

That dickhead! How did that slippery eel leave a note in Mockler's hand without her seeing it? Of all the stupid things to do. Billie handed the note back. "You sure it's from him?"

"Who else would it be?" He folded the paper back into a pocket. "He also stole a bunch of paintings."

She had almost forgotten about that. "Oh?"

"Christina's stuff," he said. Then he leaned in to share a secret. "To be honest, I was glad to see it go. She'd been painting all this spooky stuff. I'm happy to have it out of the house. I just don't know what the hell he'd want with it."

"Why does Gantry think you owe him?" she asked.

"Who knows?" Mockler tried to stifle a shudder and failed. "The thought of that sociopath in my house. Jesus."

He helped save your behind, she thought, but could never say to him. It was torture. "I saw Christina here. How is she?"

"She's good," he said, a little too quickly. "A lot better actually."

"I'm glad," she said. The lies came quick and clean now. But she needed to know. "What happened?"

"Beats me. She's just, I dunno, different now. Not so depressed all the time." He took a healthy slug on the wine. "Hell. Maybe it was all those paintings disappearing. Christ, I really do owe that English asshole."

The small laugh she gave up to his joke was fake and her gut felt queasy. Gantry said that ghosts feed on energy and foment drama within a household which gives off more energy to devour. A cyclical round of misery. By ridding Mockler of the man with the flies, she had removed the pall hanging over his home. He and Christina were clearly happier and if the detective owed anyone, it was her. The real joke was the irony of it and how she had shot herself in the foot. Typical.

"Your secret's safe with me," she said.

"That's a relief. I wouldn't want that hanging over my head." Tilting up, he scanned over the heads of the crowd. "I should probably find her before she buys up half the shop."

"Sure." A fresh ripple of panic pulsed through her belly, not ready to end the conversation. Words tumbled and crashed out. "Hey, about the last time I saw you. Uh, I'm sorry if it seemed crazy."

He cut her off. "Don't worry about that. Whatever it was, you wanted to help. That means something to me." He turned to leave, shrugging like he wanted to stay but had no choice. "Take care of yourself, Billie."

"I will. You too."

Mockler slipped into the fray of elbows and sloshing cocktails and then called back to her. "Call me if your slippery friend comes back!"

She watched him steer his date away from the guests and out the door. And then he was gone.

Billie deflated, queasy from all the lies and all the phoniness she had put out. Now that he was safely out of the picture, she allowed a tiny bubble of truth rise to the surface. She liked Ray Mockler. A lot, if she stopped to consider it. She had no idea why. Not that it mattered. He was spoken for and she would steer well clear of him from now on.

She looked over at the little makeshift bar. Tammy had stepped in after she drifted away and was doing a lousy job, completely ignoring the thirsty guests while she chatted up some guy.

Billie barged her way in, grabbed a glass and filled it to the brim with red. "Bar's open, folks, so serve yourselves," she announced before spilling wine all the way to the front door to get some air.

The night was cottony with humidity as Billie swam onto the street. She plunked herself down on the curb and watched the street. The booming racket flared up as the door opened behind her and the sound of high heels clacked smartly on the sidewalk.

She was surprised to see Jen slipping out of her own party. "Hey."

"Billie!" Jen's smile was huge and it was bubbly. She eased

herself down onto the curb, bumping into Billie. "I'm so glad you're here." Tipsy, she threw her arms around her friend.

"Me too," Billie said. "What are you doing out here?"

"I just needed some air. Did everything go okay?"

Billie said "I abandoned my post. Surrendered the bar to the barbarian hordes."

Jen laughed and then they sat quiet for a spell. A car rumbled past.

"Congratulations, Jen. For getting the shop back up and on its feet." Billie raised her wine to toast but Jen didn't have a drink so they both sipped from Billie's glass. "You should be proud of yourself."

Jen tried to shrug it off. "Thanks. You know, this might sound nutty but, in a way, I'm glad the fire happened."

"You'll have to explain that one."

"The place always had a weird feeling. It's hard to explain. It just felt odd. Or cold." Jen shook her head, the words failing to hook her meaning. "But since the fire, it's different. It feels better. Like it belongs to me."

Billie nodded her head but didn't respond.

Jen looked up at the night sky. "Sounds crazy, huh? I wish I could explain it better. There's nothing logical about it. It just feels right."

"I'm glad," Billie said.

The din from the party flared and dulled as the party-goers drifted away. The two women sat quiet for a moment. Sighing,

Jen turned to her friend and then startled. "Billie?" she said. "Why are you crying?"

Thanks for reading *Welcome to the Spookshow*. If you have a moment, let me know what you think in a review.

Books Three and Four in the Spookshow are available now. Book Five to follow. If you'd like to be notified of the next release, sign up for my newsletter at

www.timmcgregorauthor.com/newsletter

Tim McGregor is an author and screenwriter. He lives in Toronto with his wife and children. Some days he believes in ghosts, other days not so much.

Made in the USA
Charleston, SC
14 June 2016